"PARASITE?"

"When I heard John had a habit, I naturally assumed some sort of narcotic . . ."

"But the surrogate *is* a habit! A deadly one." Anthrus' eyes glittered with grim delight. "It has a narcotic effect upon its host. Once bitten by a surrogate, you're doomed!"

JOURNEY FROM FLESH

NICHOLAS YERMAKOV

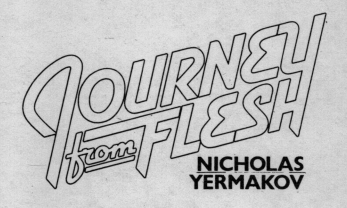

JOURNEY from FLESH

NICHOLAS YERMAKOV

BERKLEY BOOKS, NEW YORK

JOURNEY FROM FLESH

A Berkley Book / published by arrangement with
the author

PRINTING HISTORY
Berkley edition / February 1981

ISBN: 0-425-04588-9

A BERKLEY BOOK® TM 757,375

PRINTED IN THE UNITED STATES OF AMERICA

**To Norman Spinrad
and Harlan Ellison**

**With very special thanks to Richard McEnroe
and Adele Leone**

The wasp waits.
  The edge cannot eat the center.
The grape glistens.
  The path tells little to the serpent.
An eye comes out of the wave.
  The journey from flesh is longest.
A rose sways least.
  The redeemer comes a dark way.

—Theodore Roethke

Prologue

They ripped Baker's throat out before his very eyes. He heard Baker's agonizing scream, the rasping gurgle as the creatures fastened onto him, tearing and shredding. He saw Baker's hands beating weakly, uselessly, at the gangling bodies and he ran. He dropped his weapon and ran, smashing his way through the foliage, oblivious of the branches whipping at his face and cutting through his skin. *They* came after him. He could hear the rustling sounds they made, like deer leaping through the forest, as they gained on him. Unconsciously, he started whimpering, tears flowing freely as he ran.

"No, no, God please...."

He awoke, huddled in the corner, trying to crawl inside the wall. Again. It had happened again. He clapped his hands to his head, slamming it against the wall. The pain reminded him of reality. They were gone. It was over. That world was far away. They couldn't reach him here.

He pressed his hand to his heart, willing it to stop hammering.

He tried taking deep breaths to calm himself, but he knew that only one thing worked. He crawled across the floor, feeling revolted. It was disgusting. But it worked. And then, there was his crying *need*. . . .

He reached into the box and removed several translucent crystals. They seemed to flare in his hand, glowing with a fire of their own. He didn't care. The fire helped to burn away the memories.

Radu was a flamer. He lived on scraps and alcohol, whatever he could beg. His body was emaciated. He wore rags. He was forty-five years old and he looked eighty. His vocal chords were almost gone; he spoke with a rattling, croaking sound as if someone had kicked him in the windpipe. He spent his days prowling through the seamier side of the city, where the spacers liked to go because few rules were followed. He used to try to speak to them. They thought he was a crazy old man. Addled. Senile. They saw the glitter in his eyes, the cracked and festered lips, they heard his voice and knew he was a flamer, addicted to the fire crystals that only those too scared to die and much too desperate to live would take. They wanted to be rid of him, beating him if he refused to go away. At night, when he had no more energy to move, he would sit for hours inside his hole in an abandoned building, afraid to go to sleep. It was when he slept that the dreams came. The nightmares that took him back to Xerxes V.

He stared greedily at the fire crystals in his hand. He poked out his tongue and licked ruined lips.

Carefully, Radu crushed the crystals between his palms, reducing them to sparkling dust. Almost ceremoniously, he brought his palms up to his face and nuzzled, licking up the particles.

He leaned back against the wall, eyes staring at the ceiling, his rasping breath the only sound in all the world. And then, slowly, meltingly, that world began to fade away. . . .

Chapter One

I remember collecting my separation pay and taking the lighter
down to Port City, leaving the ship in orbit behind me. It felt
strange leaving the *Titus Groan*. She had been my home. But I
wanted to live in a city once again. I could afford to forget about
space for a while. There would always be work for a paramed
rated phase-shift navigator. I wanted to raise some hell.

And that I did. I immersed myself in city life; lusting, drinking,
glorious, sweaty, knock-down brawling, ridding myself of all the
stored up energy that had accumulated over the years. Port City
was accustomed to spacers running wild; it was an occupational
hazard. And there was profit to be made from it. I must have had
a good time during that first month because I don't remember
much of it. One night, I passed out in the middle of a filthy ballad
somebody was singing. I think it was me.

I awoke, perhaps revived would be a better word, to see the
vague outlines of four people standing around me. My head was
cradled in the lap of a fifth. A girl. I could tell even in that
condition. She was trying to force some liquid into my mouth and

I was gagging, spraying most of whatever it was all over her legs.

"Look, it's moving!"

"Do you think it's intelligent?"

"Don't be ridiculous. Would an intelligent being sing anything like *that*?"

"It is rather fascinating, isn't it? You think it will sing again if we buy it some more whiskey?"

"I think if we buy it any more whiskey, it'll collapse."

I was trying to focus in on the faces, but I wasn't having much luck. I tried to stand up, but the room wouldn't hold still. I fell flat on my face.

"Oh, dear, he's not going to be sick, is he? What a mess! Cilix, Irina, help him up! I won't allow him to expire without finishing that song!"

They lifted me onto a chair, but my spine had gone soft. I felt blood running down my face. I heard a loud *thunk* and realized it was the sound of my head hitting the table. I opened my eyes and saw the sympathy fir in its container begin to respond to me. As I watched it weave and sway, drunkenly, I began to feel nauseous.

They had the bartender give me a small dose of adrenalin, and after what seemed like several gallons of Terran coffee (I didn't want to think what it was costing me), I began to see straight once again. I asked the serving unit to bring me some cigarettes. They were expensive and probably artificial.

My rescuers were young bohemians. Artists. Jaded children with no goals or directions. They demanded a song, but it took some explaining. It was an old Terran chanty concerning the amorous adventures of a sailor named Barnacle Bill. Yuri listened to it all with a bemused smile. She cultivated an ethereal air. A poet. She recited some of her work. It was terrible. Jil was a painter, and apparently, a successful one. I noticed that she paid for all the others. I liked her infectious, warbling laugh and the way she joined in on the chorus. Cilix was a fallen academician of some sort, it seemed. I couldn't really tell what he was thinking; he didn't talk much. But, then again, I never could read Ophidians very well. Anthrus, on the other hand, spoke constantly. He considered himself a wit. I considered him a cynic. But I wasn't paying much attention to him. I couldn't take my eyes away from Irina.

She was slim, tall, and fair-skinned. Her skull was bare except for a tiny blossom tattooed on her cranium. Even her slightest movement was graceful. Irina knew she was beautiful and she wore it well. I wanted to hold her, to stroke her cheek, to be gentle with her. I tried not to stare, but I'm afraid it was a failed effort.

As we spoke, the gentle glow of the sympathy fir dimmed slightly and then began to flicker. Without glancing up from his wine, Anthrus smiled enigmatically and said, "John is here."

Irina tossed back her drink and announced that she was leaving, but Anthrus held her by the arm and shook his head. She sat back down uneasily. I glanced about at my companions, feeling puzzled. Cilix, Jil, and Yuri had all become suddenly glum. Anthrus pursed his lips and fixed me with his ice blue stare.

"When John enters a room," he said, "one gets the feeling somebody just left."

I noticed that several people in our immediate vicinity were, in fact, leaving. Our little group was rapidly becoming an island. It was only then that I saw John. He appeared at Anthrus' left shoulder. Our planet shivered, and its halo all but disappeared.

He was tall. The shabby surplice covered a uniform that was familiar, but I couldn't place it. The gaunt and craggy features had an almost gray pallor, and his hair was long and stringy. But the eyes were the most striking. Vacant.

"John, how nice to see you," Anthrus said, beckoning him to a chair. "Meet a new friend of ours, Alan Dreyfus, a spacer, like you used to be." He did something funny with the phrase "used to be." Some private bit of business between the two of them, no doubt. I didn't especially care for the tone with which he said it. "Will you have some wine with us?" said Anthrus.

"No, thank you," the spectre answered in a voice as tired and empty as a derelict in space. He shook my hand and it felt like touching a corpse. He sat and I stared as the fir quite literally strained away from him. Outside of the fact that he was as lost a looking soul as I had ever seen, I could not understand what it was about the man that seemed to cause everyone such concern. He didn't strike me as particularly disturbing, but the firs knew better. Every one of the sensitive plants within several meters of us was flickering like mad, and our own fir was behaving as if it had the botanical equivalent of St. Vitus dance.

The manager of the bistro approached our table, his hands clenched in massive fists.

"I have made it known to you," he said in his heavily accented English, "that I do not wish you to come here. You disturb the business, John."

"You have no right to bar this man from the premises," countered Anthrus. "He's done nothing wrong. He hasn't broken any laws."

"I have no right," agreed the manager. "You may report me if you wish."

"I shall."

"Nevertheless, he must leave at once."

Throughout the exchange, John sat motionless as if completely unaware of what was going on around him.

"If he leaves, then we all leave with him," Anthrus declared.

Of course, we all left. Having nothing else to do, I went with them. The others had all grown silent. The talkative Jil had become a sudden introvert. Cilix and Yuri both looked straight ahead as they walked, and Irina looked upset. In an effort to break the awkward silence, I asked John if he was thrown out often.

He answered, simply, "Yes."

"But . . . why?"

He said, "I have a surrogate," and then abruptly walked away.

"I don't like him" Irina said, lounging with her shoes off.

"Oh, I don't know, I find his company stimulating." Anthrus grinned. "Don't you?"

She snorted derisively and went back to doing nothing. She did it very gracefully.

"Who is he?" I asked.

Cilix paused in his preparation of the yola leaves.

"He was a merchant spacer, like yourself. A mercenary, wasn't he?"

"Ask Anthrus," Yuri replied as she carefully applied paint to her depillated cranium. "He's our expert on the walking dead."

"Walking dead?"

"Yuri is being true to her melodramatic Russian heritage," smiled Anthrus. "Yes, John was a mercenary, I suppose. I can't think who else would want to crew for the Shahin."

So that was where I had seen the uniform. "What happened to him?"

"He picked up a habit," answered Cilix, setting down the bowl of husked yola leaves.

"Is that what he meant when he said he had a surrogate?" I chose a leaf from the bowl and popped it in my mouth, feeling the delicious coolness as it melted. Anthrus looked surprised.

"You mean you've never heard of the surrogate lizard?"

I had to admit ignorance.

Anthrus leaned forward, pleased with his captive audience. "I enjoy telling this story!"

"Be kind for once," said Yuri dryly. "Make it short."

"Oh, very well." Anthrus made a mock bow in her direction. "I shall be merciful. Short and to the point. You've heard of a planet named Xerxes V, in the Julianas?"

I had. "A quarantined world."

Anthrus shrugged. "Why should that concern the Shahin? Their crews are expendable."

I nodded grimly. With their high pay came high risk.

"So," continued Anthrus, "one of John's shipmates was bitten by a surrogate while there. It came aboard with him, that is, he smuggled it in. It is a curious sort of reptile, births like a mammal. It's quite remarkable. Well, to be brief, this lizard was pregnant. It's offspring crawled into John's berth and became his personal parasite."

"*Parasite*? When Cilix said he had a habit, I naturally assumed some sort of narcotic—"

"But the surrogate *is* a habit! A deadly one." Anthrus' eyes glittered with a grim delight. " It has a narcotic effect upon its host. Once bitten by a surrogate, you're doomed. You simply cannot live without it. Its secretions are addictive. Eventually, the host dies. It depends mainly upon the host's constitution and the lizard's appetite. John and his surrogate seem to have developed a rather successful symbiotic relationship. He's been lingering for years. His parasite is very pragmatic. It knows his biological limitations."

"It knows?"

"Oh, yes, it knows! The surrogate is sentient. An intellect of a very high order. The species, as I understand it, is quite rare and indigenous only to Xerxes. Most people think its existence is a myth." He grinned wolfishly. "My friends, we simply *must* have another demonstration!"

Amidst their moans and cries of protest, he turned to me and said, "This experience you will remember!"

"Pay the man."

"Anthrus, no!" Irina showed a sudden concern. "Don't do this. *Please*."

"Why should I pay him?"

Anthrus smiled, again that enigmatic rictus. "John has a unique gift. He will reveal your innermost thoughts. In short, he will *tell* you about yourself."

Yuri took my hand, pressing it earnestly. "Don't do it. Don't listen to him."

But Anthrus knew I would. I was hooked. I paid John while Yuri cleared the table, keeping her eyes averted from our guest. Once again, a pall had fallen on my new friends. Once again, Irina tried to leave and Anthrus prevented it. I was beginning to resent his domination of her. Cilix rose to dim the lights.

"Oh, no, no, Cilix! Bring a fir!" said Anthrus gleefully. "This must be complete."

His thin lips compressed, Cilix placed a fir upon the table. Immediately, its glow began to wane. Anthrus beckoned and we formed a circle, seated round the table.

"Shall I begin?"

Anthrus looked to me to answer John. I nodded.

Slowly, John removed his faded outer surplice. Beneath it, clinging to his shabby Shahin uniform—the surrogate.

It was approximately fifteen centimeters long and bright yellow. My initial impression was that it resembled a salamander, but the head was too big. Its eyes were closed and it appeared to be asleep. With two fingers of his left hand, John gently stroked it. The lizard moved.

It detached itself from his tunic and crawled down onto the surface of the table. There was something repulsive about its movements. Yuri swallowed nervously. She looked frightened. Jil's expression was one of horror. Irina looked disgusted. And Anthrus—

But the lizard! Slowly its head turned in my direction, and it looked at me. There was nothing reptillian in those eyes. Although on a smaller scale, they were almost human in appearance. Blue. Set deep in that pyramid-shaped head. And it *looked* at me!

Then, with blinding speed, it leapt up on John's exposed right forearm, sinking its claws deep into his flesh. John winced. Again it looked at me, and then those jaws gaped. Two iridescent, snake-like fangs. Slowly, hideously, like a lover, it sank those tessellated nightmares into the soft flesh just below John's bicep.

Irina gagged and shut her eyes. The others watched in frozen fascination.

The hypersensitive fir had torn itself from its container by the roots. It lay thrashing on the table, its glow extinguished, dying.

John's eyes were closed. A tiny tear of blood welled in the corner of his mouth where he had bitten his lip. He shivered— shook—and then was still. The lizard sucked, immobile.

A fascinating change came over John. He sighed deeply. His skin was flushed, his forehead dank with beads of perspiration. The ashen gray of his complexion faded, and in its place was a robust glow of health. He opened his eyes, flashed a stunning smile, and winked. Then, taking his discarded surplice, he draped it over his arm, hiding the lizard from view.

"It disturbs some people to have to look at it, " he explained in a voice much different from the one I heard him use before. He raised a glass of wine and toasted us.

We drank. He with gusto, the rest with trepidation. He looked at Anthrus with a dazzling smile.

"Well, my predatory friend," he said, "another night of voyeurism as my brother spacer turns slowly on the spit." He winked at me. "You will get your money's worth tonight, I promise you."

"All right. So you're a fortuneteller then? What can you tell me of myself?"

He chuckled. "Only everything." Again that brilliant smile, disarming and sincere. "You're certain that you want to know?"

I nodded, skeptical. I had known gypsies, though none whose acts were quite so spectacular. He was a showman; that I had to grant him.

"You're wrong," he laughed. "I'm not an actor and this is not a farce."

I acted impressed. "Not bad. Telepathy?" I couldn't keep from smirking. He didn't seem to notice.

"Mmm, yes, I suppose you could say that. And, also, no. Let's just say I have a way of sensing truth."

Anthrus watched intently.

"Indeed?" I asked. "And what is the truth?"

He cocked an eyebrow at me. "Well, there are more truths than you know. For example, your feelings towards Irina."

I felt a tightness in my stomach. My eyes met hers and saw surprise. She did not look away.

"And she, of course, is flattered by this bit of information," John continued. "Because, you see, Irina has a hunger for much more than our friend Anthrus, here, can give her. She's thought about you once or twice. In fact, she's thinking about you now. About what you look like without your clothing. Shall I tell her?"

I think I blushed. Anthrus threw back his head and laughed.

"Don't let his laughter fool you," said John. "He really doesn't like you, you know."

"That's right, I don't." Anthrus had a strange look on his face. "I don't like you at all. But then, I don't like anyone. Now our Irina, well, she devotes herself to passion, don't you, my love?" She was looking at me, not him. "So you like our new friend? Well, go on, enjoy him. He's relatively young and twice as strong as I am, no doubt. Go on. But I shall hate you for it. Perhaps you'll let me watch?"

"That isn't funny, Anthrus," I snapped.

"It wasn't meant to be. You see, we have to tell the truth tonight. Otherwise, John will catch us in our dissembling. Because he *knows* the truth. And John is never, ever, wrong."

"He's right," John said. "I never am. And that explains your earlier confusion as to why I'm so universally disliked. It isn't that I am, as you so aptly pictured me, as lost a looking soul as you had ever seen. Most people find tragic losers reassuring in a way. They feel superior in seeing someone worse off than themselves. The simple fact is that no one can bear to hear the unadulterated truth about themselves. Nobody really wants to hear the truth when lies are so much more attractive."

"And the truth about yourself?"

"You did not pay for that."

"I'll pay you now."

"I'm not that hungry. Besides, tonight is yours. I have much to tell."

And so it went. A brutal session of encounter. Alan Dreyfus stripped and flayed. John laughed, he smiled, he charmed and told me things about myself that were so deeply buried that my conscious mind had never thought to resurrect them. And, finally, there was a stirring underneath the surplice. The lizard crawled back up his arm and took its place upon his chest. It shut its eyes and moved no more. The surrogate—sated—slept.

And, as I sat there stunned, John's effervescence faded. The spark diminished in his eyes till once again they glazed. The skin resumed its ghastly pallor. The life was gone, the shell remained. With a tired, croaking voice, the spacer thanked us. Then he stumbled through the portal and was gone.

I said, "I think I'd like to kill him."

And Anthrus chuckled. "But you can't. He's too compelling. Who among us, after all, can kill the truth?"

I found it difficult to look at Irina, sitting with Anthrus' gracefully clawed hand covering her own. I was not normally given to prejudice, but watching them, I felt more strongly than ever before that the Terran girl belong with me, with one of her own.

"I certainly wish I had psi powers as effective as his," I said, trying to keep the irony out of my voice.

Cilix thoughtfully stroked the stem of his goblet.

"You still don't understand, do you?" He was regarding me with that never blinking Ophidian stare. "John has no psi powers. He is not an empath or a gypsy or even a very perceptive human being. John is a pitiable derelict. That is all he is and all he ever shall be."

"But, then, how——'

"The surrogate," answered Yuri. "It speaks through him. It has no vocal chords of its own, nor does it have any kind of telepathic ability. As John said, he—it—*senses* truth. And it uses its host to communicate."

"You look startled," Anthrus grinned. "I told you that the lizard possessed an intellect of a very high order. Small wonder Xerxes V was placed under quarantine!"

"I feel sorry for him," Jil said, softly. Her voice had taken on a meek and gentle quality. "I wish that there was something we could do to help him."

"Your sympathy is very touching," said Anthrus flatly, "but it would only cause you grief to interfere. Nothing can be done.

He is an undesirable. Where can he go? What can he do? John really lives only when the surrogate's teeth are in his veins. Tonight he shone and glittered; he radiated truth and brilliance and provided us with much amusement—"

"Speak for yourself," interjected Yuri.

"—and for all we know, he's better off that way. You see what he is like in normal circumstances. Won't eat more than is necessary to barely stay alive, won't drink, won't laugh, won't even cry as humans do so often . . ."

I saw Irina wince.

". . . why, without the lizard, he would die! He told me so himself. His apathy may be his normal state! After crewing for the Shahin, I wouldn't be surprised if that were so. And, if that's the case, well then the lizard saves him! And, you must admit," he looked at me and smiled maliciously, "thanks to him, we all know all your inner thoughts and secrets."

I watched him as he smirked and gloated over how he had manipulated me.

"I must admit I am surprised though," he continued. "I know you hated what you heard tonight. I know it must have hurt you deeply. And yet, you're unashamed. How is that possible? I was under the impression that I knew human nature well."

He turned his strangely beautiful face to Irina and chucked her chin gently with his fragile fingers, having sheathed his claws.

"We must speak of this tonight, Irina. We really must discuss our friend. Why is he unashamed? *Your* reactions were rather different, as I recall."

I sought solace in the quiet, moonless night. Standing naked on the balcony, I felt the warm northern breezes on my skin and I breathed in deep lungfuls of the humid air. The others slept. I stood alone and smoked, thinking and looking at one of Jil's paintings, not quite finished. It rested on a metal stand in the corner of the balcony and glistened in the soft light. I turned down the illumination so that I could see the painting's luminescent glow. It was a study of a face. John's face. The eyes were sad, unlike the glazed and lifeless ones of the model.

"I wonder if you feel anything at all?" I asked the painting. "What's it like being a surrogate mouth for a parasite? I wonder what you see when you look into someone's soul?"

"I often wonder that myself," said Jil. I jerked, involuntarily, feeling faintly embarrassed. Silly. After what they heard. . . .

She sat behind me in the shadows. She had been so still I hadn't noticed her before. I stared at the red fire of her eyes, two glowing dots that floated up as she rose and came towards me.

"This one will sell," I gestured at the painting. "But to a stranger, one who hasn't met your model. It's the eyes. The sort of look one sees in poets, I suppose."

"I don't think that I will sell it," she said. She, too, had undressed to enjoy the evening breeze. Her fur rippled in the gentle wind. "This painting gives me . . ." she hesitated. "There is no word for it in English." She made a sound no human throat could copy. "It's just one word, and yet it means so many things. I really can't explain."

"No need. I didn't understand it, but the sound conveyed the meaning. And I agree." I grinned. "Whatever it means."

She smiled pensively.

"You're not yourself tonight."

"You mean I'm different from when you first met me. That is because I don't have on my public face."

"Your what? Your public face? What's that, a role you play, you mean?"

"Not really. More like . . . assumed discretion. You know something of my people?"

"A little. Mostly only what I've heard."

"We wear two faces," she explained. "One which we 'present' from day to day to those around us, in order to accommodate their actions. The other is for family and friends. The private face. It loses a little in translation."

"I see. It's not so different really. Most humans do the same. Only more covertly. And some of us get trapped behind our masks."

"Irina will have you, if you want her," she said. "But be careful."

"You mean Anthrus?"

"No. I don't."

I didn't quite know what to say to that.

"I know you want a lover," Jil said, "but you need a friend."

Before I could reply, she placed two fingers on my lips and held them there.

"You shouldn't sleep tonight," she said. "Stay here. Watch the night and think about the things the surrogate has told you. Few people really know themselves. Confronted with such knowledge all at once, it's easy to deny the truth. It's simpler not to face it. That is why John is hated, even though the man, himself, is blameless. You should not hate a man for things said by a voice that he cannot control."

She left me so that I could be alone. I felt the need to walk. I dressed quietly, so as not to wake the others.

Port City never slept. It had too many diverse life forms to accommodate. There were five "standard" languages spoken and the city was subdivided into different environments. Anyone who did not fit in had to adapt as best they could, but there were even facilities to help accomplish that—provided one could pay. It was an exciting city. The new Rome to which all space routes led. But, like the original, this new Rome had its share of decadence and desolation. I had been attracted by the decadence. What I found instead was something else entirely.

"Where are we going?"

Irina.

"I thought you were asleep. I'm sorry if I woke you."

"I'm a light sleeper. Not like Anthrus."

"Why did you follow me?"

"Can't you guess?" She linked her arm with mine as we walked. "Don't tell me we need John here to tell us all about each other." There was an unpleasant edge to her voice.

"You're beginning to sound like Anthrus."

"Must we talk about him?"

"Why not? The three of us don't have any secrets from each other anymore, do we? The surrogate saw to that."

"He disgusts me!" I was surprised at her vehemence. "How anyone can allow himself to fall to such a state...."

As she spoke, I suddenly realized that this was my opportunity. I should have been taking advantage of it, but I wasn't. I kept thinking about what Jil had said. We walked awhile in silence. Awkward silence. Irina was the first to break it.

"What's the matter? Don't you want me anymore?"

I never thought I'd have to think before I answered such a question. "I...I'm not sure. I suppose so."

"You *suppose so*? That's a fine thing to say! I could be wrong, but do I detect a certain lack of enthusiasm?"

"I'm just confused. I thought I knew myself inside and out. Oh, I knew I had a lot of shortcomings, but—"

"Are you still thinking about John? Forget him! He's just a bum. He isn't important, you shouldn't let him get to you."

"He seems to get to you, though. Anthrus must have arranged for the two of you to meet before, didn't he? A private session, with just the three of you?"

I felt her arm tighten.

"No."

"No?"

"Not just the three of us."

Of course. The others would have been there too. Anthrus would have seen to that. It also explained his earlier statements about the human capacity for shame. The experience had been a painful one for me. For Irina, it may have been truly humiliating.

"Why do you let him treat you that way?" I asked. "Why do you stay with him? You aren't a masochist, are you?"

"You don't have to be insulting. If you don't want me, simply say so."

"Would you return to Anthrus?"

She stopped and faced me. "Yes."

"Then I can't think of a single good reason why I should want you."

"*Svolotch*!" she swore in Russian. Her hand darted up at my face, and I felt a sharp stab of pain as the long nails did their work. There was a warm stickiness just above my left eye. She may have meant to blind me in her spite, but I had already seen enough. I left her standing there.

The juice of the berries from the harlequin bush, unfermented, is a deadly poison. But when pressed and processed into wine, the berries have an anesthetic quality. I was feeling no pain.

I had wandered into the sealed section of the city that had been set aside for the Frilissi whose auditory membranes are so sensitive that theirs is, to humans, a virtually mute culture. What I perceived as silence was comforting to me. I had wanted to go someplace where I could be alone and I have found in the past that nowhere is one so alone as in a crowd of total strangers.

I rubbed my thumb and forefinger together softly, and an attendant appeared at my side. In his own language, I subvocalized my request for more wine. He was pleased to see the pains I took not to let the slightest whisper escape my lips, and he did his best to imitate a human smile even though it must have been uncomfortable for him. To a Frilissi, the baring of teeth is an offensive act. I thanked him for the compliment he paid me. He started.

The thick fibrafoam flooring prevented me from hearing any footsteps, but someone had actually approached so silently that not even he had heard. It unsettled the Frilissi greatly. Only one species known to man could move that quietly when they wanted to, and we had no name for them. We couldn't speak their language, so we called them by the adjective which most closely described their appearance—feline.

Jil sat down and waited quietly until I had finished my wine. She did not know how to subvocalize and we could not otherwise communicate without causing severe pain to the Frilissi, so we merely sat and watched each other. It felt nice.

I needed the wine to deaden my emotions so I could think. I thought about how much Anthrus, Irina, and I had in common. Like the surrogate, we were manipulators. Users. Small wonder Irina hated John so much. Seeing the ultimate victim must have been unpleasant for her. For me, too. Hate was a convenient surrogate for guilt.

I couldn't remain in the Frilissi zone for long. Although I couldn't hear it, the ultra high frequency pitch of their conversation was giving me a migraine. I paid my tab and we left. It looked like it was going to rain.

"You tracked me," I accused Jil. "Why?".

She was embarrassed. She must have smelled my clothes right after she left me on the balcony to be able to pick up my scent so easily. She must have suspected I would leave. But why should that have concerned her?

"You weren't going to come back, were you?" she asked.

"No, but that still doesn't answer my question. What made you think I was going to leave? And why track me?"

It started raining. Jil made as if to look for shelter, but I grabbed her by the shoulders. She didn't resist. We looked at each other for a long moment.

"Jil . . . I'm just some guy you picked up off the floor."

She looked down. The rain was matting her fur. She brushed

at it absently. She looked like a drowned cat and I felt like laughing.

"I'm going to smell funny to you," she said.

I burst out laughing. She looked up in surprise, and then she started laughing too. Our eyes met again and suddenly I wanted very much to kiss her. I did.

"Do you want to go back?" I asked her.

She shook her head. "I want to go with you."

"But your paintings?"

"I only want the one." I knew which one. "I can get it later. There's a hostel not far from here. We can get a room."

I had been with females of every sort, yet I was surprised to find myself feeling so exhilarated. It was as if I were about to have a new experience. But then, that's exactly what it was. I had never gone to bed with a friend before.

Like children, we ran through the downpour, dodging shuttle-craft and turbines, splashing in the puddles. I tripped and fell, sprawling. We were both completely soaked and I couldn't remember when I had laughed so much. Then, as I was getting up, I saw what I had tripped over. It was John.

He was lying on his back in the street, his eyes wide open. He was dead.

Jil made a little mewling noise and looked away. I knelt over his body, brushing the straggly hair out of his face. His neck was broken and he had been lying there for some time. I was brought back to reality. Someone had killed him. No one would ever know why and no one would care. Just another night in Port City.

Jil screamed. Too late, I noticed that his surplice had been blown back by the wind and that the lizard wasn't there. It was climbing rapidly up my leg. I tried to beat it off, but it was too fast. I saw Jil running towards me and I yelled at her to stay back. And then I felt excruciating pain. I sank to my knees, tearing at the thing, but it wouldn't let go. I screamed, half with pain, half with fear. A flood of searing heat flowed through me. I felt dizzy. Weak. I heard Jil calling my name. I could feel her hands touching me, trying to pry the creature loose, but she sounded very far away. I could feel myself sweating. Warm. It was *so warm*. So relaxing and pleasant. Let me go, Jil. Leave me alone, it feels good.

I pushed her away roughly. I hadn't wanted to, but it was all right. It didn't matter. Nothing mattered. Don't cry Jil, please. . . .

She doesn't understand.

How can I explain? It really doesn't hurt so much, it. . . .

You can't explain. She'll never understand. She doesn't want to. Forget her.

No. . . .

I felt like I was coated with warm vaseline. My skin had a consistency I never saw before. What a wonderful thing, my skin! Funny how I never noticed it before. The way the tiny little hairs on the back of my hand resemble a wheat field. . . .

And there's an area where the thumb and forefinger join, in that little webbed part between the fingers—I could see a vein throbbing! Tiny, miniature eruptions of blood, coursing through there, just below the skin . . . pump. Pump. Pump. Pump. Pump. Pump. . . .

My head seemed to be moving. Really wish it would stop, most distracting . . . Jil? Is that you? I couldn't seem to focus my vision. What? Why . . . she was slapping my face. Stupid thing to do.

Make her stop.

Right. Make her stop. Was it raining? Somehow, I seem to remember rain. Strange. The sun was shining.

Variegated fields of indigo and scarlet, sanguine skies besmirched with gridelin and glowing golden birds.

Beautiful, isn't it?

Mmmmmmmm. . . .

There was a village. Primitive. And people toiling in the gardens by their homes. Bandy-legged people, with protruding eyes and gawky elbows. Frog-like. Docile. Calm. Serene. And each one with a lizard clinging. . . .

No, wait!

It was gone. I wanted to see more. The rain was trickling down my face, commingling with the sweat. The street was empty. I could hear traffic in the distance. Traffic and the dripping, plopping sound of rain. I was prostrate in a puddle. My vision cleared and I could see my predecessor, decaying in the damp. Poor John. And, now, poor me.

With a sloshing, I raised myself to hands and knees and tried to gulp some air into my lungs. My head was hanging down between my shoulders, dear God, it was so heavy it was all that

I could do to lift it. I did. And I saw Jil.

She was lying on her side, a stream of stark vermilion coloring the pavement by her face. Her lips were gashed, her pointy teeth were chipped, and the knuckles on my hand were cut and swollen.

It was clinging to my shoulder. Watching me. I began to heave.

I thought that I would literally spew my guts out onto the street. My stomach kept contracting and I was racked with shivers. I crawled over to where Jil was bleeding in the rain. She wasn't badly hurt, but I had knocked her senseless. In a fury, I snatched for the *thing* that was clinging to my arm. I felt the lizard's fangs, two heated razors slicing deep. Again, I screamed. I never knew so many different feelings in so short a span of time. Frustration, hate, helplessness and pity, rage and ecstasy, futility and fear and sweet, serene contentment. And, somewhere, between the dreaming and reality, I think, perhaps, I cried.

The bed was soaked with sweat. And there was an odor. It wasn't pleasant. It was coming from me. My eyes felt like rusty hinges as I tried to open them. I heard a familiar voice say, "Look, it's moving."

Deja vu. Anthrus' smirking face faded into focus. I shut my eyes again.

"Strange, how ironic life can be, isn't it?"

There was the sound of a slap and a yelp of pain. I opened my eyes again to see Anthrus clutching the side of his head. Jil was standing with her back to me, her arm raised to strike again. There was a flicking noise. Anthrus showed his claws. And then Cilix was between them saying, "Don't."

I watched them with detachment. Jil turned to face me. She did not look pretty. I had done more damage than I thought. "How do you feel?"

My mouth moved of its own accord. It said, "Weak."

Cilix had shepherded Anthrus out of the room. We were alone. No. We weren't. *It* was with us.

"Sorry," I mumbled. I didn't mean it.

She shrugged. It was a human gesture. Yet somehow she made it look natural.

"I tried to...." She looked away. "I tried to...to take that thing away while you were sleeping."

It was resting on my chest, quiescent.

"You wouldn't let me."

I stared at her. I heard what she was saying, but it didn't seem important.

She sighed deeply. "Every time I came near, it...it would do something, I don't know what...or how. You wouldn't let us near you."

I had beaten Cilix. Also Yuri. She was with Irina, crying. And I had hurt Jil. Again. So? So. Anthrus was right. Life can be ironic. I had come full circle. Wasn't this where I came in?

"Stop it! Stop it!" Jil half-screamed, half-sobbed.

Why? What was...I had begun absently stroking the lizard with two fingers of my left hand. It watched her. And then it looked at me. Its gaze was very direct. Very comforting.

Cilix burst into the room as the lizard began crawling slowly, lazily, up my chest. I was dimly aware of Jil, straining against Cilix's grasp. She was hysterical. I wasn't paying very much attention. I wished that *it* would hurry....

The sounds of sobbing faded. I felt the heat. I shut my eyes. It was so wonderful, and all I had to do was simply lie there. The pain was part of it. The burning and the soreness...I'd come to know the soreness well. My arms inflamed from all the places where it bit me, my neck a mass of scar tissue from when it feasted at my jugular, my skin erupting, breaking into eczema and oozing, itching, I lived a scabrous existence in a semi-darkened room.

I heard its voice, I knew its truth, I saw its visions. I lived the story of the quarantine. I heard the voices from the past. The saga of the Zharii—the froggish gangly people with the penetrating eyes.

"What do you mean they're not intelligent? Are you insane? Their level of—"

"I'm telling you, sir, they're *not intelligent !* There is no sentience! We've been communicating with the lizards!"

And that was the beginning. It was then that they began the persecution.

But you were killing them....

We were controlling them.

Voices, Distant voices....

"It's the ecology. The Zharii breed like rabbits. The lizards are their predators."

"Good Lord."

"We may be able to teach them zero population growth, or something, I don't know how it will work. . . ."

They tried. It cost them dearly.

Yes. It had, indeed. The Terrans had deprived some of the lizards of their Zharii mounts. The results were catastrophic. I saw torn and bleeding bodies. Or what was left of bodies. Shredded flesh and entrails. Leaping maniacs with salivating mouths and fiendish groping fingers. . . . I couldn't beat them off! I couldn't . . . couldn't. . . .

Something grabbed me. Someone. Cilix. Jil was lying on the floor, a bloody spattered mess. And there was Yuri. And Irina. Yuri kneeling by Jil's side, Irina with a dagger.

"*Sookin sin!* I'll carve the bastard!" She lunged and Yuri caught her arm.

"Let her," Anthrus said. "She's nursed a hate for him ever since he turned her down. Go on. Put the poor fool out of his misery."

"No. . . ." Jil moaned faintly from the floor. "No, please! It's not his fault. He didn't mean it. I'm all right. . . ."

I could see into the depths of all their souls. Irina had it in her mind to kill me. If not now, then later. Anthrus felt himslf a cuckold, in spirit if not in fact. Irina's lust for murder evoked in him a sexual excitement. Yuri was both disgusted and afraid, but she felt pity. Cilix thought of me as a disease without a cure and he wondered how best to isolate me. And Jil. . . .

Jil loved me. I knew it as an irrevocable truth. And I had the answer to a question I once asked a painting. When you look into someone else's soul, you feel despair.

The walls were bare. The light was minimal. The bed was hard. The floor was cold. Jil and I were hiding. Part of me wanted her to leave and part of me wanted her to stay. So I did nothing. I didn't know what I wanted.

Irina knew she couldn't kill me. The surrogate would sense it. So, faced with an opponent who would know her every move well in advance, she made the most logical one. The authorities in Port City don't take kindly to spacers wandering about with dangerous life forms, carrying deadly infections. The lizard qualified as both. As she was reporting us, we fled.

They wouldn't look too hard for me. So long as there was no

real danger of a spreading of infection, they would be content to look the other way, as they had with John. At best, it was a clear cut case of violation of quarantine. But Irina had made a formal complaint. The police would have to make at least a token effort to arrest me.

Because of me, Jil too was technically a fugitive. She had sold the remainder of her paintings. Except the one. It was propped up in the corner where she slept, curled up like a wounded kitten. She sometimes stared at it for hours.

I didn't know which one of us looked worse. Poor Jil was emaciated, bruised, and battered. And I was afraid to look into a mirror. I didn't want to know.

It seemed that I could not control my rages. The surrogate wanted to be rid of Jil. In my more lucid moments, I screamed, I cried, I pleaded with her to leave me. But she refused. The surrogate and I both knew that it was useless. So I sank back into an apathetic daze.

From time to time, Cilix and Yuri would stop by to bring us food. Yuri would sit with Jil, trying to console her, to talk some sense into her. Cilix never said anything. But then he didn't have to.

The surrogate and I were beginning to arrive at a harmony of sorts. I no longer suffered chills or bouts of vomiting after the visions. I grew accustomed to the pain and I was no longer bothered by the stench. Somehow, I felt that John had handled it all better. I couldn't find the strength to fight it, or the will, so I just lay there, helpless, trying to accept the situation. Deep down inside, I couldn't. But I tried not to think about that. There was nothing I could do. Someday, maybe soon, I'd die. And then I would be free.

But the surrogate was not content.

Day by day, it struggled for control of my personality.

Do you want to be like John?

I am like John.

You're different.

I'm the same.

You won't accept me.

Have I got a choice?

I want you to be functional. Not like John. He was an empty vessel.

I had to laugh. It wanted me to be functional. Not like John. Playing fortuneteller wasn't good enough for me. No, I was meant for some loftier purpose. The surrogate was practicing upward mobility.

I can't think for you all the time. It's tiring.

What do you want from me?

Accept me.

Leave Jil alone. Stop hurting her.

I felt a drop of moisture on my cheek. I opened my eyes. Jil was looking down at me. She was crying.

"I can't bear what it's doing to you."

I sighed. I felt very, very tired. "Go away, Jil. Please. There's nothing you can do."

She shook her head. "There must be something!"

"Kill me."

"I've thought of that."

"I know."

"Yes. I know you know. *It* knows. It knows that I can't do it, too. It hates me."

"*I* hate you, Jil. Go away."

"You're lying!"

"Have it your way."

"You love me! I know you love me!"

"You're being used, Jil. I'm using you just like this thing is using me. Can't you see that? Look at us! We're like Anthrus and Irina! Please, Jil. I don't want to live off your grief."

"No! No one is using me! I won't allow myself to be used!"

"Jil. . . ."

"Listen to me! You're not using me. You can't. You won't. You could have used Irina. She wanted you to, but you wouldn't. You could have used John, to get back at Anthrus for what he put you through. But you didn't."

She kneeled at my feet, holding onto my knees, resting her head upon them, a Juliet mourning her catatonic Romeo.

"I can't fight the creature for you. I would, if I could. You have to fight it for yourself."

"I can't, Jil. I need it."

"It needs you!"

"I'm not free, Jil."

"You're wrong. You are, you just don't see it."

I was too tired to argue. But not too tired to beat her again that night. The surrogate gave me strength. My nightmare was the morning.

All night long I dreamt of the Zharii. Masquerading monsters they were fiends that only surrogates could tame. Again, I saw them attack the Terrans. Only this time, I was shown the counterattack.

I saw the Zharii slaughtered by the thousands. And the lizards along with them. My night was one vast sea of blood. I saw the seared and blackened reptiles twitching in their death throes, and I heard the high-pitched squeal of their agony. I felt my own flesh burning, crackling, crisping. I choked and gagged on the acrid smoke. I retched as all my inner senses were assailed by the massive spectacle of death. I came to, screaming. Jil couldn't hear me.

I had bludgeoned her unconscious with her painting.

I don't remember leaving. There was money in my pocket, but I don't know where I got it. I ate a hearty meal for the first time in what seemed like years. The surrogate was hidden underneath my jacket. I had washed though I could not remember washing. I was still a pretty miserable spectacle, but at least I had the energy to walk and I didn't smell so much.

Much of my mind was blank. I simply wasn't thinking. I was walking in a daze, dimly aware of taking one step at a time, vaguely knowing that I had a destination, yet not knowing what it was. I had left Jil lying in a crumpled heap upon the floor. Her painting was ruined. Along with much of her face. She wasn't dead, perhaps because I still had just a spark of my old self within me, but she would never look the same again. I ran. I ran because I didn't want to kill her.

The spaceport loomed before me. I entered through its massive gate.

There would always be work for a paramed rated phase shift navigator. I had wanted to raise some hell. Well, I had found hell. It must have been painfully obvious. Although there were plenty of berths for a man of my special talents, I couldn't seem to find one.

In spite of all the pains I had taken to make myself appear presentable, I still looked like a corpse. Captains have a tendency to be a bit particular about the physical health and emotional stability of their navigators. I must have looked like a bad bet although I really can't say that I could blame them. I had exhausted almost all the possibilities by the end of the day. I still had one chance left and I wasn't crazy about it. There were those who didn't mind employing the services of the flotsam and jetsam of space. The Shahin.

I had never been a mercenary, and I once swore that I would never sink so low. But I had sunk a lot lower than I had thought was possible. I had to get away. And there didn't seem to be any other choice.

As I waited to see the Shahin commander, I thought about the future. It didn't seem as though I had one. If I played my cards right, there was a chance that my habit might escape detection. Who knows how long John had been able to keep his surrogate a secret? At any rate, I would jump ship at the earliest opportunity. Perhaps I'd be lucky enough to find my way to a deserted planetoid where I could hide until they gave up searching, and then I could live out the remainder of my days in peaceful solitude. Peaceful? No. I didn't think the lizard would allow me any peace.

Finally, I was admitted in to the office of His Excellency Lord Commander Hhargoth. The ceiling was high. Even sitting down, Lord Commander Hhargoth dwarfed me. His red-flecked yellow pupils watched me with an expectant gaze. I hesitated, then managed a salute, Shahin-style, closed fist extended, then opened to display an empty hand. His Excellency seemed satisfied with that. He grunted, gave a curt nod, and proceeded to peruse my papers.

He was frowning. It wasn't a good sign.

"Is something wrong, Your Excellency?"

He looked up, slowly. "These are *your* papers?"

It was simple enough to check. He knew that as well as I did. The question was rhetorical.

"If they are forgeries, then they are very good ones," he said, his eyes not leaving me for an instant.

I still did not reply. He was baiting me. My appearance was, of course, the reason. The man standing in front of him could hardly be the navigator documented in the records.

It was clear that he suspected narcotics of some sort. He was looking at my neck. The high collar of my jacket did not quite hide the scars. I saw his breathing quicken.

"Remove your jacket."

"Forget it, Excellency. If you'll just let me have my papers, I'll be—"

"Remove your jacket!"

I thumbed it open. Moving with uncanny speed, the lizard leaped!

Hhargoth was even faster. He was on his feet and reaching for his sidearm with a yell before the creature landed on his desk. He rushed his first shot and missed, ruining the heavy quartzite desk. The surrogate realized its error and jumped back on me. It dug into my arm and I was off and running. White pain exploded in my brain!

I never faltered. I charged headlong into the lieutenant, bowling him over, and I kept right on going. I breathed in gasping sobs, knocking into people as I ran. I didn't stop until I passed the spaceport gate. My wind was gone. I stumbled heavily, regained by balance, and lurched away into the crowd. I was wheezing like an asthmatic. I was being stared at. I reached for the wall of a building to steady myself, but I fell against the building. There had been nothing to reach with. My left arm was gone from the shoulder on down. I stared in disbelief at the charred and crispy flesh.

"Oh, God. Dear God, why me?"

My vision blurred. I stumbled on. I found a quiet alleyway and there, surrounded by gray walls, I sank down to the ground and cursed the day that I was born. I felt feverish. Again, I reached with my left hand to wipe the sweat from my forehead. Nothing happened. I began to giggle. I stuffed my one remaining fist into my mouth to choke off the hysterics. I bit down upon my knuckles until I tasted blood. I was so cold that I couldn't keep from shaking. And I was sweating too. I vomited. The slime drooled down upon my chest. I didn't wipe it off.

My demon was clinging to my leg. It had been badly frightened. Eyes wide-open, it was twitching its tail nervously from side to side. Its plot had backfired.

Belatedly, I realized that running had never been my idea in the first place. I had only acted as the lizard had intended. Like a chessmaster, it had plotted out its moves and I had taken every gambit. It didn't work with John or with that other nameless crewman because they were only pawns. But as a navigator, I could have been a bishop. Right up there with the king. A phase-shift navigator works in close proximity with the commander of his ship. And the lizard needed a commander. And not just any commander, but one who didn't give a damn about the quarantine. One whose home world's power placed him just a bit outside the law. I had to go through hell just so that no other crew would take me. Through me, the lizard almost had its Shahin. I would have been abandoned, left to die, and the lizard would be surrogate to the captain of a ship.

The light was fading fast. I didn't have the energy to move. I wanted very much to sleep, but I was afraid to close my eyes. I might never open them again. How had Hhargoth known? If they ignored the quarantine, then perhaps my surrogate was not the only one. . . .

There was a silhouette at the entrance to the alley. Someone had stopped and was standing there, hesitating. I scuttled like a lobster, creeping back into the dark. The silhouette came closer. Whoever it was was moving erratically as if drunk. It looked too short to be Shahin. And then it called my name. I whimpered. It was Jil.

Words cannot describe the way she looked. I crawled away from her, just like an insect, until there was no further room to crawl. And then I huddled like a baby, my one arm covering my head, my legs drawn up beneath me. That's how she found me, calling for my mother.

"Why did you go? Why did you leave me, why?"

I threw myself upon her and I cried. I held on to her as if she was the last thing that was real in the universe. She held me, cuddled me, and stroked my hair. And then she saw the ugly wound where my left arm had been. Her feline howl was heart-rending.

Gently, slowly, she helped me peel off my jacket. The material at the shoulder had been cooked into the flesh and it came away with a stretching and a crackling sound. Blackened bits of skin flaked off onto the ground and pus oozed from the wound.

She wrapped the jacket around me and held me as I shivered. The night was quiet. Almost. A long way off, I heard somebody scream. I felt a movement. The surrogate was climbing up my leg. I groaned. Perhaps it wasn't very hungry. I had nothing left to give.

Jil released me. She looked exhausted. She sighed. For the first time, she spoke directly to the creature.

"No," she pleaded softly. "He's hurt. He can't. You'll kill him. Please. Take me."

And she held out her hand.

The lizard stopped. It turned and looked at her. And it decided. It crawled onto her hand and started climbing up her arm.

I don't know what possessed me or where I found the strength. With my right hand, I swiped at it and knocked it off her arm. And then I lunged. I dove upon it. I grabbed its hindquarters with my fingers and I roared and dug my teeth into its neck.

There was a buzzing in my ears. It squealed and thrashed between my jaws and I bit down with all the strength that I could muster. Cold, pungent blood spurted into my mouth. I gagged, but I did not let go. I was like an animal, goaded into a frenzy that I could not control. I growled and shook my head, tearing at its flesh. I swallowed and bit down again. I ate half of it before it died.

I lifted up my head, my jaws dripping, and belched. Jil stared at me with horror, then she doubled over and vomited. I began to tremble violently and, in a matter of seconds, I was having convulsions. The street hit my chin and I passed out.

Chapter Two

Hhargoth slammed his fist into the wall, creating a sizeable hole. Lieutenant Lokhrim flinched slightly. He had seen the commander angry before, but this was the first time he had ever seen His Excellency lose his temper.

"I want that Terran found!" Hhargoth rumbled.

Lokhrim stood totally immobile, ramrod straight, a silent black obelisk. It was his fault that the Terran had escaped. His fault that a surrogate had been admitted to His Excellency's chamber. Others had died for less grievous dereliction.

The man had looked terrible, as thin as an Ophidian, a pitiful excuse even for a Terran. Still, the Shahin had recruited men who looked far worse. Men who, after a bath and a hot meal, began to look like something. Lokhrim had guessed nothing more than that the Terran had fallen on hard times. Only men with no principles or no other choices accepted service with the Shahin. Few questions were asked.

"I want to know," said Hhargoth, pacing the room like a caged animal, "what that lizard was doing here in Port City. How did it get here? How *long* has it been here? What did it intend to do? *Are there any others?*"

Lokhrim felt relief. His Excellency's words meant that he was still needed. At least, it was a stay of execution. And, if he performed his duties well, perhaps the unpronounced sentence would be commuted.

"It must have been smuggled in aboard one of our ships, Your Excellency," he said. "It will not be difficult to find out which one. I doubt that more than two or three ships, at most, have made the passage from Xerxes directly to Port City in recent years. It is not, as you well know, the usual route."

"No, it is not," agreed Hhargoth. "You will obtain that information for me instantly. I will have the commander of that ship shorn and broken. And he'll live out his remaining days with *humans*."

Lokhrim felt his blood turn to ice. For a Shahin, suicide was unthinkable. Death was infinitely preferable to banishment and loss of honor. But, never to see a Shahin face again. Never to hear a Shahin voice. Sent to a world where there was no honor, where they feared and hated Shahin. He would certainly go mad. And he, himself, had feared execution. His fears had been conservative.

"As of this moment, Lokhrim," Hhargoth said, "you are relieved of your lieutenancy in my command. You will resume the rank of *xothol* in my household." Lokhrim's shoulders tensed and his face jerked, briefly, as if he had been slapped. It had taken him most of his life to work his way up to a ship's lieutenancy. Now, he was once again a bondwarrior, the class to which he had been born. "You will give your full time and attention to this assignment. If at all possible, I want that Terran and his surrogate taken alive. If not, destroy them. Are there any questions?"

"Yes, Your Excellency."

"Ask."

"We still have the Terran's application for service. With your permission, it would expedite matters if the papers were processed. In this way, we could inform the local authorities that we are searching for a deserter and we would be left unhindered."

"Good. You have my permission."

"One thing more, Your Excellency. In matters such as this, discrete inquiry is often very useful. The lesser men would speak more readily to one of their own than to one of the people. I have in mind a certain mercenary who has been under your command for several years now. It will require some bargaining, but his services would be most helpful."

"Use your own judgment," Hhargoth replied. "I am interested in the result, not the method. Have you finished with your questions?"

"Yes, Your Excellency. I am finished."

"You are dismissed then."

Lokhrim saluted, turned on his heel, and left the chambers. There was no time to lose. "I am *not* finished," he thought to himself. "There is still hope. I am not finished yet!"

It was very dark in the bar. Steiger liked very dark places. They made him feel comfortable.

"Your name Creed Steiger?" asked the bar manager, his voice coming from the speaker of the serving unit that had floated silently up to his table.

"Who's asking?"

"Funny company you keep, Steiger. There's a Shahin here asking for you."

"Zat so? Send him on over."

There was a short pause. Then the voice resumed. "Your friend prefers to wait for you outside," it said. "I sort of prefer it that way too, actually."

"In that case, he's going to have a long wait," Creed said, "because I'm not finished yet."

"I've taken the liberty of instructing the serving unit to prepare your tab, Steiger."

"I don't think you understood me. I said I wasn't finished."

"I think you are, Steiger," answered the bar manager, still speaking through the serving unit. "It won't be necessary for me to instruct the unit to evict you, will it?"

"No," replied Steiger, "it won't." He removed the sidearm from its holster and blasted the machine. The thermal charge slammed its way through the unit, superheating it, and causing a violent explosion.

Several minutes later, another unit floated into view. It seemed to hover, hesitantly, several yards away from Steiger's table. Creed aimed.

"Please don't shoot," said the bar manager, through the second unit's speaker. "These things are expensive as hell. Take anything you want, on the house. I just don't want any more trouble."

"Thoughtful of you," said Creed. "I'll have another bottle of *baharri*. Make sure it's cold."

"Anything you say, sir." The unit floated away.

"Sir!" The corners of Steiger's mouth turned down in a grimace. "It's nice to have respect." He laid the sidearm on the table.

"Respect and fear are two different things, Steiger. Still they are related."

Lokhrim had materialized out of the darkness. Creed looked up at the flat obsidian colored face, at the red-yellow eyes that glowed in the dimness. The long, raven black hair was not worn loosely as was the normal fashion for ship's officers. Instead, it was worn in a pony tail, held together by a single, burnished golden ring. The surplice was gone as well. In its place, Lokhrim wore a close-fitting jorskin tunic with no sleeves. The heavy braxite wristlets below his heavily muscled forearms were engraved with the Lord Commander Hhargoth's crest.

"Well, well," said Creed. "Look who's been busted. What happened, Lieutenant... or should I say, *xothol* Lokhrim? You forget to salute or something?"

Lokhrim reached out with a meaty hand and aiming his weapon at Steiger, picked him up by the throat, lifting him clear of the table. "Your insolence is truly unbelievable, even for a Terran." Almost casually, he threw Steiger against the wall. As he picked himself up, Creed produced the sidearm he had retrieved from the surface of the table.

"What we have here," said Creed, "is something my ancestors used to call a Mexican stand off. Your move."

"An excellent strategic ploy," said Lokhrim. "You might even have killed me."

"Oh, I don't want to kill you, Lieutenant," said Creed, rubbing his throat with one hand while keeping the Shahin covered with the other. "I don't hate you, you know. I just dislike you a lot. You're a good soldier, but I never did like officers."

"Yes," said Lokhrim, "I seem to recall that you killed three of them. Terrans. Your own race."

"Well, *those* guys I hated. They were just too damn stupid to be allowed to live, that's all. They weren't good soldiers. You, on the other hand, you're a good soldier. Only you're not an officer anymore, and that makes it open season. I'll make a deal with you. I'll put down my gun, you put down yours, and we'll settle this thing the good old-fashioned way. What do you say, Lieutenant? I've wanted a crack at you for the past two years."

"You're insane," said Lokhrim. "A human is no match for a Shahin in unarmed combat. I could easily kill you."

"Yeah, but you won't. *You* came to *me*. That means you need me for something. I don't know what, but whatever it is, I'm no good to you dead. You might bruise me a little, maybe break a bone or two, but you won't kill me. Whereas I don't have that limitation."

Lokhrim smiled. "You have no honor, Steiger. You are contemptible. Still, there is something about you that I like, a little. If you survive, I must try to find out what that is."

The Shahin put aside his gun. Creed Steiger holstered his. He cracked his knuckles and moved forward.

Fourteen tables, six serving units, an undisclosed number of chairs, and one heartbroken bar manager later, Creed Steiger lay draped limply over the wreckage of the holojuke, one eye swollen shut, his nose broken, his mouth bleeding, his body, though relatively undamaged, badly battered.

"Is that enough of a 'crack,' Steiger?" asked Lokhrim, himself not entirely unscathed. His knuckles were barked, his face was bleeding at the cheek where Steiger had slashed him with a broken bottle, and a trickle of blood ran down his calf where Creed had bitten him.

"Unnnnh!" moaned Creed. "I'll quit if you'll quit."

"Oh, I'm not nearly tired yet. I want to be certain that you're satisfied."

"I'm satisfied, I'm satisfied. Hell, I'm not satisfied, I'm dying. Whatever you want, Lokhrim, we'll work it out, okay? Only stop with the piledrivers."

"Agreed. It was foolish of you to fight with me, Steiger. You knew we were unevenly matched."

"Yeah, well . . . it seemed like a good idea at the time."

"You fight well," said Lokhrim. "Dishonorably, but well. For a Terran."

There was no answer.

"Steiger?"

Lokhrim lifted Creed's head up by the hair. He was unconscious. Lokhrim frowned. "I hope I haven't damaged him," he said. He lifted Creed Steiger easily, threw his body across his shoulder, and strode out of what was left of the bar.

"Where did you find this?" asked Hhargoth, staring at the contents of the container before him.

"In an alley, not very far from here," answered Lokhrim. "I have had several teams conducting a search throughout the city. So far, they had yielded no results, save this. They found it quite by accident."

Hhargoth stared at the pulpy remains of a surrogate lizard. It appeared as though it had been chewed, half of it eaten. He felt uneasy.

"Is it the same one that attacked you, Your Excellency?"

"I can't be sure," Hhargoth replied. "Perhaps some vermin killed it."

"I doubt it, Excellency. It is possible that it was already dead before it was eaten, but the teeth marks are too widely spaced for any known city-dwelling vermin. I believe the teeth marks are human. Some derelict, perhaps, who was starved for food and would try eating anything."

Hhargoth's entire body tensed. If that was true. . . . Lokhrim didn't know. None but the elite knew. What they all had feared had finally come to pass.

"Find me that Terran."

"Yes, Your Excellency. I have men searching—"

"I do not care how many men it takes," he said tersely. "I want him found. I want him found and I want him killed."

"Yes, Your Excellency. Your order stated that he should be taken alive, if possible—"

"That order is rescinded."

"Yes, Your Excellency." Lokhrim reached for the container with the lizard's remains.

"This stays with me," said Hhargoth.

"Yes, Your Excellency." Lokhrim pulled his arm back to his side.

"You are dismissed."

Lokhrim saluted and left. Hhargoth stared at the container for a long time. Then he rose from behind his new desk, crossed to the other side of the room, and dumped the lizard's carcass down the incinerator tube.

Alan Dreyfus. Alan Dreyfus. He fixed the name firmly in his mind. If Alan Dreyfus had eaten the surrogate, he was now the most dangerous Terran alive.

I awoke to the sound of voices, speaking softly. I was in a bed, covered with a heavy blanket. Both the blanket and the sheets were fresh. They felt good against my skin. I was in a small compartment. It looked run down, but it was clean and bore no resemblence to the fetid hole I had been living in, if you could call that living. At least I was still alive. I felt peculiar. I recalled my last grisly meal and the gorge began to rise in my throat. I coughed and hacked, trying to banish its memory.

"Alan!" Jil rushed to my side.

"What happened?" I asked her, propping myself up on my elbow. "How long was I unconscious?"

A familiar voice said, "Two weeks." Cilix.

"*Two weeks*?" It seemed impossible.

"We thought you were going to die," said Jil.

"Two *weeks*!"

"You were delirious," said Cilix. "You babbled incoherently and you were feverish. You remember nothing?"

"No, nothing." I felt dazed. "Where am I?"

"In a small compartment I rented in the North Port district," replied Cilix. "We should be safe here."

"Safe from what?"

"From whom," corrected Jil. "The Shahin have been looking for you. And me. It seems we're fugitives. I don't suppose you know anything about that, do you?"

"I'm afraid I do," I said. I told them everything that happened from the last time I saw Jil until I passed out in the alley. I told them how Commander Hhargoth had seen the marks on my neck and instantly guessed the truth.

"The lizard tried to attack him," I said, remembering what

happened. "But Hhargoth *knew*! Otherwise he could never have reacted so quickly. The surrogate would have left me for the Shahin then and there."

"I thought that whatever happened to your arm had something to do with the Shahin," said Cilix. "They came looking for you, it couldn't have been long after your visit to Hhargoth. Anthrus and Irina did not know where you were, though I suspect that Anthrus would have gladly told them if he had known. Yuri and I knew, of course, but we kept silent. As soon as they left, I made my way to the room where you and Jil had been staying. I knew that if they had so easily traced you to the commune, it would not be long before they found you there."

"The room was empty when he got there," Jil took up the story, "so he broke in and waited. He took a terrible chance, Alan. If the Shahin arrived before we did, they would have known that he was helping to hide you. Fortunately, I came before they did."

"She carried you," said Cilix, a rare trace of a smile on his face.

Jil couldn't have weighed more than one hundred pounds. The fact that she was able to lift me and carry me all the way back to that room, even given the emaciated state that I was in, was astonishing. I didn't deserve her.

"I'm sure that I was seen," said Jil. "I just wanted to get you home and call a doctor. It never occurred to me that anyone was looking for you. I'm sorry, Alan."

I couldn't believe she was apologizing. After all she had done and after all that I had put her through. . . . I put my arms around her and hugged her to me. "Jil, those are two words you're never going to have to say to me for as long as you live."

"Don't say that yet," she said. "I wasn't able to get you any medical attention. Cilix said it would be too dangerous to take you to a hospital."

"And he was right," I said. "That would be the first place they would look."

"It isn't quite as simple as that," said Cilix. "There were other considerations, Alan. A doctor would have asked too many questions."

"It's just as well," I said. "I'm not sure I want to know how long I've got to live."

"You may have a great deal longer to live than you suspect,"

said Cilix. "You didn't let me finish. At first, while you were sick
with fever, we tried to do everything we could to help you and
it all seemed futile. Your fever lasted several days, perhaps three,
perhaps four. Jil and I lost track of time after a while. Then, on
either the fourth or fifth day, the fever broke and you fell into a
coma. That was when we thought we had lost you for certain.
But you surprised us. Tell me," he said, interrupting himself,
"how do you feel right now?"

"Strange," I answered. "Weak, I guess, a little hungry. . . ."

"How strange?"

"I don't know. Peculiar. I've never felt this way before; I can't
describe it."

"But you do not feel as though you've been in a coma for the
better part of two weeks."

"No," I replied, puzzled. "No, I don't. I don't understand."

"Neither do I," said Cilix, "but I am fascinated. Look."

He reached out and whipped the covers away from me. I
gasped. Nothing he could have said would have prepared me for
what I saw.

The scales and the flaking of the eczema were gone, as were
the many bruises. The pale, discolored skin looked pink and
healthy and there were no sores. The wounds and scars caused by
the lizard's fangs were gone. Not a trace of them remained anywhere. The charred and blackened skin just below my shoulder,
where my arm had been, had fallen away and the wound was
healing, covered over with fresh, new tissue.

"It isn't possible," I whispered.

"That was what I said," Cilix agreed. "Jil is not familiar with
human biology, so she saw nothing out of the ordinary. I said
nothing at first. I was sure I was mistaken. She kept showing me
how you were getting better, and I kept refusing to believe my
eyes."

"He said that it was impossible for a human body to heal itself
so quickly and so thoroughly," said Jil, as if hoping to have me
contradict him.

"He's right," I said in a dazed voice. "It *isn't* possible. *Nobody*
can heal that fast."

"And yet you have," said Cilix. "You told us at one time that
you had a paramed rating. What would be your *professional*
opinion?"

"I don't know," I said. "A paramed is a long way from being a doctor. Still, I've been in situations where I've had to operate on men or else they'd die. I've seen some wild things in my time, but never anything like this. I could conduct some tests, I suppose, but I don't have any of the necessary equipment. I can't even do a simple blood test."

"But you have healed!" said Jil, not understanding. "Is that so terrible? Why are you so concerned? It's wonderful!"

"Yes, darling, it's wonderful, all right, but it's not normal. For this to have happened, some incredible chemical changes must have taken place in my body and I can only guess at what must have happened. Ingesting that damn lizard...." I shut my eyes against the memory. "It must have done something to me. Some sort of a mutation must have taken place."

"My thoughts, exactly," agreed Cilix. "Where are we to get the equipment that you need?"

"Okay, wait a minute, first things first," I said, sitting up in bed, amazed at how well I felt. "The tests can wait a while. Whatever is happening to me, there's not much that I can do about it. But I can do something about the Shahin being after us." I looked at them both, thinking that a short while ago I didn't even know them. Now Jil and I were bound to each other inseparably and Cilix had proven himself a true friend. In a way, it was worth going through all this for such love and friendship. But I wouldn't want to do it again, not for anyone or anything.

"We've got to get off-planet," I said. "The longer we stay here, the greater the danger of our being found. Cilix, they know about Jil, but you're not even involved with me, so far as the Shahin are concerned."

"I am involved with you so far as *I* am concerned," he said.

"I don't understand," said Jil. "Why must we run? Can't we just explain to the Shahin that the surrogate is dead?"

I found myself chuckling. "Have you ever tried explaining *anything* to one of them?"

"Alan is right, Jil," said Cilix. "It would be pointless. To a Shahin, only the judgment of another Shahin has any real value. They regard all other races as inferiors. They have been forced to compromise somewhat by taking others into their service as mercenaries, something which they regard as an economic convenience. Yet this has resulted in their becoming even more prej-

udicial toward those not of their kind. Even if we could convince
them that the surrogate was destroyed, Hhargoth would still order
Alan killed for what he's done, even though Alan meant no harm.
No, there is no possibility of our coming to any kind of terms
with them."

"You speak as though you really know them," I observed.

"I served with them once," he answered.

"You were a mercenary?" Jil asked, amazed. "*You*?"

"The subject is closed," he said in a tone that indicated he was
not proud of it.

"I have no love for them myself," I said. "But Hhargoth knew
about the surrogate. He recognized the signs immediately, and he
was fully aware of just how dangerous it was. That really bothers
me. He knew all about a creature that few people have even heard
of, a creature from a quarantined world. And the surrogate knew
enough about the Shahin to know that if anyone would not respect
the quarantine, they wouldn't"

"You think the creatures want to break the quarantine?" asked
Cilix. "You believe it was a plan? That they are that sophisticated?"

"Yes. To all three questions. Cilix, that thing was using me.
Not just for sustenance, but using me, like a . . . a stepping stone
of some sort. From John, to me, to a Shahin . . . there was *reasoning* there. Those creatures are dangerous, and the fact that they
are sentient makes the danger even greater. The Shahin know
about them, *all* about them, I'm sure of it. And yet they've said
nothing. They've told no one. Why? What's in it for them?"

Cilix sat very still, staring at me with his unblinking gaze.
"I see," he said. "There must be some profit in it for them, that
is their constant motivation. They have been to Xerxes V before."

"Why would they go to a quarantined world?" asked Jil. "Why
would they expose themselves to danger needlessly?"

"The Shahin are a suspicious people," Cilix answered. "If I
were to quarantine a world, they would want to know why. If I
were to tell them it was dangerous, they would demand to know
how and in what way. And if I were to answer that, they would
feel it necessary to find out for themselves. I might be lying. I
might be keeping them away for a reason. There might be something there I don't want anyone else to have. That is how they
would think, for that is what they, themselves, would do."

"Or have done," I added.

"I understand," said Jil. "Hhargoth knew you were possessed by a surrogate because he's seen it before. The Shahin have been attacked by the lizards before, yet they keep it quiet because they have discovered something on Xerxes V that they want." She shook her head in disbelief. "It's incredible," she said. "What could possibly be there, what could be so valuable to them that they could justify the risk of. . . . It's horrid!"

"That's got to be it," I said. "And they're not stupid. By now, they know that if I'm still alive I must have figured it out for myself. The only way they're going to stop looking for me now is if they think I'm dead."

"Because as long as you're alive, there's not only the threat of the lizard, which is still in possession of you so far as they know, but there is also the added threat that you'll discover they were hiding something. And you will tell someone else, as you have told us. And eventually, someone will find out just what it is they're trying to hide," Cilix nodded solemnly.

"Which is precisely what I intend to do, " I said. "I'm going to find out what they're trying to hide and I'm damn well going to find out what's happening to me. And before we leave here, there are several things we've got to do. It'll be risky, but this is a big city. The Shahin might have a lot of pull here, but they don't own the place. Jil, I want you to do some research for me. Find out everything you can about Xerxes V, see if there are any records, documents, anything. I want to know as much as possible about that first Terran mission there. Who was the officer who issued the quarantine order? Have the computers run a scan on surrogates, lizards, Shahin, Xerxes, anything you can think of that might relate to what's happening to me. Check medical records concerning mutations of the blood and spontaneous remissions, anything that pops into your mind.

"Cilix, try to find out if there are any other spacers currently in Port City who have served with the Shahin at one time or another. Use any kind of dodge that you can think of, but be discreet. We'll all meet here tonight. Be careful, okay?"

"You can't be thinking of going out yourself!" protested Jil. "You've been very ill. You're not strong enough. . . ."

"I'll be fine, Jil. If you really want to help me, be as thorough as you can down at the library and keep out of sight of any Shahin."

"What will you do?"

"I'm going to pay a call on someone who seems to know more about surrogates than any of us. The one who started all this. He won't like it very much, but Anthrus is going to have to answer some questions."

The commune was a shambles.

Anthrus lay, bleeding, on the floor. He had been beaten to a pulp. At first I thought he was dead, but then I saw that he was breathing. How long he would continue to breathe was a question that was purely academic. I could tell that he was dying. I felt it.

"Anthrus," I kneeled beside him.

He moaned softly. His claws grasped weakly at the floor. His fragile Cetian bones had been shattered. Blood was everywhere. It was obvious that he had been lying there that way for quite some time.

"Anthrus, it's Alan. Can you hear me?"

He coughed weakly, and I had the strangest feeling. It was almost as if I could experience the feeling of my ribs poking through my lungs. There was no pain, but . . . an awareness.

"Anthrus! What happened? Who did this to you?"

He coughed again. He lifted his head slightly and looked at me, his eyes unfocused. I could tell he couldn't recognize me. His face was a sheer ruin. Whoever did this to him must have been a sadist, a psychotic.

"Anthrus, talk to me. Tell me, where's Irina?"

He whispered something barely audible. It sounded like, "With him."

"*Who*, Anthrus? Who did this?"

He was sinking fast. His eyes were glazed and he was having difficulty breathing. Red foam flecked his lips and there was a rattle in his chest.

"L-Looking for Alan . . . ," he wheezed.

"This *is* Alan, Anthrus. *Who* was looking for me? Was it the Shahin?"

"Terran . . . ," he whispered. I could barely hear him.

"A *Terran*? Are you sure?"

"Terran . . . l-looking for Alan . . . I didn't know . . . didn't know. . . ."

His eyes closed and I could feel that I was losing him. I reached out and shook him. It was like shaking a bag of bones. Everything seemed disjointed. "Anthrus!" He winced with pain and opened his eyes again.

"Dying . . ."

"Yes, Anthrus. You're dying."

For a moment his eyes seemed to focus, and I saw a look of recognition there.

"Alan?"

"Yes, Anthrus, it's Alan."

"L-look different . . . better. . . ."

"Yes, I'm better. The surrogate is gone."

"Gone?"

"Gone."

He reached out to me and I picked his head up gently, cradling it in my lap. "Both . . . dying," he whispered.

"Maybe."

He nodded. "Dying. Radu said. . . ."

I seized on it. "Who's Radu, Anthrus? Who's Radu? Was he the one that did this to you? Is he the one who's got Irina? Answer me, Anthrus!"

Anthrus coughed again. The rasping was becoming a death rattle. And then, amazingly, he smiled. "Strange . . . ," he said. "Ironic. . . ." His voice almost completely went away. "This time," he whispered, "you are . . . picking . . . me . . . up from the . . . floor." He actually chuckled.

"Anthrus, *please,* snap out of it! You've got to tell me, who is Radu? Is he the Terran? Did he do this?"

He opened his mouth and tried to speak, but no words came out. He gasped for air and a horrible sound came from his throat. I felt like choking, my own throat muscles involuntarily constricted.

"*Anthrus!*"

And suddenly I was holding a lifeless lump of battered flesh. It was over. He had escaped his pain. A Terran had done this to him. A tall, blonde, muscular Terran. And a man named Radu. A spacer. He had told Anthrus about the surrogates.

I froze.

How did I know that? How did I know that the Terran and Radu were two different men? How did I know that one was tall, blonde, and muscular while the other was a spacer? Anthrus had never answered my last question. He hadn't said a thing! I tried to concentrate and found that I could "recall" what the Terran looked like though I had never seen him. He was, indeed, tall and blonde with a muscular body. He had a hard, ruthless face with thin lips and a sharp, slightly hooked nose. His eyes were blue. He looked as if he had been beaten recently.

What was this? What was happening? I felt suddenly weak. Confused. Was this some sort of side effect of possession by a surrogate? Had I retained something of its empathic powers? Telepathy! But, no, that couldn't be. Anthrus was dead. You don't receive telepathic messages from dead men: human, Cetian, or otherwise. It just doesn't happen that way. Yet I could suddenly remember exactly what he had looked like, this psychotic Terran. And he had been looking for me. A mercenary in the pay of the Shahin? It was possible. I could think of no other explanation.

I sat there, Anthrus cradled in my lap. What had happened here? I tried to concentrate again, tried to remember. I shut my eyes.

It came in flashes. Yuri, answering the door... Yuri! I had forgotten all about her! Bits and pieces, unconnected, memories like dreams that seemed to dance just out of reach the moment that I tried to grasp them. Irina, screaming.... Anthrus, being struck repeatedly....

I remembered what it felt like. I shook my head to clear it. I didn't want to see if I could recall what it felt like for Anthrus to die. I wasn't ready for that. I wasn't even ready for what had already happened!

The surrogate had said that it had a way of "sensing truth." I thought back to the visions it had given me. The images of Xerxes V and the Zharii. I had been sharing its memories. And just now I had shared with Anthrus what had happened to him. After he had died. The memories did not come to me until after he had died. That was not telepathy. It acted like telepathy, and yet it wasn't. And the lizard, speaking through John, had denied having any telepathic powers.

"Let's just say I have a way of sensing the truth."

And now, whatever it was, I seemed to have it too. Only, what was *it*? How did *it* work? Most important, would I be able to control *it*?

Anthrus had said that we were both dying. That had been my

belief as well. Yet I felt strong. And my body had healed with amazing rapidity. It didn't make sense. Something didn't gel. Anthrus had been my only source of information regarding the surrogates. And now it seemed that he might well have been wrong. Or misinformed. I had to find out who Radu was. I had to find out for certain what was happening to me. And if I would survive it.

There was one other problem. Both Yuri and Irina were gone. The man who had killed Anthrus had Irina, possibly Yuri as well. There was no telling what he would do to them. I owed Irina nothing, certainly. But Yuri was completely blameless. Whatever was happening to them now was happening on my account.

It would soon be dark. Jil and Cilix would be waiting. I gently lowered Anthrus' head down to the floor and left. I didn't like Anthrus, but it was the first time anyone had died because of me. And, strangely, I seemed to understand him now.

There was a surprise waiting for me when I returned. Yuri was there. Jil was trying to comfort her, Cilix had not yet returned. My first thought was that Yuri had been followed, and I had a spasm of panic. But if that were true, it was probably too late and there was little I could do about it if anything. Yuri looked up at me, fear in her eyes. Jil visibly relaxed.

"I thought you'd walk right into it," she said.

I shook my head. "No, he was already gone when I arrived." I looked at Yuri. "Anthrus is dead."

She had been prepared for it. She nodded silently. I could see she had been crying. "And Irina?"

"She wasn't there. Anthrus said she was with *him*. What happened, Yuri? Anthrus . . . couldn't tell me very much."

It began happening again, even as she was telling me, haltingly, how the mercenary had come seeking information. I started to remember it all as if it had happened to me.

The Shahin had come to them before seeking me, so they had known I was a fugitive although they weren't sure why. The Shahin had told them I deserted after signing one of their service contracts. Anthrus had readily agreed that such might have been the case. He had told them that I had a surrogate, and they had been very surprised that he had known. Obviously they had known themselves, but thought that I had kept it a secret. Cilix was not co-operative, refusing to answer their questions. After all, they were not police and, as such, had no authority. Yuri also had said nothing. Irina, bless her heart, told them exactly what she thought of me and what they could do with me once I was found. And Anthrus was his usual charming self, glib as always, promising to let them know if I ever showed my face around there again. They had seemed satisfied and they left. But something must have happened to change their minds.

The next time, earlier today, in the morning, the Shahin had sent a Terran mercenary. I saw him a little differently this time. As Yuri spoke, I did not recall his face as vividly. She had opened the door and he came rushing in, slapping her out of his way. He went straight for Anthrus, knocking him down as he was rising from his chair. He asked one question and one question only "Where is Alan Dreyfus?" He kept on asking it, violently. Irina tried to stab him with her kinjhal, but he disarmed her easily, knocking her unconscious in the process. Yuri had panicked. She fled. He didn't even bother trying to stop her.

The Shahin had made an error. For some reason, they had decided that Anthrus and I were closely linked and that he was hiding me or at least knew where I was. The truth was as close as Yuri, only the mercenary ignored her, thinking her insignificant. But if Yuri was insignificant to them, Irina certainly wasn't. Irina herself was the reason. There was something about a knife-wielding woman that would appeal to such a man.

"What happens now?" asked Jil.

"We wait for Cilix to return. As for Irina, well, forgive my lack of gallantry, but I'm not about to offer to surrender myself in exchange for her safety. She's vicious and she tried to kill me once and I have no doubt she'd try again if she had the chance. Besides, I rather doubt the mercenary would let her go. They sound like they were made for each other."

Yuri didn't say anything. Jil looked at me sadly. She sighed and her ears drooped slightly. She seemed to shrink into herself.

"You've become very bitter," she said. "Or perhaps you're just trying to convince yourself that you are. A lot has happened to us in a very short time. I never dreamed that anything like this would ever happen to me. I never thought that I would be hearing myself saying this, but in real life, I suppose, there is no nobility in gallantry. Only death. If you offered yourself in exchange for

Irina, they would only kill you. And they would probably do whatever they wanted to with her anyway. I feel sorry for Irina, but I would rather have you safe."

There was, of course, nothing else to do. I never liked Anthrus. And Irina, well, she gave me an attack of lust such as I'd never had before or since. She was an animal—beautiful, but deadly. And she would have used me and thrown me aside when first we met. Later, she tried to kill me and, given a chance now, she'd sell me out in a second. I didn't have anything to feel guilty about. So where was the bad taste in my mouth coming from?

When Cilix arrived, we all compared notes. Jil had been thorough in her research. She had brought back a great deal of information concerning the Shahin. Information, of course, that the Shahin did not mind others having. Still, it could prove useful. There was nothing in the banks that related to surrogate lizards. Officially they did not exist.

But the most interesting piece of information was actually non-information. There was data in the banks concerning Xerxes V. Only it was classified. Jil had found the name of the ship that made the voyage. I had told her, having learned from the surrogate, that the first ones to land there had been Terrans, so she went through every likely ship of Terran registry, both past and present, scanning their logs. It was a mammoth task and, even with the library computer, it had taken her all day. But she finally found what she was looking for. The *Iron Dream*, under the command of Captain Andrick Dios, was the first ship to visit Xerxes V.

"And the log readouts on *that* particular voyage were—"

"Classified," said Jil. "Any reference to Xerxes V was simply marked, 'Quarantined, Information Classifed.' It's in there somewhere, but we'll never get it out without the proper code."

"At least we have something to go on," I said. "We've got the name of the ship and of her captain. Thanks, Jil. You've done well. Cilix?"

"I have spent the day listening to scuttlebutt," he said "I was able to learn of only three spacers, besides myself, currently in the city who have served with the Shahin. There may be more and probably are, for all I know, but three I know for certain. One is Xanfru, a Cetian. No one has seen him recently, but it is doubtful that he has shipped out since he is a cripple. Another is a Terran named Creed Steiger. He was seen to take part in a rather violent altercation with a Shahin bondwarrior, a *xothol*. Doubtless he is no friend of the Shahin, although he has evidently been in their service for quite some time. The last is also a Terran, Radu Zoltek. Word has it that—"

"*What did you say?*"

"The third man is also a Terran, named Radu Zoltek. Why? Does that mean anything to you?"

"Anthrus said something about a man named Radu before he died."

"He must be the one who killed him!" Jil exclaimed.

"No," I said, not wanting to explain how I knew, not yet. "No, he's not the one. Anthrus mentioned his name in connection with the surrogates. I believe he first learned of them from this Radu. Either that, or he first saw John and then went to this Radu Zoltek for further information. He never mentioned his name to any of you?"

They all shook their heads.

"Radu Zoltek's description does not fit that of the man who killed Anthrus," said Cilix. "Zoltek is said to be a half-crazed old man. Not at all like the man you said you saw," he turned to Yuri.

"What about that other one?" I asked. "The one who had the fight with a Shahin. That, in itself, sounds suicidal. Humans are no match for Shahin, not physically, anyway."

"Creed Steiger," said Cilix. "It's true that the fight was one-sided, but I am told he gave a good accounting of himself just the same. The combat was unarmed, even though both were armed with Shahin thermal weapons."

"*Both* of them?"

"I thought of that too," said Cilix.

"The Shahin don't let you keep their weapons if you leave their service."

"Perhaps this man's having the weapon was the issue," suggested Cilix.

"Then why didn't the Shahin simply kill him? I don't understand. There is no honor for a Shahin bondwarrior in engaging in unarmed combat with a human. It would be like fighting a child."

"I was unable to establish all the facts," said Cilix. "However, the Shahin *xothol* was seen to carry this Steiger from the premises."

"And he wasn't dead?"

"No," replied Cilix. "Which suggests to me that the *xothol* needed him for something. Do you agree?"

"Creed Steiger," I said, sounding out the name slowly. "Creed Steiger. What does he look like?"

"Tall, well-built, blonde. A hook-shaped nose, blue eyes—"

"*That's him!*" said Yuri.

"We're making progress," I said. "The next step is to find this Radu Zoltek. Find out what he knows and get off-planet fast."

"We can make further progress without even leaving this room," said Cilix.

"What?"

"We have to find out what changes are taking place within your body," he said. He picked up his satchel and removed a black case from it. "I trust you know how to use this," he said, "or I stole it for nothing."

"A medipak! Cilix, you're a genius!"

"No, I am a thief. Since I've met you, Alan, I have been growing more and more disreputable. I certainly hope you appreciate it."

"Oh, I appreciate it, all right. Everything's here. Enough to perform minor surgery. I'll need your help, Cilix. Radu Zoltek's going to have to wait a short while. This should not take long."

It took much longer than I thought it would. Mainly because I kept repeating the tests. The results were undeniable, but I simply couldn't believe what they were telling me.

Yuri, finally overcome with exhaustion, fell asleep. Jil curled up beside her. They both looked so peaceful. It was hard to believe how much they had been through.

"Well?" said Cilix. "What is it? You have repeated all the tests several times. They're inconclusive?"

I sat back, stunned. "They're conclusive. You were right from the very beginning."

"I was right about what? I do not remember."

"You said, when I thought that I was dying, that I might live a lot longer than I thought I would. You probably had no idea just how literally right you were."

"I meant that your body was healing, not decaying as you seemed to think."

"I know. I thought that I might have mutated somehow, or that some sort of virus or fungus was taking over, but it wasn't any of those things. I still don't know the entire answer. There are things happening to me I simply can't test because there are no existing tests for them. Something is happening to my mind. It's almost . . . *meta*physical. I seem to be growing more and more sensitive to other people."

I told him about the strange "memory" phenomenon, the almost telepathic relationship that seemed to spring up from time to time, coming and going, without my being able to exercise any control over it.

"Sometimes," I told him, "when I feel it happening, I can intensify the experience by concentrating on it, but I can't seem to consciously bring it on."

"John was like that, sometimes," said Cilix. "Only he had the surrogate. Without it, when he was not directly under its influence, he was no different from any other . . . derelict."

"That's what I can't figure out. With the lizard, I had similar flashes of cognizance. But now that it's gone, it would seem logical for the sensitivity to be gone as well. If it were a lingering side effect, it would logically decrease, Instead, it's increasing. I just don't know what's happening."

"But you said the tests were conclusive."

"As far as what's happening to me medically, from the point of view of known science, yes they were. Remember, just now I said that you were right to think that I would live longer than I thought? Well, I'm probably going to wind up living longer than any human being has ever lived before, unless I'm killed first."

"What do you mean?"

"I'm only guessing, since I don't have the remains of the lizard to analyze, but it's pretty foolproof guessing under the circumstances. There's just no other foreign substance except the lizard that's been introduced to my body lately.

"Something in the chemical composition of the lizard must have triggered a reaction in my body. Not a mutation, technically speaking, since it . . . well, it enhanced a latent potential which was already there. Normally, if you cut me, I'll heal eventually, unless the cut is a fatal one. New cells are growing all the time. Except, in my case. I've developed one step further. The reason why I healed so quickly, Cilix, is that I have developed the ability to *regenerate*!

"Epithelial cells regenerate constantly in humans. Muscle tissue regenerates after heavy exercise; it's literally torn apart, only to grow back bigger and stronger. If I started heavy exercising now, there's no telling *how* strong I could become. Imagine the sort of regeneration I'm capable of now, Cilix. I could build an entirely new body for myself. *I'm already growing a new arm!*"

"Are you certain? There's no mistake?"

"Why do you think I double-checked and triple-checked and quadruple-checked everything? I couldn't believe it either!"

It would not be very long before I had my arm back again. No, not my old arm, a new one. Stronger. How long would it take? Two months, perhaps? Less? And if I started training, say, with heavy weights, was there a limit to the growth I could achieve? Given enough time, it was quite possible that I could even match a Shahin's strength. No wonder they were so anxious to find me.

"Cilix, my friend, I believe we've stumbled on the Shahin secret."

He nodded. "I believe you're right," he said. "An awesome secret, indeed. They will have to kill all of us now."

Chapter Three

I had come full circle.

During my first month in Port City, I must have made the rounds of every bar and sex emporium on the lower west side, stimulating some parts of my body and numbing others. Now I was doing it again, only this time, it was different. I was looking for a man. A half-crazed old man named Radu Zoltek. And, at the same time, I knew I was being hunted. By the Shahin and by a renegade of my own species, a killer named Creed Steiger.

We stayed together, Cilix, Yuri, Jil, and I. It was, perhaps, not the safest thing to do, but we didn't want to take a chance on being separated. Two of our number had already fallen to the enemy. Together, we felt more secure. Yuri, especially, was afraid to be left alone and she was concerned for Cilix. Jil flatly refused to sit and wait for word of our progress, not knowing where we were or what was happening. I had made a token effort at convincing them all to remain behind, but I was just as happy having them all with me. There was strength in our unity.

We drifted in and out of little hell holes, places where most spacers carried weapons. We had none. But all of us were becoming adept at surviving. And the trouble with carrying a weapon is that it's easy to succumb to the temptation to use it. On several occasions, Jil and Yuri were accosted. Once or twice, things had come dangerously close to disintegrating into violence, but we had been lucky. I saw my "former life" from a new perspective. It seemed hard for me to believe that there was a time, not so very long ago, when I actually used to enjoy frequenting such places. Now, my nerves were constantly on edge and I was feeling jumpy. Paranoia had set in; I spent half the time looking over my shoulder. My every instinct screamed at me to give it up, to run away, to get off planet and get as far away as possible from spacers and Shahin alike. But then, I'd never know the truth.

It was difficult at times to keep my mind on the task at hand. At first, I asked all of the questions, buying spacers drinks and drugs, whatever would make them more amenable to conversation. A great many of them needed little or no prodding. I could understand that, being a spacer myself. It can be a lonely, boring way of life. That is why excess is so often a common factor. The profession attracts a certain type of person. The crews are carefully selected, based on experience, health, and extensive psychological profiling. Even with a skill as readily in demand as mine, I was frequently denied a berth because the computer predicted a possibility of conflict between myself and another member of the crew. And, on still other occasions, crew members that already had a berth were grounded because the commander's need for someone with my qualifications was greater than his need for another crew member with whom I possibly would not get along. It was something one simply had to accept. Each crew would be together for a great length of time. They were a family of sorts. Carefully selected to maintain a balance.

I should have been completely in my element. I knew these people and understood them. But I wasn't quite the same any longer, and they sensed it.

My mind would wander.

It was difficult to concentrate. My sensitivity seemed to be constantly increasing. My vision was becoming more acute, as was my sense of hearing and my sense of smell.

I noticed virtually everything. The whorling patterns created in the room by the thick, narcotic smoke. The dust particles float-ing in the air. The shimmering beads of moisture on the glasses, discolorations in the surface of the bar. I found myself focusing on details in faces, on snatches of conversation picked up from across the room, on the garish interplay of holojuke projections, on the acrid odors all around me. It was like being trapped in a sensorium, assailed by a myriad of tactile experiences, adrift in sound and taste and sight. I would discover myself drifing off, no longer paying attention to whomever I was speaking to; instead, I was intent on something else which had attracted my attention.

At such times, I would often be brought back by someone touching me or repeating something if they realized I wasn't really with them anymore.

Jil was the first to notice my apparent distraction.

"Alan, are you all right?"

"What?"

"Are you all right? Is something wrong?"

"Oh, yes, I mean, no, nothing's wrong. I think. I don't know."

"Is something happening to you again?" asked Cilix.

"I'm not sure. I just can't seem to keep my mind from wan-dering."

I was looking at the most ordinary things as if I had never seen them before. Jokingly, Yuri suggested that perhaps I was undergo-ing male menopause. The least little thing would set me off. I alternated between irritability and complacency. One moment, I was full of energy, bursting with vitality and speeding as if on an amphetamine high, the next, withdrawn, silent, contemplative, feeling a profound exhaustion.

In one such fit of detachment, I caused a disastrous confron-tation.

I was asking a young spacer about Radu Zoltek, trying to establish if he had ever frequented that bar. The young man had been unable to supply me with any information, but he had launched into a long polemic concerning the relative merits of different sexual fetishes. Such conversational segues, total non sequiturs, occur frequently in such places. The man was prob-ably a sadist of some sort, and my contact with him revolted me. I simply withdrew, focusing all my attention on a disfunc-tioning serving unit. Idly, I speculated on what might be the matter with it.

"Hey!" The young spacer grabbed me roughly by my arm. "I'm *talking* to you!"

"Oh, I'm sorry, what did you say?"

"You weren't even listening!"

"Yes. I mean, no, I realize I wasn't, I was...distracted."

"Distracted, hell, you were asleep! I don't like it when people don't pay attention to me, I take it personally, you know?" He kept jerking my arm.

"There's no need to feel that way; it's nothing against you really. I'm just a little tired, that's all. I've been sick, that's all."

"Yeah? Well, you're going to feel a lot sicker in a second. What are you on, anyway?"

"I'm sorry?"

"You look like a floater to me. I can't *stand* floaters. It's a disgusting habit." He grabbed me by the shirt.

"Take your hand off me, please. I'm not a floater. I assure you, I'm not taking any drugs...."

He shoved me roughly and I fell off my chair onto the floor.

Jil was between us instantly. "Leave him alone," she said. "Can't you see the man's a cripple?"

"Well, what have we here?" The spacer's voice oozed contempt. He reached out and snared Jil by her waist. "I've never had a feline female. I'll bet that fur feels soft as silk."

"Let me go," she said. I started to get up, but he lashed out with his foot and caught me in the chin. I fell back down, tasting blood. It had grown quieter inside the bar as all eyes watched to see what would develop. The spacer tried to kiss Jil, but she twisted away from him.

"Leave her alone," said Cilix.

With his free hand, the spacer grabbed up a bottle and flung it at him. It caught Cilix in the head and he fell down. I was halfway up by that time, but he booted me in the chest and then placed his foot across my throat, all the while holding a squirming Jil tightly with one arm. Her own arms were pinned in his grasp and she struggled uselessly against him. He slowly increased pressure with his foot as I tried vainly to dislodge it with my one hand. He clearly meant to kill me. Slowly.

"Let him up or die," a strange voice said. I couldn't see who it was from where I lay. There was a second's hesitation, then the foot was removed from my throat. I coughed and started trying to get up.

"You stay out of this," the spacer said to the stranger.

"Let the feline go, as well."

"This isn't your conc—"

"I'll kill you, Stanzki." Said with a perfectly controlled, even voice.

The spacer let Jil go. She moved instantly to my side and helped me up.

"I'll get you for this," the spacer hissed, and I saw for the first time who our rescuer was. A cripple. Like myself. Only this man had no legs. He sat in a Mali chair, hovering several feet away from us. He was very slight, a Cetian, as Anthrus was. In his right hand, he held a thermal gun—a Shahin sidearm. Yuri stood nearby, a broken bottle in her hand, uncertain what to do.

"Get out," the Cetian said.

Stanzki hesitated, then moved towards the exit. The Cetian rotated his chair, keeping the spacer covered every step of the way. Scowling, Stanzki stepped outside. The Cetian didn't move, keeping his back to us.

"I'd like to thank you . . ." I began. Suddenly, the portal opened and Stanzki stood there, a stinger pistol in his hand. He never had a chance to fire. The Cetian's eyes had never left the exit. He was prepared. He incinerated Stanzki where he stood.

The chair flashed around and the Cetian covered the bar with his weapon. "Anyone object?"

No one spoke. Then someone laughed and gradually the noise in the bar resumed its former level. Only then did the Cetian lower the gun. "Are you injured?" he inquired.

"No. No, I'm all right, thanks to you, friend. You saved my life. And my friends' as well."

"We crips have to stick together," he grinned. "Come on, let's have a drink." His chair revolved and floated off towards an empty table. We followed.

We sat and the Cetian's chair sank to the floor. Jil looked none the worse for wear, but Cilix was going to have a big bump on his forehead. A serving unit, the half-broken one, came over and the Cetian ordered a a cold pitcher of *baharri*. My mind was on that gun of his.

"How did you lose your arm?" he said.

I hesitated. Jil glanced at me apprehensively. "I don't really like to talk about it," I replied.

The Cetian laid the thermal gun on the table. "Wasn't one of these, by any chance, was it?"

It began to happen once again. I knew that I could trust him. He knew who I was, but he wouldn't turn me in. His name was Xanfru. He was a mercenary who had served with the Shahin. He still did—in a clerical capacity.

"Yes," I said. "It was one of those. As you obviously knew."

He nodded. "You're Alan Dreyfus. And the feline must be Jil. I fear I do not know the others."

I saw the alarm on their faces and I hurried to reassure them. "It's all right," I told them. "We have nothing to fear from him." I introduced Yuri and Cilix.

He nodded at them. "My name is Xanfru," he said. They recognized the name. He was the one Cilix had mentioned earlier. They masked their recognition well, however. We were learning. "You're right, Alan. You have nothing to fear from me. Although I'm curious how you knew that."

"I don't know," I lied. "You saved our lives. Somehow, I just feel that I can trust you."

"I don't really think you're that naive," he said, "but never mind. It's not important. What *is* important is that the Shahin want you dead. Perhaps you'll tell me why?"

"You don't know?"

He shook his head. "I'm not testing you, I really don't. You must know that they're looking for you. Hhargoth ordered your capture. You are officially listed as a deserter. That order was recently rescinded. You are now to be killed on sight. And anyone with you as well. I'm not certain how they intend to justify that, but that will be a purely administrative problem. To be taken care of after the fact."

I looked at Cilix. "You were right. You're all in danger now because of me. I didn't think they'd go so far."

"You do not know them very well, I see," said Xanfru.

"I don't understand," said Yuri. "Why should you care, one way or another? You're one of them, aren't you?"

"I make my living from them," replied Xanfru. "But I don't owe the Shahin anything. Because of them, I lost my legs. Fortunately, whatever else their faults are, the Shahin have a concept of honor and duty. Of obligation. I saved an officer's life once and the result was this..." he gestured to where his legs should have been. "They felt that they owed me something for that act of sheer stupidity on my part. I agreed. I was retained for clerical duty. It's all I have now. A cripple is not much use as a spacer. But I'm not one of them, girl. I'm not *that* crippled."

"I'm sorry."

"Don't be. I don't want pity and it was a reasonable question." He turned to me. "And you still haven't answered mine."

I told him everything. What had happened, what I knew, what I suspected, and what I hoped to learn. He listened carefully. When I finished, he remained silent for a long moment.

"You do not seem to be a fool, Dreyfus," he said, "but if what you say is true, you have to be a lunatic. The information you have given me is enough to initiate a mercantile court of inquiry. The Shahin will stop at nothing to destroy you in order to prevent that. But you've stayed planet-bound. Why?"

"There's still one thing I have to do," I told him. "I have to find a spacer by the name of Radu Zoltek."

"I know him," Xanfru said. "He is half insane, a flamer. What could you possibly want with him?"

I told him about Anthrus. "He was a Cetian, like yourself. But there, the similarity ended. It was through him that I met John. Whatever information he had concerning surrogates, Anthrus got from Radu Zoltek. Zoltek was *there*. He can tell me about Xerxes V."

Xanfru looked thoughtful. "I do not understand why the Shahin would allow a human to set foot on Xerxes V if your guess is correct. It would compromise them. The secret could get out. I will have to see what I can learn of this."

"Xanfru," said Jil, "you've already done enough for us. Please, do not expose yourself to further danger on our account."

He smiled wistfully. "My motives are not completely selfless." He glanced down at his chair. "If there is just the smallest chance that I could grow my legs back, the risk to me is justified."

"You know Zoltek," I said. "Where can I find him?"

Xanfru shook his head. "You will not. I now have a vested interest in your cause. If there is a chance that ingesting a surrogate lizard will affect me as it did you, I won't allow you to jeopardize your own safety. *I* will find Zoltek and bring him to you. You may stay in my quarters. They are somewhat cramped, unfortunately, but the Shahin would never think to look for you there. They have passed the word about you, Dreyfus. I recognized you from their description. It would only be a matter of time before someone else did too. Someone not as readily sympathetic as one cripple to another."

"You're right," I said. "And I don't want to endanger my friends. I've caused them enough grief already. There is one more thing, however, something that I have to warn you about. The Shahin have employed a Terran mercenary to find me. You should watch for him, he's highly dangerous, a killer."

Xanfru frowned. "That would be Lokhrim's doing. Hhargoth despises Terrans. He doesn't trust them. Thinks they are inferior. Lokhrim is the one who communicated the order to kill you on sight. He has good cause to seek your death. Because of you, he lost his lieutenancy. Hhargoth reduced him to the rank of *xothol*, bondwarrior. He was disgraced. Do you have any idea who this mercenary is? Perhaps I know of him."

"His name is Creed Steiger," said Cilix. "He has already murdered Anthrus and abducted Irina. He is blond, he—"

"I know Creed Steiger," Xanfru said. He exhaled heavily. "He is an animal. He is also a fine soldier."

Xanfru's quarters were, indeed, cramped. But they were not uncomfortable. There was a military sense of order in the small compartment. Mementos of Xanfru's career as a mercenary spacer were everywhere. A small glass case contained his decorations. It was difficult to think of the fragile, courtly Cetian as a soldier, but then I had seen the way he dealt with Stanzki.

He apologized for the spare accommodations and the lack of food, but he served us a vintage Abraxan brandy from a bottle that he must have been hoarding for years. I protested, knowing full well the value of the brandy, but he wouldn't hear of it. He said that it was rare for him to entertain guests, and he insisted that we drink a toast to his walking again someday.

We drank. "Tell me about Steiger," I said.

"There's a great deal to tell." I noticed that he had developed the mannerism of rotating his chair slightly as he spoke. "We both served aboard the Terran Guildship *Triton* many years ago. I held the rank of corporal, and he was an enlisted man even though he was senior to me in terms of service. I had heard that he went to the academy on Dyson, which meant that he should have been an officer. I never did find out what happened, but I knew that Steiger hated officers with a passion. He was often insubordinate, but he got away with it because, for one thing, he was a brilliant soldier. Also one of the finest systems specialists I had ever seen. I suspect he has a doctorate in computer science and probably one in military science as well, though I was never able to confirm that. I suppose it would be a simple matter to look up his records, but I hesitated to offend him. That was the other reason his frequent insubordination did not result in his court martial. He was feared by officers and noncommissioned officers alike.

"As for the enlisted men, he was their champion. They would listen to him before they followed an officer's orders. Our commander was a flexible man. He had come up through the ranks and he believed in leadership by example and respect. A man like Creed Steiger can be an asset if you know how to handle him. The trouble started when the *Triton* got a new commander.

"He was a young captain about Steiger's age. He had his own ideas about how a ship should be run. By the book. The academy way. Spit and polish. He was, as the old Terran expression goes, a 'military asshole'. He brought his own executive officer with him. Rumor had it they were lovers. The exec was of the same temperament. A young lieutenant on the crew soon perceived their susceptibility to sycophancy and the three of them formed their own little clique. The lieutenant was quick to point out to them that Steiger was a nonconformist, a troublemaker.

"Steiger had nothing but disgust for the three of them, but he acted shrewdly, never giving them the chance to make an example of him. He managed to find a way to go over their heads and request a transfer. Had it gone through, there's no telling what he would be doing today. Perhaps he would not be a mercenary, but I somehow doubt that. It seemed to be his destiny.

"We were ordered to Ixanthi to put down a guerilla war being waged against the braxite miners. Ironically, the Shahin were behind that. Their intent was wage a limited jungle war against the miners and force them to forsake their claim, thereby leaving the territory open for them to move in. Ultimately, they succeeded.

"The assignment meant combat duty, something which Steiger thrived upon. He was a veteran. But, as for the three officers, it was to be their first combat assignment. It proved to be a disaster.

"If they had their way, they would have defoliated half the planet. Fortunately, their orders were specific on that count. It was to be a land war, nothing else. If the Shahin gave them provocation in space it would have been another matter, naturally, but the Shahin are not fools.

"Steiger fought brilliantly. Loving every moment of it. With more men such as Steiger, we could have driven out the Shahin's mercenaries in a month or two. But never were there three officers more ill suited to command. Because of their incredible incompetence, sixty-seven men were killed, literally sacrificed in a strategic ploy that backfired. Steiger was one of a handful of survivors.

"The only reason there *was* a handful of survivors was that Steiger disobeyed orders. No one in his right mind would have blamed him for disobeying. But the triumvirate needed a scapegoat and Steiger was elected."

"He was court martialed," I said.

"No," said Xanfru. "He killed all three of them."

"The man has to be a maniac," said Cilix.

"He has been called that," Xanfru said. "Not by me. There are a lot of things that I could call him, that would not be one of them. He was pushed too far. Certainly a court martial would not have meant the end of his career, although there would have been serious repercussions. The threat of court martial, I believe, had nothing to do with his killing those three officers. Steiger simply felt that they deserved to die for what they did. He passed judgment and executed the sentence. After that, he went over to the Shahin, who may not like Terrans, but they could appreciate a man of his talents. And afford him some protection. There are no extradition agreements between the Shahin and anyone else. It would seriously hamper their ability to draw on the mercenary pool. Needless to say, if he ever leaves their service, Steiger will become, as you would say, open game. And obviously he can never return to Earth."

"You make him sound like an innocent victim," said Jil.

"Not at all. I only told you how he came to serve with the Shahin. As I said, it was probably his destiny to wind up a mercenary. Few wars are actually fought anymore. There are some sporadic conflicts here and there, some internecine rivalries, some so-called police actions similar to the one on Ixanthi which I described to you, but Alan can tell you that the day of the soldier of fortune is long gone. Battles are now fought on the political and economic fronts for the most part. Steiger is a misfit. An atavism. A useless weapon in a time of peace, in a manner of speaking. And now you tell me he is an assassin in the pay of the Shahin. I would say that he has finally found his calling."

"You have not seen each other since that time?" asked Cilix.

Xanfru shrugged. "It is a large city. And the Shahin employ many mercenaries. Until you mentioned his name, I did not even know that he was here."

"What was your relationship with him like?" asked Jil.

"We knew each other, but we were not friends. As I said, I have great respect for him as a soldier. Creed Steiger is the sort of man who will always be alone. It is difficult to guess how he might have changed over the years. Certainly it is intriguing to speculate about how he relates to Shahin superiors. But then, if anyone could handle him, Lokhrim would be the one.

"The two of them together make a formidable team. Finding Radu Zoltek should be the very least of your concerns. I can manage that. If I were you, I would give some serious thought to how you are going to manage leaving this world. If *my* task was to hunt you down, the first thing I would do would be to station soldiers at the spaceport. And I am not as resourceful as Creed Steiger. We were seen together. A one-armed man, a Cetian with a thermal gun and no legs, a feline, an Ophidian, and an attractive Terran girl—that does not make for an inconspicuous combination. And Steiger will be thorough in his search. With any luck, he will not learn of our meeting until after you have a chance to speak with Radu and plot your escape."

"And if he does?" asked Cilix.

"If he does, I will simply have to think of a story to tell him."

"Suppose he doesn't believe you?" said Yuri.

"Then I will learn how much value he places on our having once been shipmates."

Creed Steiger was drunk.

The Cetian, Anthrus, had not known where Alan Dreyfus was. Steiger had resorted to beating him only because he felt certain the Cetian knew something. He had judged correctly that the Cetian had no backbone, no stomach for violence. A few well placed blows and he would spill it all. And that was how it started.

Anthrus had sniveled, crawled and begged, all according to Steiger's expectation. The girl had attacked and he had easily disarmed her, knocking her unconscious. He had struck Anthrus a few times only to add to the Cetian's terror. It had worked. Panic-stricken, Anthrus had begun to whine and blubber, promising to tell him everything he knew about Alan Dreyfus. And he had started to do exactly that. He had told him how they met, what sort of man Dreyfus was, how he had tried to take the girl, Irina, away from him. He had started telling him about the former mercenary, John, and the strange lizard called the surrogate. Steiger had listened carefully, inflicting no more harm. But then the girl revived.

She had moaned softly, and she sat up shakily, rubbing her jaw where Creed had struck her. And then she saw Anthrus. Saw him totally humiliated. She looked at him with disgust. . . .

That look was what did it.

How well Steiger understood that look! The Cetian had looked at him defiantly, and he refused to tell him anything more. And Steiger started beating him again.

It was all for nothing. Wasted energy.

With every blow that fell, the Cetian glanced back at the girl to see how she was taking it. And she watched it all, staring, fascinated. It was all a show just for her benefit. It was as if the Cetian took a perverse pride in showing her just how much he could take. What a relationship they must have had! By the time Steiger realized the Cetian knew nothing of Alan Dreyfus' whereabouts, it was too late. By the time Steiger realized that he was being used, a pawn in some insanely masochistic game, Anthrus was as good as dead. His own fists were covered with the Cetian's blood and he knew that Anthrus would not survive the day. The beating that would have hospitalized a human for perhaps a day or two at most was fatal to the fragile Cetian. And the girl had watched it all. Her one attempt at the defense of her mate or lover thwarted, she simply watched, accepting. Her face was calm. Expressionless. But her eyes burned with an unholy fire. The bitch was actually excited by it all.

He had left the limp and battered Cetian on the floor, then he had gone to her. She looked up at him with no expression whatsoever on her features. Then he backhanded her viciously across her mouth. Her face turned under the impact of the blow. When she looked back at him, her expression had not changed. Blood ran from her mouth where her teeth had split her lip. She went with him quite willingly.

His fury mounted on the way back to his quarters. By the time they reached his compartment, he hated her. He did not say a single word to her at all. He didn't even look at her. She simply followed him. And when they were home, she stood before him, shoulders squared, staring at him, challenging him. Her full lips were twisted in a sneer. Daring him. He took her.

She fought back, clawing at him with her long fingernails, biting him, spitting in his face. He raped her brutally. More brutally than he had ever taken any woman. She was a hellcat in his bed, but even as she struck him with her fists, her tongue responded to his kisses, her legs gripped him tightly, her vaginal muscles closing on him like a vise. She thrusted back at him, pulling at his hair, clawing at his back, snarling and, when she came, she screamed.

And when he pulled out of her, drained, she laughed.

Lokhrim stood before the captain in his quarters, irritated that a human was seated in his prescence. Still, it was proper protocol. The *Titus Groan* was, after all, this man's ship. But it galled him, just the same.

"How may I help you, *xothol*?"

The address was formal and the tone was polite, but the executive officer and lieutenant stood behind him at parade rest. Both were armed. Lokhrim had voluntarily surrendered his own sidearm without waiting to be asked when he boarded the lighter that brought him to the ship. He had been careful to learn the correct behavior aboard a Terran Guild vessel and was following it scrupulously. He had learned the Terran way of saluting a superior and the proper forms of address, phrases such as "Permission to come aboard, sir," and so forth. It all seemed like so much pointless ritual to him, but this was a matter of diplomacy. Terrans were said to be touchy about such things. He would show them that a Shahin knew how to comport himself.

"Until recently, a man called Alan Dreyfus was under your command," said Lokhrim.

Captain Seraphim Kovalevski regarded the Shahin coolly. "Are you asking me or telling me?"

Lokhrim masked his annoyance at the human's impertinence.

"It is a matter of record," he said in a carefully neutral tone of voice. "A ship this size would require a complement of many men. It would be presumptuous of me to assume that the commander would know them all by name."

Kovalevski nodded. "Continue, please."

Lokhrim fought to keep his features expressionless. Was there no end to this humiliation?

"Alan Dreyfus applied for service with..." he almost said "the people." He had to be careful not to antagonize the humans. "...The Shahin and was accepted." He saw the look of surprise on the Terran's face. "His current status is that of a deserter. He is wanted for crimes against the Shahin. I have come to ask a courtesy. We believe that he is in hiding. It is possible that he may contact you and attempt to avoid pursuit aboard this ship."

"And you want me to contact you if he does so," Kovalevski said.

"We would be grateful if you would do us this courtesy."

"I see. Will you answer a question for me, *xothol*?"

"Sir?" The word almost stuck in Lokhrim's throat.

"What is the Shahin policy regarding the return of Terran deserters?"

Lokhrim had expected that question. He had asked it himself when Lord Hhargoth instructed him to confer with the commander of the Terran Guild ship. It was a singularly unique case. Unusual and unpleasant; precedents were being set.

"You are aware, of course," Lokhrim replied carefully, "that there are no formal agreements in effect in this regard. In the past, it has been 'Shahin policy' to accept into service any qualified spacer who applied. The judiciary matters of other states and powers are none of our concern. Still, I am certain that Terran authorities would not knowingly aid a criminal. I make no accusations. I merely wish to make my point. You lose nothing by turning a fugitive over to the Shahin and you gain, let us say, diplomatic advantages." Lokhrim finished with a sneer, "And I believe it *is* Terran policy to further the cause of peace?"

Kovalevski lit a cigarette as he considered his reply. It was astonishing what disgusting habits these Terrans cultivated.

Kovalevski nodded slowly, exhaling a thin stream of smoke. "I see your point," he said. "*Touché.*"

"I fear I do not understand the meaning of that word, Captain. If you would be so kind?"

Kovalevski smiled tightly. "As a soldier, you should appreciate that particular expression. It is derived from fencing, a Terran art of swordplay. A primitive art, but it has its own rewards. It means that you have scored a 'touch.' In other words, you gave as well as you received, in a manner of speaking."

Lokhrim was mildly surprised. "A sentiment worthy of a Shahin," he said, then cursed himself as he realized his blunder. The Terran smirked. "I ask your pardon," Lokhrim said, nearly choking on his words. "It would seem that you have scored a 'touch' yourself, Captain. It was not my intention to offend."

"No offense taken, I assure you."

"It is a good expression, this 'touché.' I shall remember it."

"In a way, it relates even more closely to what we are doing at this moment," Kovalevski said. "You and I are engaged in taking each other's measure with verbal swords. There are Terrans who enjoy that sort of thing. I find it tedious. I have a feeling you do too. Please understand that *I* mean no offense when I *also* point out something that is, shall we say, a matter of record?"

"Understood."

"Shahin do not like humans. Humans are not especially fond of the Shahin. In fact, you probably do not relish this present discussion. I find it bearable. Interesting, in point of fact. You have obviously taken some pains to present yourself properly. I respect that. But I see no point to this strained politeness. I prefer to speak my mind plainly. If you would do the same, we could dispense with waste. Feel free to speak bluntly as a Shahin. You obviously have in mind some sort of proposal. Let us get on with it."

Lokhrim met his gaze. The human seemed to be sincere. And Lord Hhargoth *did* instruct him to accommodate the Terrans.

"Very well," Kokhrim said, dropping his deferential tone with relief. "If you wish. I will also speak bluntly. You will stand."

The men behind him shifted suddenly, and Lokhrim tensed, anticipating a reaction. Kovalevski rose to his feet. "Alright," he said. " Anything else?"

"You will extinguish that obscene thing."

One of the men behind him swore. "At ease, Lieutenant," said Kovalevski evenly. He put out the cigarette. "Alright. Consider your own courtesy returned," he said. "Now I have something to say. On my ship, *I* give the orders. Not a Shahin bondwarrior." Lokhrim flinched. "You were ordered to come here. It is not the practice of a Terran commander to deal with messengers. I will make an exception in this case. Any deserter from a Shahin mercenary force is welcome on my ship, providing he submits to scanner interrogation. I don't want scum on my ship. The Shahin have no such compunctions. Am I to believe you are here to offer me some sort of deal?"

Lokhrim fought to control himself. His voice was full of studied calm as he answered.

"Lord Hhargoth has instructed me to say, in whatever terms you find acceptable, that we are particularly anxious that this deserter, Dreyfus, be returned to us. If you do this thing, I am empowered to tell you that the Shahin will consider entering into an agreement of extradition with the Terran government. We will provide your authorities with the names of every Terran currently in our service. From this list of names, you will be allowed to choose ten. These ten will be exchanged for Alan Dreyfus. You will communicate this to your Terran embassy and reply directly to me. You, yourself, will so reply and not a *messenger*." He spat the word out.

"*Jesus* Christ!" said the officer behind him. "*Sir*, are you—"

"One more outburst from you, Lieutenant, and you're grounded. As an enlisted man. Is that clear?"

"Yes, *sir*!"

"You must want Dreyfus very badly, indeed, *xothol*. What has he done?"

"That is none of your concern."

"In that case, you are dismissed."

Lokhrim turned rapidly and strode from the room. The young lieutenant was taken unprepared and did not have time to move aside. Lokhrim swatted him away with a casual sweep of his arm. The lieutenant was thrown in a heap on the deck, staring at Kovalevski with dismay. The executive officer had not moved.

Kovaleski sighed. "Get up, Charlie. And thank you. I appreciate your restraint. If it makes you feel any better, when I was your age, orders or no orders, I would have shot him on the spot."

"I should follow him. . . ."

"No need. The O.D. will see that our 'guest' leaves the ship safely."

"Skipper, you're not going to do what he asked, are you?"

"I have no choice. The formal request concerning an extradition agreement made it official. I'll have to communicate with the embassy. I have no doubt that they'll accept the terms."

The exec spoke for the first time. "I don't believe Alan signed on with the Shahin. It can't be true."

"It has to be," Kovalevski replied. "They wouldn't dare to lie about such a thing. It would be an open and shut case of piracy, a charge the Shahin have carefully skirted."

"Yes, you're right, of course. But I still can't believe it. *Why?* He has a berth here anytime he wants it. He knows that! A Shahin mercenary, for God's sake! I just can't believe it!"

Kovalevski raised his hands and began to massage his temples. "Nor can I, Mustafa. Something must have happened. I'm afraid to even speculate. I will delay my communication to the embassy as long as possible. Mustafa, I am placing you in command of an unofficial landing party. Assemble as many men as we can spare. Find Alan and bring him back here. I'll see what I can do to arrange a berth for him on the first outbound ship."

"Right away."

The two men left together. Kovalevski remained alone in his quarters. He was about to commit his first illegal act in all his years of service. It would certainly mean court martial. And probably the end of his career as a line officer. At the least.

"God *damn* it, Alan," he said softly. "What the hell have you gotten yourself into?"

When Steiger returned, he found Irina lying on his bed, crying.

"What are you still doing here?"

She looked up at him, then sat up in bed, wiping her eyes. "Where would I go?"

"You're unbelievable."

"You took me. Now you take care of me."

"You're crazy."

"Tell me you don't want me."

"I don't. . . ." Even with a tear-streaked face, she was astonishingly beautiful. Her every motion was practiced, calculated to be sensual. It was a reflex with her. He *did* want her. She made him hungry.

"You see?" she said.

"I see that you're going to be a royal pain in my ass," he said. "And probably other places too. I killed your man. Doesn't that bother you at all?"

"Yes."

"And you still want to stay with me?"

"Yes, you need me."

"Wanting you is not the same as needing you."

"That isn't what I meant," she said. "I can help you find Alan Dreyfus. I know him, what sort of man he is. All you have is his name. And a description. I can give you more than that."

"What's in it for you?"

She shrugged. "I have no place to go. The others all left. I'm all alone. And I don't like being alone."

"Why are you willing to sell your friends so cheaply? Did Dreyfus kick you out of bed?"

She stiffened and her eyes gave him all the answer he needed.

Creed laughed. "Boy, have I ever got *your* number! You're one of a kind, you are. A real original. I've met some pretty tough characters in my time, but you've got them all beat, hands down. You're really hard."

She stood, her hands clenched into fists.

"*Sit down!* I'm not impressed. And turn it off. You want to stay, then stay. But you're going to be an obedient little toy. You turn it off when I say so, and you turn it on when I say so."

She sat down slowly. Her face was flushed with scarlet. God, thought Steiger, what a pair we are!

"Parasite," he said.

"And what does that make you?"

"I know what I am. I don't pretend to be anything else."

"And that makes you proud?" she asked scornfully.

"I didn't say it did. I don't lose any sleep over it though. Get me a drink."

It was hard to believe that Radu Zoltek was only in his forties. He looked like an old man. He also looked strung out.

"Delivered, as promised," said Xanfru. "Good luck. You'll need it."

A moment later, I understood what he meant. Zoltek was a dying man and he knew it. His vocal chords were practically burned away by fire crystals. Perhaps one word in ten was intelligible. He gibbered at me weakly, pawing at my clothes, looking into my eyes as if he hoped to see something familiar there. He acted like a lost dog.

"Radu," I said, "can you understand me?"

A torrent of croaking and wheezing. Jil looked at me and shook her head in resignation.

"Radu, can you tell me about Xerxes V?"

I was unprepared for the psychic emotional shock which set my mind reeling. I slumped forward and grabbed Radu for support. Dimly, I heard Jil's exclamation of alarm and I felt Cilix beside me, holding me steady. Beside me, Zoltek jerked under the same compulsion.

It continued.

Baker was much faster than I was. It was all that I could do to keep up with him. He only slowed down when we were well into the forest and away from the landing field. He waited for me to catch up and we both stood, breathing heavily and grinning. We were going to make it. They'd never catch us now.

All that time spent swallowing their insults, bowing and scraping, getting them to trust us, had at last paid off. It was the perfect opportunity.

Our orders had been to remain with the lighter. They were orders we had never intended to follow. We had both waited too long for this chance and they had given it to us. It was the perfect time and the ideal place.

It was an Eden. The sky was flushed with pink and all the colors of the rainbow were in evidence. It was a fresh, unspoiled world, a garden planet with a warm, seductive climate. Saffron colored birds with giant wingspans flew in flocks above the tree-tops, filling the air with their ululating cries. Fruit-bearing trees were all around us and another ten miles distant was a river. Quarantine world, indeed! The Shahin had lied to us. Counted on our fear and blind obedience to keep us waiting in the lighter until they returned. There was something here they wanted no one else to know about. Mineral deposits maybe, or something of even greater value. No matter. We would find out what it was. They would search for us certainly, but their patience would give out and they would leave. And we would stay. Free at last from orders, duties, and routine. Free to live the simple life.

We made our break!

We delved deep into the forest, proceeding at a slow and easy pace, heading towards the river we had seen from the air. Beyond the river, on the other side, perhaps a day or two's hike away, was a range of mountains. And on the other side, a valley with a giant lake.. Everything a man could ask for. We could be pioneers. Hunters, trappers, mountain men, anything we wished! Living off the land. We had a whole world in which to hide.

Eventually I called a rest and sat down beneath a thick-boled plant. Baker couldn't rest. He was anxious to go on. He was stronger than I was and he was fired with frenetic energy, pacing back and forth and calling my attention to this plant and that tree, speculating on our new home.

It came from up above, where it had been perching in a tree, waiting for a chance to strike. It brought him to his knees and he yelled and flung it from him, but then another came from out of nowhere and both of them attacked him. It happened so quickly that by the time I was on my feet, they had brought him down. He screamed and I saw one of them sink its teeth into his throat. He thrashing, gurgling horribly as I stood frozen in my terror. He beat at them weakly, but I saw the blood and I knew that he was done for. And then a third one came into view, a thin and gangling creature with a hairless head and bulging eyes and I noticed for the first time the reptillean parasites that clung to the three of them.

I bolted through the jungle, oblivious of the branches that struck my face and scratched me. I tripped over roots and scrambled to my feet and ran again. Bawling like a baby, I pushed my body to its limit, running as I had never run before. One of them was closer than the others. I heard it land just behind me, and somewhere I found the energy to put on a final burst of speed; but then, a moment later, I felt it clawing at me and I screamed and turned around and smashed it hard. It fell and immediately another sprang to its feet. I was desperate now and waded into the fight. I held one of the creatures by its spindly neck in my hand and was using its blunt head to beat off the pack. Between my fingers its parasite squirmed and spat. Afraid that it was going to lash at me, I threw its broken body to its brothers and attempted to jump back. As I fell, I saw the monster explode in a mess of blood and entrails. I covered my eyes to shield them from the carnage and found cover among the bodies that already littered the forest floor.

I felt a hand close around my arm and I lashed out with my fist. I was hauled to my feet and dealt a punishing blow that made

*my head ring. A Shahin face began to fade from focus and, in a
moment, I had forgotten all my troubles.*

"Dear God" I whispered. And then I saw Radu; his cough had
begun to rack him again. Protectively I put my arms around him,
burying my hands in his hair and stroking his head affectionately.
His desperate loneliness was over at long last. I felt his tears dropping on my neck and I squeezed him to me. He coughed and I
felt something wet and warm flowing down my neck.

"Alan, he's bleeding!" Cilix exclaimed.

I knew. He continued coughing, shuddering as I held him,
retching blood on me. He was frightened.

"Go on, Radu," I said. "Don't be afraid. Let go. Let go."

He heaved once again and it was over. I held a corpse. There
wasn't a sound from any of the others. None of them understood
what had happened, but they all somehow felt its import. Cilix
was the first to move, rising and taking Radu's body away from
me.

I didn't want to let him go. I felt as if I had lost a brother.

Chapter Four

The tall black man entered the hostel and walked over to the desk. He smiled engagingly at the woman seated behind the counter.

"Don't tell me you're taking care of business by yourself? Things couldn't be that bad, could they?"

She smiled back. "Not at all. The clerk went on the blink last month and I didn't get around to having it serviced right away, so I took over myself. Been doing it ever since. I like it. It keeps me busy. I'm afraid I won't be able to oblige you with a place to stay though. There simply isn't any room."

"Well, that's all right," he said, still smiling. "Actually, I was looking for an old shipmate of mine. I thought he might be staying here. His name is Alan Dreyfus. A Terran."

"Just a minute, I'll check." She ran the name through her computer. "No, I'm sorry, there's no one by that name in residence currently."

Mustafa pursed his lips thoughtfully and sighed. "Well, I'll be honest with you. My friend's in a little bit of trouble. You know how it is, it's a matter of credit. Poor Alan drank up all his money, see, and if he's staying here, it could be under an assumed name." He held up a small holocube and showed it to her. "This is Alan."

She looked at it and shrugged. "I don't know. There's such a high turnover here, there isn't any way I could remember faces. Let me check for you; it shouldn't take very long." She studied the cube, then programmed the description into the computer after inquiring about Alan's height and weight. She then scanned all the faces that fit the description. It took perhaps three minutes. "No, he isn't here. If it's a matter of credit, I could run it through to central, but I'd need an official clearance." She said it hopefully.

"Oh, I could get one, I suppose," said Mustafa, "but it would really be an inconvenience. I'm very anxious to expedite matters. I'm sure you understand. The clerk normally authenticates a clearance order before running a check, isn't that correct? And seeing that your clerk is temporarily incapacitated, isn't there a possibility of an error due to its malfunction?" He managed to slip her the money very casually.

"You know, it's funny you should say that," the woman replied with a wink. "I've had a lot of trouble with that unit. I really should replace it altogether."

Mustafa lit a cigarette and waited. He didn't have very long to wait. There was an intermittent tone and the woman read the result of the check off her screen.

"Your friend has moved around some," she told him. "It looks like he's down on his luck, like you said. His last recorded residence is in a sleazy little place on the lower west side of the city." She gave him the address. "If you're going to go looking for him there, I would suggest that you go armed."

"Thank you very much," he said. "I'll be careful. You've been a great help."

She winked at him again. "Stop by anytime. It gets a little lonely around here, if you know what I mean."

Mustafa winked back. "I might just do that, lady. Thanks again."

They all responded to his signal, converging on the tiny compartment. They bypassed the unattended clerk, an old, decrepit model, and broke into the room. It wasn't very hard. The compartment had already been the subject of forced entry.

"Jesus Christ," said Charlie, "why would anybody in their right mind want to stay in a stinkhole like this?"

"I don't know," Mustafa said, "but he was here. And we found the place, *without* going through the proper channels. Don't forget, the Shahin have him listed officially as a deserter. If we know he was here, then so do they. Now, Alan isn't stupid. He's probably far away from here by now and chances are he's met someone who's helping him hide. We have to find him before they do. Spread out through the area, but watch yourselves. Stay out of trouble. The last thing we want to do is let the Shahin know we're looking for him. Ask around, someone must have seen him. The spacers would talk to us before they spoke to one of them, so concentrate on them. If he was seen *with* anyone, try to find out who that was."

"Suppose he's left the city?" one of the men asked.

Mustafa shook his head. "Not very likely. He can hide out better here, and he knows his only chance of avoiding capture is to ship out as soon as possible. He may be trying to get in touch with us. That's what I'd do. Let's move. The minute any one of you finds out anything, get on the horn. Right. Go."

The men left the building, spreading out and heading in different directions.

It was an incredibly large city and they were searching for only one man. One man who did not want to be found. But Alan was family.

Kovalevski felt the same way even as he realized that he could not possibly forestall communicating with the embassy any longer. As far as he and any other Terrans were concerned, the embassy was Earth. It would have been impossible for governmental business to be conducted from the home world over such long distances. Wherever there was a Terran embassy, there was a little piece of Earth, a mandate *in loco parentis*. It was a far from perfect system. Each embassy answered, ultimately, to Earth, but by the time that orders and revisions and new laws and amendments reached the far flung outposts, the men and women who authored them were long since dead. And, more often than not, the orders and laws became either irrelevant or were superseded. So, final authority lay with each ambassador. An ambassador's word was not to be taken lightly. It was, literally, the word of the Terran Guild.

Each ambassador was assisted by a court of advocates. The advocates, by three quarters majority decision, could negate the word of the ambassador. Advocates and ambassadors alike were appointed for life or until the arrival of new officers, whichever came first. In the event of death, positions were filled by computer selection based on assessment of qualifications of all Terrans currently under the jurisdiction of that embassy. It was not possible to refuse selection. Mandatory retirement was required of any embassy officer or official failing to meet the periodic medical and psychological scan qualifications, and a new selection was made. It was not possible to refuse retirement, nor was it possible to avoid the periodic scans.

While this system had its imperfections, it was more often than not the rule that the officials of the embassies were the most qualified and, in a manner of speaking, the most superior Terrans in each jurisdiction. Superior in certain aspects, that is. Patricia Character was one such official.

She was the ambassador in Port City but not the sort of person one would invite to a social gathering. She considered such gatherings essentially boring, terminally vacuous, and needlessly time consuming. Nor was Ambassador Character the sort of person one would turn to as a leader. The ambassador had no ambitions in that regard and lacked the necessary temperament. But what the ambassador lacked in ambition was more than compensated for by a great facility for logic and deliberation.

Sixty-three years earlier, Character had coolly assessed the opportunities in Port City, discovering, at length, a profession that seemed to her to offer the maximum in wages for a minimum of effort. She became a prostitute.

She secured a position with a reputable sex emporium and worked four hours each day. She did not enjoy her job. But then, the question of enjoyment never entered into it. Prostitution was merely a means to an end—that end being a satisfactory bank account and sufficient independence until a better opportunity presented itself. Such an opportunity arrived with the death of the incumbent ambassador. When Patricia Character was notified of her selection, she was not surprised. She merely acknowledged the computer selection with a curt nod, a brief "I could do that," and assumed her office. Now, sixty some odd years later, the embassy functioned like an old, well-oiled machine.

"I appreciate your seeing me on such short notice, Patricia," Kovalevski said. An aide had earlier advised him of the ambassador's predilection for informality. She was not interested in ceremonies or honorifics. Only in the matter at hand.

The old woman sat ramrod straight, smoking a cigarette. Kovalevski was surprised to recognize the aroma of a Balkan blend, a very strong tobacco which flourished well in the orbital farms. It was the type most favored by local spacers. She smiled at him.

"Short notice, my ass," she said in a pleasantly husky voice. "You've been sitting on your hands for days now with this Shahin proposal."

Kovalevski was startled. Visibly so.

"Yes, I knew," she said.

"But . . . then, why. . . ."

"Why didn't I contact you? And tip my hand that I have an informant? You know what the Shahin do to spies?"

"I see," Kovalevski nodded morosely.

"Sit down," Patricia said. "Seraphim. An unusual name for a soldier. Is there something short for that?"

"My friends call me Sim."

"Well, then, Sim . . . I won't hold it against you. I'm sure there's a very good reason for what you did. Is this Alan Dreyfus a close friend of yours?"

"Yes, he is. I . . . I think it would save a lot of time and unnecessary explanations if you told me what you *do* know of all this. You seem incredibly well-informed."

"It's my job," she said. "All right. It's a reasonable request. I am informed that the Shahin, in the person of Lord Hhargoth, are very anxious to get their hands on one Alan Dreyfus. They claim that he is a deserter, but I checked and learned that his application for service was processed on the very day that he is supposed to have deserted. That still makes it legal, of course, but I find it suspicious. It is also suspicious that he was crippled in an attack on Hhargoth."

"*What?*"

"That's what I said," replied Patricia wryly. "Somehow, I can't seem to picture anybody in his right mind attacking a Shahin. Still it wouldn't be the first time. As a matter of fact, another such incident occurred only recently, involving a human and a Shahin *xothol.* Hand-to-hand combat, no less! A damage claim has been filed, protests, etc. etc. Something strange is happening around here, that's for sure. I'd like to get to the bottom of it."

"You said Alan was crippled. How?"

"His left arm has been burned off at the shoulder."

"Good God."

"What's so special about Alan Dreyfus?" Patricia asked.

"I don't know," said Kovalevski. "Your informant didn't tell you?"

"My informant has an unpleasant habit of playing both ends against the middle. It's a touchy situation."

Sim was tempted to tell her that his men were combing the city in an effort to find Dreyfus, but he didn't dare. There was too much at stake. Patricia Character was a very compelling woman. He *wanted* to trust her, to confide in her. And that, he realized, was precisely what made her dangerous.

"You know, Sim," she said, "I've been thinking. About what I would do if I were in your shoes. If it were *my* friend who was in trouble."

Kovalevski put himself on guard.

"I'd want very much to help my friend, I think. With a ship on layover and idle hands available, I might even consider sending a landing party out to try to find him before the Shahin do. To try to help him get away before the ambassador has time to act on the Shahin's offer. It's a very attractive offer, you know. Still this is all speculation, of course."

"Of course," said Kovalevski.

"I don't need to consult the advocates to know that they'd jump at a chance to negotiate an agreement with Hhargoth. Hhargoth knows it too. I'm doing everything I can to discover why they want your friend so badly. Did you know that orders have been issued for Dreyfus to be shot on sight? And anyone with him as well?"

"No, I didn't."

"I'd have been surprised if you had. You know, Sim, I'm really very curious to find out why it's so important for them to have Dreyfus dead. What has he learned from them?"

"I'm curious about that myself."

"Mmmm. I've always believed that negotiations are better conducted from a position of strength. Suppose, just for the sake of discussion, that Alan Dreyfus surrendered to the embassy. Suppose that the information he has turns out to be of greater value than an extradition agreement with the Shahin. Do you think that's possible?"

Kovalevski nodded. "Not only possible, but probable, knowing the Shahin as I do. But let me suppose, again for the sake of discussion, that Dreyfus does surrender to the embassy and that his information, whatever it is, is either of little value, which I doubt to be the case, or... or *supposing* that he divulges this information to you and, having received this information, it is decided by either yourself or the court of advocates to turn him over to the Shahin anyway? Chances are excellent that you would be able to prevent their knowing that you have this information they are anxious to conceal and, at the same time, you would be able to negotiate an agreement from, as you say, a position of strength. Theoretically, how does that sound?"

The ambassador regarded him thoughtfully. "It sounds like an interesting theory. While we're speculating about all sorts of things, Sim, what do you think would happen to an officer who knowingly hindered embassy negotiations with a foreign power?"

"I would rather not speculate about that, if it's all the same with you."

"Mmmm. In that case, *I* will. I should think that a court martial would probably be convened at the earliest opportunity. I don't think I need speculate what the result would be. However, *if* the accused officer was able to, shall we say, plea bargain with certain evidence, information that could provide the embassy with an edge over a certain foreign power, then it's possible that certain of that officer's transgressions could be... overlooked?"

Kovalevski nodded. "But there is no certainty in that, is there? That officer, whom we have invented for the sake of discussion, would still be taking his chances, would he not?"

She nodded. "He would, indeed."

"Hmm. Very interesting. Well, Patricia, I must say, it's been stimulating. I've already taken up a great deal of your time. I must be getting on about my business. Again, my apologies for the er... unavoidable delay in conveying Hhargoth's offer to you. Strange that he didn't make the offer to you, himself, isn't it?"

"Perhaps he thought there would be a possibility of negotiating with a certain officer first."

"Yes, I see. Of course."

"Goodbye, Seraphim."

"Bye, Patricia." He turned to leave.

"Oh, Sim?" He turned, again. She grinned at him. "Don't get caught, okay?"

Charlie Faen asked a lot of questions. The young lieutenant was very persistent. So intent was he on his task that he didn't notice the man who had been following him. Part of his carelessness was caused by his excitement at having located someone who remembered a man answering to Alan's description, except that he had only one arm. But the spacer had been certain. He had positively identified Alan's likeness in the holocube, saying that the reason he remembered him so well was that he had been in company with an Ophidian and a striking feline female. Charlie was exuberant. He imagined himself finding Alan without any help from the others. His fantasies were abruptly shattered by a sharp blow to the back of his neck.

He revived in an abandoned building, smelling urine and refuse. He found that his hands were in restraints.

"Good morning, Lieutenant," said the tall, muscular blonde man sitting several meters away on a pile of rubble. "It *is* morning, by the way. I hit you a little harder than I realized, I'm afraid. You've kept me waiting quite a while."

"What do you want?"

Creed shrugged. "Nothing much. A few answers, that's all. Feel up to talking?"

"Who are you? What are you after?"

"The name's Steiger. Creed Steiger. Mean anything to you?"

"Should it?"

"Not necessarily. And I don't want anything from you, not personally, anyway. But you *have* been asking a lot of questions about Alan Dreyfus. I'd like to know why."

"You a friend of his?"

"Maybe. What's he to you?"

"If you're a friend of his, if you know where he is, you'll take me to see him. Alan's in a lot of trouble."

"I know all about that," Steiger said. "But I still don't know why I should take you to him."

"Ask him. Tell him Charlie Faen. He'll know me. We were

together on the *Titus Groan*. Tell him that it's very important that I see him. I can help him."

"Okay," nodded Creed. "I'll ask him. For your own good, I hope you're telling me the truth."

"Hurry," Charlie said urgently. "There isn't much time."

"Right," said Steiger. He smiled at Faen. "Don't go away now."

He left the young lieutenant and strolled over to the nearest cafe, where he enjoyed a slow, leisurely breakfast. When he returned, Charlie Faen was sitting, leaning against a wall, waiting.

"Well?" he asked anxiously.

Steiger nodded. "He knows you, all right."

"So you'll take me?"

"Not just yet. He might know you, but *I* don't. You still have to convince me. I don't want to see Alan get hurt any more. You said that you could help him. How?"

"I told you, we were together on the *Titus Groan*. I can help him get away, get off-planet. If he stays here, the Shahin are bound to find him sooner or later. One of them came to see the captain, Kovalevski. That's how we found out he was in trouble. They want him so badly, they've made a formal proposal to the embassy. Extradition agreements. We give them Alan, they'll give us any ten men the embassy asks for. They'd have to be crazy not to jump at a chance like that. If we can find him and bring him back to the ship before the ambassador gives her okay, he's got a chance to make a break for it. We're all pulling for him, the old man too. But we're running out of time!"

"They actually said that, any ten men? Just for Alan?"

"You better believe it. One of Hhargoth's own bondwarriors delivered the message. They actually thought we'd just hand him over if he came to us! Don't you see? It's his only chance! You've got to take me to him!"

"How many of you are there?"

"Fourteen. We've been spread out all over the place, trying to find him. And we can get more too. Whatever it takes to protect him. *Now* will you take me to see him?"

"Well, now, I'd like to," said Steiger, "I really would, only you see, I don't know where he is."

"What?"

"See, *I'm* looking for him too, only I represent the other side."

"You son of a—"

"Ah, come on, now, Charlie, don't be that way. It's just a job, you know. I've got nothing against the guy, hell, I don't even know him. But you and I have got this little problem, Charlie, and I'm going to have to think about it some. You see, if the Shahin are really serious about this extradition thing, it puts me in a bit of a spot, 'cause I'll bet you anything that when the embassy gets around to making up that list of ten names, mine'll be right up there, at the top. And that just wouldn't do, no sir."

Charlie started thinking—fast. "You oughtta know the way they operate," he said. "You do their dirty work for them and they turn right around and sell you out."

"It does look that way, doesn't it?"

"So now you see who you work for," said Charlie with disgust.

"Yeah, well, I'm not too thrilled with them myself. Still, beggars can't be choosers."

"Why not come in with us? Back with your own kind? I'm sure that if you—"

"No, I'm afraid I couldn't do that, Charlie. See, I killed three men, three officers. It was a long time ago, but somehow I just don't think they'd be willing to forgive and forget. No, I appreciate your offer, I really do, but you see what a position I'm in. Caught right between a rock and a hard place."

Faen had run out of ideas. He sat silent.

"I guess Hhargoth really does want Dreyfus pretty badly. I didn't know about that extradition thing. Appreciate your telling me. But, you see, Hhargoth wants Dreyfus dead. And, if he's dead, there won't be any agreement. And that'll take me off the hook, won't it?"

Charlie swallowed heavily. "Then you'd better kill me too. Because if you kill Alan, there won't be any place for you to hide."

Steiger laughed. "Oh, Charlie! This is a big universe, there're millions of places to hide! Hell, look at Alan! Sounds like he's got half the population of the city looking for him and we can't even find him. Look, let me give you some free advice, okay? I'm a little older than you are and I've been around some. I've even seen some action. I know how you feel, believe me. I felt the same way once. You know what happens to heroes, Charlie? They die, that's what happens to them. And if they get lucky, somebody pins a piece of tin on 'em and maybe a promotion goes with it and then what? You get to go out and be an asshole again, and sooner or later your number comes up. And if it doesn't, if you get really lucky, you get to live long enough for people to forget all about you and everything you did. Remember Neil Armstrong, Charlie? No? I didn't think you would. You want to know who he was? He was the first man on the moon, Earth's moon. He was a hero. But how about Benedict Arnold? Yeah, every schoolboy knows who he was and he lived two hundred years *before* Armstrong. And you want to know something else? *He* was a hero too. Only nobody remembers that. Nobody cares. They remember the bad guys, Charlie. Sure, I could kill you now. I could even let you go and give you back your gun and I'd still kill you. I do it well, Charlie. I've got experience. So I could kill you and let you be a hero. And you'd be dead. And who would care?"

"I would care." Charlie stared at him defiantly. "My friends would care."

"Oh, that's just great. They'd all hoist a few to your memory and talk about what a brave man you were and how nobly you died. Military camaraderie's a wonderful thing. I miss it terribly."

Charlie regarded him thoughtfully. "You know," he said softly, "I think you really do."

"Don't be a hero, Charlie," said Creed. "It's not much fun."

"What are you going to do with me?"

"I'm going to let you go. You've told me everything I wanted to know, kid. I'm going to keep your piece, of course, but there's not much point to my killing you, is there?"

"We'll find you, Steiger."

"That shouldn't be very hard. I'm not in hiding. Look, I'm dropping the key over here on the ground. By the time you crawl over and get yourself free, I'll be long gone, so don't bother trying to follow me. I've got work to do and you'd only get in the way."

"Steiger!"

Creed turned. "Yes?"

"Let us find Alan Dreyfus. If we can get him before the embassy acts, we'll put him on the first outbound ship, beyond reach of the Shahin. No Alan, no extradition agreement. You'll be safe."

"It's an idea," said Steiger, "except that if I let you boys have him, I'll never find out why Hhargoth wants him so badly. I've become real curious about that. And then there's one other little thing."

"And that is?"

"If Alan Dreyfus gets away, I don't get paid."

"You're playing a very dangerous game, Xanfru," I said.

"I don't know what you mean; what game?"

We spoke quietly. The others were all sleeping. Xanfru didn't sleep much. For all practical purposes, we were alone and it was just as well. I didn't want the others to hear this.

We had been living like virtual prisoners. Cilix occassionally ventured outside to run errands for Xanfru in meager exchange for his harboring us. Yuri had grown paranoid. She was given to nightmares. Her greatest fear was that Creed Steiger would find us. It was all that Jil could do to help keep her calm.

The pressure on Jil must have been incredible. For several days, I had not spoken. Ever since Radu died in my arms, ever since that unbelievably powerful coupling experience, I had been in something like a fugue state. I had been dimly aware of the others around me, trying to get through to me, but I could not respond. I perceived everything around me through some thick, mental haze. There was a sort of dull unreality about it all. I remembered Jil and Cilix desperately trying to get me to talk to them and Xanfru telling them to leave me alone.

"Go away from him," he had said, "he isn't ready yet." One cripple's empathy for another.

Tonight, all night, I was aware of him sitting there in that chair, motionless, his gaze never leaving me for an instant. He watched me with intensity, with hunger. It was something I could feel.

I wasn't wholly human anymore.

I had been struggling to understand what was happening to me. Trying to find a name for the insane game in which I had, somehow, become a pawn. It was necessary to play it out to the natural end.

To move is to win.

It was also necessary for me to empty myself so that I could become filled again. Alan Dreyfus, the spacer who had come to Port City for release had, indeed, at last *been* released. I was different then. I wondered, briefly, who I thought I was.

"Alan? You haven't answered me. I don't understand, what are you talking about, what game? Are you all right?"

I watched him for a long moment.

"Yes. I'm fine."

"Good. I'm relieved. I was beginning to think that—"

"I'm curious about what you're going to decide."

He frowned. "About what?"

"About whether or not to turn me in to the ambassador."

"What are you talking about?"

I smiled and shook my head. "Give it up, Xanfru. I *know*."

"How? How could you possibly—"

"How could I help *not* knowing? You're literally shouting it at me. It's really eating away at you, isn't it?"

He looked away from me.

"I didn't know at first. I really didn't. I had a very strong feeling about you, that you could be trusted, that you sincerely wanted to help us. And you did. Then.

"It's a funny thing, I seem to have nothing but strange encounters with Cetians lately. That's a feeble, morbid sort of joke, I'm sorry. You hate the Shahin, don't you? Hate them for robbing you of your legs. Even though it wasn't really their fault. I was a way of getting back at them. But it's different now, isn't it?

"You've been watching me. You've seen what I can do. You've seen my arm growing back, little by little, right before your very eyes. And you want it too. You want your legs back and you want to be powerful. But you don't even have the vaguest notion of what it's *really* like. You just want a lizard of your very own to eat. Only you're not sure that I can get one for you or what my next move is going to be. I might find a way to escape and that would leave you right where you had been before, except that you would know there had been a chance to transcend your present existence and you lost it. And that fear is tearing you apart.

"On the other hand, you might be able to bargain with the embassy. I might fail. The embassy has power. The ambassador has power. Will she promise you a lizard in exchange for me? Will she be able to deliver? Or will you be used and left out in the cold? Tell me, Xanfru, what are you going to do?"

He sat tensely, like a coiled spring, resisting.

"Why don't you talk to me, Xanfru, instead of screaming with your mind? Give in and let me help you decide.

Xanfru seemed to go limp in his chair. "It does all *that* to you? You can even read minds?"

"No, not really, Xanfru. The surrogate once told me that it had a way of sensing truth. I understand that now. For example, you could think a lie, but I would know it was one. I'm really *with* you, Xanfru. I feel very close to you, even though you've been thinking of betraying me. Kind of love thine enemy. It's very difficult to hate when you really know someone and are a part of everything that is their experience. If you'll let me, I can show you."

His chair floated away from me, hesitantly. "No. No, get out of my head. I don't want any part of it."

"Now you're lying to yourself. You do want to be a part of it. You already are, believe it or not. You're just questioning how much you're willing to pay. How much? What's in it for me? What is it going to cost me? Will it be worth the price? The struggle between 'for' and 'against' is your mind's worst disease."

"You're insane."

"Yes, that makes it very convenient for you, doesn't it? You're afraid because you don't understand what's happening. But once you point a finger, once you isolate it, categorize it and give it a name, then it all becomes very simple. Then you can act. Then you can justify."

"I don't have to justify anything to you. I saved your life, remember?"

"Yes. I do. Why not let me save yours?"

As soon as I asked the question, I knew that he would be unable to make the committment. His chair whirled around and he fled. I made no attempt to follow. He could easily outdistance me anyway. Without meaning to, not in that way, I had helped him make his decision. Now, it was time to run again.

I woke the others.

"Alan!" Jil threw her arms around me and hugged me close. The others crowded around. We all touched each other. I knew now that I was up to it.

Without preparing them, without giving them any warning, I began. It came as a shock. Yuri tried to pull away at first, but Cilix held her tightly by the hand. He understood. It was like having sex with three people at the same time, only it was better. Sex, good sex, is not all that difficult to find. When sex is good, the physical chemistry is very satisfying and, more uncommonly, the emotional involvement can make the experience truly special and unique. This went far beyond that.

This was, essentially, complete unification. On every level. We four were one.

It was over very quickly, in actual time, but it seemed to take a lifetime. Four lifetimes. In reality, it was one single, piercing flash of cognizance, shared between the four of us. When it was over, all of us were crying. Not Cilix, of course, whose eyes were structured differently, but even his normal semblance of control was shaken. We held each other tightly, rocking together gently in the aftermath of communion.

Yuri touched my cheek and kissed me on the lips. There was no need for her to say anything. She didn't need to explain her fears and her anxiety. And I didn't need to tell Jil how much I loved her. She knew. She really *knew*. It was the greatest gift I could have given her. As she had given it to me.

"What an amazing society the surrogates must have," said Cilix, "if they can all unite together in this way. It's terrifying."

They all knew that Xanfru had gone to betray us. That had been a part of the experience which I communicated to them. The unknown was still before us, as it always was and always will be, only now, there was unified acceptance. We would somehow ride it out.

I felt sad for Xanfru.

"Where do we go now?" asked Jil.

I smiled wryly. "I don't know. We can't stay here. Xanfru has gone to the ambassador. And I have no way of knowing what she will do. If I could have some time with her, I believe that I could make her understand, but I don't know that she will give me time. Hhargoth has offered her a lot for me. I'm afraid to take the chance. There is one man who would help me, but I don't know how to get to him. My old captain, Kovalevski. But trying to reach the ship would be like running a gauntlet. It's too dangerous."

"So," said Cilix, "for now, we run."

"We run," I said.

"I'm sorry," said Charlie Faen.

"It wasn't your fault," said Mustafa. "He tricked you. You had no way of knowing that they had employed a mercenary, one of our own people. It could have happened to any one of us. At least, we know. His name was Steiger? Creed Steiger?" He turned to face his men. "Remember that name," he said. "Creed Steiger dies." They all nodded solemnly.

"What's our next step, sir?" asked one of the men.

"Back to the spaceport," said Mustafa.

"We're not giving up!" another protested.

"No, we're not giving up. But I've had word from the captain. We rendezvous at the spaceport. This time it's all out. Only a skeleton crew is being left aboard the *Groan*. The old man and every member of the crew, all of them are coming down. Whatever Alan got himself into it's big, that's all I know. We move now."

At the spaceport, the entire crew, save for the small complement left with the ship, gathered in a large meeting room. Kovalevski stood up to address them.

"All right, ladies and gentlemen," he said, "Here's where it stands. The word is out, as they say, on one of our people. The Shahin want Alan Dreyfus dead. They claim he signed up with them and deserted and it all looks very official and proper, but I don't buy it for a minute. I've met with the ambassador. The Shahin have offered to negotiate an extradition agreement and, to show their 'good faith,' they're willing to hand over any ten men the embassy chooses in exchange for Alan. By now, the ambassador and the court of advocates will have had time to reach a decision. I have no idea what that decision will be, although I can make an educated guess. I do not want to know. I will have no way of knowing. As of a short while ago, the *Groan* has experienced a massive equipment failure. All communications are out. Naturally that means us too. You understand what I mean?" He scanned the faces to see that they did. "Good. Putting it quite bluntly, ladies and gentlemen, my career is on the line. Chances are better than even that we will all be renegades before this is through and I am telling you that up front, just so you will know.

"We are all taking a very big chance. I believe it's worth it. Alan has learned something, somehow, that the Shahin are willing to bend over backwards to make sure he doesn't have a chance to tell anyone. Most of you know what the Shahin are like. Work it out for yourselves. I don't know what it is, but it must be pretty important for them to go to these lengths.

"Alan is in hiding somewhere in this city. The Shahin are looking for him with official sanction since, legally, and I use that word loosely, he is a deserter. Covertly, they have employed at least one Earthman that we know of. His name is Creed Steiger." He proceeded to relay Charlie's very accurate description. "Steiger's dangerous. A renegade. A deserter himself. His record shows that he has killed three officers. He's a veteran and he's good. Watch yourselves. If any of you sees him, *terminate* him. Do I make myself clear? Good.

"There is no way, repeat, *no way* that the embassy will not be aware of our actions. The ambassador is very sharp, and she already knows what I've planned to do. If we can find Alan and convince him to share what he's learned with us so that we can, in turn, communicate that information to the ambassador, there is a chance, *just* a chance, that we might get away with this—if the information is valuable enough and I have no doubt that it is. But, and I stress this, there are no guarantees. The ambassador refused to commit herself. It's all a game, ladies and gentlemen, and the name of that game is politics. If we succeed and what Alan knows is worth something to the embassy, we might pull it off. If not, we all hang. And if *that* happens, I'm telling you right now, so all of you will know, I'm turning pirate."

Kovalevski waited for the reaction to die down. It took a little while.

"It is not a decision I have arrived at lightly. You may not agree with me and I respect your right, in this case, to dissent. So. Now you all know." He took a deep breath and realized, for the first time, that his hands had been trembling. He stuck them in his pockets. "This is your one and only chance. If there are any of you here now who, for whatever reason, want out of this, I want to know now. The people on the ship have already heard my little speech. They have made their decision. Anyone not wishing to go along will be returned to the *Groan* and held, albeit comfortably, *incommunicado*. The records will show your dissent. The records will also show that you were forcibly detained and prevented from communicating with anyone. In short, it will be arranged that there will be absolutely no grounds on which you can be prosecuted. And no hard feelings, at least not on my part."

He swallowed nervously. "If we get away with this, you'll be welcome to stay or, if you so desire, obtain an honorable separation. Either way, no animosity. All right. If any of you want out . . . step forward now."

There was an undertone and a noticeable hesitation, then six people stepped forward. One of them was Charlie Faen.

"I'm sorry, sir," he said quietly. "I'd back you up in anything, you know that, but piracy? If it comes to that. . . ." He shook his head. "No. I can't. I just . . . I guess I just haven't got it in me. I'm sorry."

"It's all right, Charlie. Nothing personal, I don't blame you. Take the others and use the lighter to get back to the ship. One of the people who stayed behind will bring it back down. We'll need every one of them if we have to get back to the ship in a hurry."

Charlie nodded. The corners of his mouth turned down. "Sir? Just do one thing for me. Get that Steiger for me," he said bitterly. Hating himself, he knew that Steiger would have approved of what he was doing now.

"I'll do my damnedest," said Kovalevski. Charlie snapped to attention and saluted him. He returned the salute and the six left for the lighter.

All the others had elected to remain with him. Every single one of them stood, watching him, waiting for him to give the orders. It was a vote of confidence such as he never could have expected. They were all laying it on the line with him. Many of them were young with great prospects ahead of them. Yet they were willing to throw it all away. For the "old man."

He felt proud. Overwhelmed. He started to speak, but his voice cracked and he stopped, looking down, clearing his throat awkwardly. When he looked up again, all of them were smiling.

He brought them up short by calling them to attention. "I want Dreyfus found. And I don't care how. You're all armed. Use your own discretion, but don't get violent unless you have to. I don't want any innocent people hurt. Work in pairs or threes or by yourselves, any way you like. But get the job done.

"Now, keep in touch. Work together. And good luck."

Chapter Five

"So," said Lokhrim, "Xanfru is a traitor."

The Cetian had been seen entering the Terran embassy. That put everything in a new perspective. How much did he know? There was no way of telling now. He would not be fool enough to return to them. If he did not know, then the ambassador would certainly be aware that her embassy was being watched.

It had been a mistake to contact the Terrans. He knew that from the first, but it was not for him to criticize Hhargoth's judgment. His Lordship had an almost hunted look about him. The way Alan Dreyfus had been leading the Shahin by the nose had become a personal affront. Lokhrim longed for the old days before this indignity had come upon them.

His sole duty consisted of directing a massive search for Dreyfus. The people under his command were tense and sullen. It was a unique situation, officers and soldiers having to answer to a bondwarrior. He didn't like it and neither did they. They hated the constant contact with humans that their search demanded.

Other races as well, but humans were the most despicable. And yet, of all the humans he had known, Creed Steiger was the only one whom he could tolerate.

Creed. The word meant a faith or a belief strictly adhered to. The name fit him well. Steiger was true to his own peculiar system of values. The opinions, judgments, rules, and regulations of others did not concern him. He remained above them all. The man was born fighter, a warrior. Although Lokhrim could not say he liked him, he had respect for him. And that was something he would never have thought that he could feel for one not of the people. The humans could not appreciate a man like Steiger. Lokhrim could.

And Alan Dreyfus. What sort of man was he? Lokhrim thought back again, as he had many times before, to the time when he had first seen him. A miserable specimen of humanity. Ravaged, emaciated, a seeming derelict. A man who barely seemed to have the strength to stand. And yet he had managed to avoid capture for so long. Clearly, he had misjudged him.

The obvious answer was, of course, the surrogate. Under its control, he would be much more than a man. Lokhrim had never been to Xerxes V, but he had heard stories, as had all the Shahin. Stories of the war. The war which was being fought in secret, undeclared, forever escalating. The lizards were becoming more and more adept. It would have been a simple matter to wipe them out, to defoliate their jungles and to raze their planet, but it would serve no purpose. The Shahin were limited in what they could do because they needed the cursed creatures, needed them for the chemical derivatives which were manufactured on the home world, the treatments that helped to make their soldiers the most feared warriors in the universe.

There was the matter of the dismembered lizard which his men had found. His Lordship seemed to believe that it was the same one that attacked him, the one that lived off Dreyfus. It was possible that it was not the same creature, but highly unlikely. So then, where was the danger? According to all that he had heard, Dreyfus should have died without the lizard. Yet they had not found his body and he had been seen, or so it was claimed, in the company of an Ophidian, a feline, and another Terran. The obvious conclusion, the *only* conclusion, was that the bite of a surrogate was not fatal. Yet he had been told otherwise. It was puzzling.

It had never before occurred to him to question the word of his superiors. It was unthinkable. And yet. . . . And yet he could not help wondering why His Excellency wanted Dreyfus killed. If the lizard was dead, where was the threat? What didn't he know? Lokhrim was troubled.

The screen on his desk alerted him to an incoming call.

"I just called to thank you," Steiger said.

"To thank me? Thank me for what?"

"For being such a devious sweetheart. For trying to sell me out, you creep. What's the idea, don't you think that I can get the job done?"

"I fail to understand—"

"That little trick you pulled with the extradition treaty or whatever the hell it was. Ten men of their choosing for Dreyfus. Who do you think they'd pick first, *xothol*? Yours truly, that's who. I oughtta go down there and wring your blasted neck!"

"You have tried that once already, Steiger. I seem to recall that you did not succeed."

"I'll try to do better next time."

"The extradition agreement was not my idea," Lokhrim said, wondering why it seemed necessary to justify himself to a Terran. "I was following His Excellency's instructions."

"Yeah? Well, it was a real smart move, let me tell you. It's liable to backfire right in his face."

"What do you mean?"

"I mean that the crew of the *Groan* have taken things into their own hands. They're down here looking for Dreyfus. If they find him before you or I do, you can just kiss him goodbye. They'll bring him back aboard and smuggle him out on the first outgoing ship. That's just what I would do if I was in their place."

"You do not think the ambassador will agree to the exchange? I know for a fact that Kovalevski has communicated with the embassy and—"

"Oh, I'm sure he has. And I wouldn't be surprised if they agree to your terms. That's liable to make things a bit uncomfortable for me. But you don't know Character. She's a sharp old bitch. She will have figured out by now that the only reason you people want Dreyfus so much is that he knows something. Something that can hurt you. She'll just look the other way while the crew from *Titus Groan* runs amok in the city, breaking regulations trying to find Dreyfus. It's called friendship, Lokhrim. Something you wouldn't understand. Character will give Kovalevski enough rope to hang himself. Then, when he gets Dreyfus, she'll spring the trap. Either Dreyfus passes on what he knows or Kovalevski and his entire crew go up on charges. Either way, she wins. You screwed up, Lokhrim. You screwed up badly."

"That is not for you to judge. In light of this information, however, I would suggest that you redouble your efforts to locate Dreyfus."

"Oh, I'll find him, all right. He can't stay in his hole forever. He's going to run. And the minute he does, I'll be right there. Only now I'll be tripping all over a bunch of crusaders, thanks to Hhargoth. The only reason I haven't found him yet is that somebody's hiding him. It could be a Cetian. There was an incident—"

"Xanfru!"

"What?"

"The traitor cripple, Xanfru," Lokhrim said. He filled Steiger in on what had transpired. It seemed so obvious, he cursed himself for not guessing it earlier.

"I know him," Steiger said. "Where does he live?"

It was a simple matter to obtain his address. "I will send help," Lokhrim said.

"You just keep your people out of my way," replied Steiger. "If Dreyfus gets past me, he's all yours. But I get first crack."

The screen went blank.

Patricia Character had been awakened from her sleep by the arrival of Xanfru. With a vitality belying her age, she splashed cold water on her face and dressed. She moved quickly. She was angry.

She received Xanfru in her office, then motioned to her aides that they were to be left alone. Xanfru was dangerous, but privacy was necessary. And of course she was not completely defenseless.

"You fool!" she spat at him. "Why did you come here? Why did you ignore procedure? You've ruined everything! Didn't you know the embassy was being watched?"

"I have Alan Dreyfus!"

"What do you mean, you *have* him? Where is he?"

"In my compartment. He's been staying there in hiding."

"You idiot! Why didn't you tell me sooner? Do you think he's stupid enough to stay there and wait for us to come and get him?"

"If you move quickly, there's still a chance—"

"Shut up!" She activated the screen and snapped out quick commands. "You simple ass. The Shahin will be there long before us. You're useless to me now."

"Not quite," said Xanfru. "In fact, I'm more valuable than you ever realized."

"If you have something to say, say it."

"Alan Dreyfus is still of some use to you in order to negotiate with Hhargoth. But that is all you can use him for. What the Shahin do not know is that killing Dreyfus will solve nothing for them. What he knows, *I* know."

"I don't believe you."

"Can you afford not to?"

"You're bargaining with me."

"Absolutely. You can have my knowledge for a price. A very, very reasonable price. It will not even deplete the treasury one iota since it is not in money."

"All right. I'll listen. But this had better be good. What's your price?"

"I won't tell you. Not until you agree to meet it. In writing, with your official stamp."

"What *is* this? You expect me to agree to your terms without even knowing what your terms are? *Officially* agree? Do you think I'm crazy?"

"Oh, no. Not at all. I told you, it is a very, very reasonable price. A small thing really. I am placing myself entirely in your capable hands, trusting you to act in good faith. After all, if you refuse to grant me asylum, I am just as good as dead. And then, conveniently for you, there will be no one left to pay the price to, will there?"

They sat there, staring at each other for a long moment. Patricia nodded. "All right." She called in one of her aides. "How do you want me to phrase it?"

Xanfru shrugged elaborately. "Very simply. Something in the nature of... in exchange for, uh, 'services rendered' to the government of Earth or the Terran Guild or however you wish to say it, you agree to pay me whatever price I ask in whichever commodity I specify. Words to that effect."

The aide smirked. His smirk changed to a stare of disbelief when Patricia said, "You heard him. Draw up the document."

They waited in silence while the aide prepared the "receipt." Patricia lit a cigarette, then, as an afterthought, offered one to Xanfru. He floated closer to her and took it, allowing her to light it for him.

"It's really a disgusting habit," he said, smiling. "It affects my system even worse and much quicker than it does yours. I very rarely indulge. However, I do not think that I will have to concern myself with matters of my health much longer." He grinned and Patricia frowned at him. What was the little Cetian getting at? She drummed her fingers on the table nervously, stopping when she realized that he had noticed it. He grinned at her.

"Be patient, Ambassador," he said with a sly smile. "It should only take another moment or two. I promise you, you will not regret our little deal."

"I very rarely regret anything, Xanfru," she said flatly. "If you're playing some sort of game with me, you'll be the one with regrets."

He only grinned in reply.

The aide returned; with an uneasy glance at Xanfru, he handed her the document. She read it quickly, nodded, and dismissed him. She then signed it, stamped it with her official seal, pressed her thumb into the sensitized lower right hand corner, and inserted the document into the sealer. She handed it to him a second later, watching as he looked it over carefully.

"This will serve, I think," he said.

"Enough with this charade," she said. "I've done as you asked. Now, name your price."

Xanfru looked up at her innocently. "I want you to provide me with the means to regenerate my body."

She stared at him. He looked serious. "And how am I supposed to do that?"

"You'll be able to do it very easily with the information I am about to share with you. Not immediately, of course, but I am willing to wait."

"I've been waiting," she snapped. "And I'm getting tired of it. What the hell are you talking about?"

"I'm talking about the Shahin's most closely guarded secret," he said. "Something that, unless I miss my guess, not even the

Shahin themselves know the full extent of. The elite know, but they haven't even told their own people. And *that's* what really frightens them. The truly ironic thing about it all is that you Terrans could have had it for yourselves. You were there first. Only you saw fit to quarantine the planet. Dreyfus is a poor, blind trusting fool. He told me everything. He went through hell to learn the secret and, even then, he only discovered it by accident. It really is a very fascinating story. As I understand it, he came to Port City for the same reason any spacer comes here. He wanted to get drunk. . . ."

"At last," said Steiger. "He's running."

The compartment was empty, but it was clear that they had been there. Now it would only be a matter of time. They had nowhere left to go.

He whirled as the door opened behind him and an armed man entered. In a brief second, Creed saw others behind him, at least two, perhaps more. The man's eyes widened in surprise and he started to bring up his weapon as Steiger shot him in the chest. It was messy. The others retreated quickly, interposing the door between them and Steiger. Steiger flattened himself against the wall, but they did not fire. They were embassy men.

There was a detachment of Shahin outside, but they were out of sight and they would not become involved. They were only interested in Dreyfus. Steiger could not count on them, nor did he expect to.

There was no other way out.

"*Shit!*" The complicated legalities that kept him safe from prosecution for the murder of those three officers so long as he was in the service of the Shahin no longer applied. He had now committed a capital offense within the local jurisdiction. He was in legal no-man's land. In other words, fair game.

"Give yourself up, man," came a voice from the other side of the door. "You don't stand a chance!"

"Hmmm. Now where have I heard *that* one before?" he murmured.

"We've got you dead, whoever you are! You're outnumbered! Come on out!"

"Jesus. Oh, what the hell, I'll play." Then, shouting, "C'mon and get me, coppers!"

"You can't stay in there forever!"

"I can sure as hell try!"

"We'll wait you out!"

"Okay by me!"

He edged around the room and found a bottle, then poured himself a drink.

"Are you coming out?"

He sipped. "Mmmm. Not bad. Hey, listen. I've got some pretty good Abraxan brandy, here! There's about half a bottle left! Why don't we have a drink and talk it over?"

There was no response.

"No, huh? Oh, well, waste not, want not." He drank straight from the bottle. As he drank, he tried to remember the layout of the building. He was near the front part. Logically, there should be room for three or four other compartments between where he found himself and the outside wall. And the silicon-base walls were not all that thick.

"Hey, you guys want to hear some music?" he yelled. He walked over to Xanfru's sound system and flicked it on, turning up the volume all the way. Then he leveled his weapon at the opposite wall and fired several quick bursts. The music did not quite drown out the sound. He leapt through the gaping hole in the wall into the adjoining compartment. He fired back through the hole and killed the first man in the door. Then he turned and ran.

He easily lost his pursuers in the city streets. It would soon be dawn. He needed time to think things over. He had one thing in common with Alan Dreyfus now. They were both running. He didn't know how Dreyfus felt about it, but he didn't especially care for his predicament. No, come to think of it, they had more than one thing in common after all. There was still Irina.

He slipped into a crowded club. Sin City, the spacers liked to call it. It was a shame he'd have to leave. He had grown to like the place. He ordered a brandy, not quite as good as the bottle he had left unfinished behind him. That had been a little careless. He should have brought it along.

What to do about Irina? He couldn't take her with him, that much was certain. Besides, that girl was poison. He had no illusions about her. She'd stick it to him at the earliest opportunity as soon as she thought she couldn't use him anymore. Quite a girl. He really liked her in a way. She sometimes reminded him of himself. He checked the thought. No, he was mean, but she was meaner.

Like it or not, Lokhrim was his only hope of escape. He might help him. For a Shahin, Lokhrim really wasn't a bad sort. He thought back to the fight they had. Pretty one-sided, all in all, even though he had managed to get in a few licks. He grinned and wondered what they fed them on the homeworld to make them all so tough. Yes, Lokhrim might well help him get off the planet. But he would have to dispose of Dreyfus first. An ellusive prey. Even though he didn't know the man, he was beginning to like him in a perverse sort of way. Now he had to contend not only with the crew of the *Groan*, but with Character as well.

"Hmpf! What goes around, comes around," he said. "Here we are again, Steiger against the world. *Plus ça change, plus c'est la même chose*. It's like pissing in the wind."

"Steiger?"

He turned in response to the soft, seductive voice and twisted, without even thinking, as he saw the woman's gun. She fired and he felt it hit even as he kicked out and knocked the weapon, spinning, from her hand. Then he lunged and grabbed her, pulling her close, spinning her around so that her back was up against his front. One hand pinched her larynx as the other held his gun. Sure enough, she was not alone. Two others were with her, both men. He looked down at her shoulder and saw the insignia of the *Titus Groan*.

The room emptied very quickly. "Okay, put 'em down," he said. The two men dropped their weapons. The woman was choking from the pressure he was applying to her larynx. He relaxed his grip, but only slightly, just enough to barely let her breathe. He didn't know how badly he had been hit. There was no time to check. It hurt though.

"Jesus, this really isn't my night," he gasped.

The two men stood, watching him uncertainly. He could easily kill them both. It was the logical thing to do. He wondered why he wasn't doing it. His hand wavered. It felt very heavy. He felt his knees begin to buckle.

"Ohh, *fuck!*" he said and collapsed to the floor.

The woman coughed and bent over, picking up his gun. She leveled it at him. One of the men plucked it from her hand.

"Finish it!" she said.

The man shook his head. "Uh, uh. We're not going to start playing *that* way. He had us cold and you too. And, besides, he gave Charlie a chance, remember?"

"Yeah. You're right. What do we do with him?"

"We let the old man decide. That is, if Steiger lives that long."

He was awake, but his eyes were closed. Despite the drugs, he was still in a great deal of pain. I could feel him struggling with it. He opened his eyes and looked at me.

"Dreyfus."

"Hello, Creed."

He shut his eyes and chuckled. Briefly, almost imperceptibly, his eyes shut even tighter in a short, involuntary wince. Then he opened his eyes once more and saw Cilix.

"The Ophidian," he said, nodding slightly. "The others?"

"We're all here," I said. "Yuri, the girl you've seen once before, didn't want to come. Jil is with her."

"Jil? The feline?"

I nodded.

I opened myself up to him for an instant and immediately shut him out again. It was too much for me. How he could take it was beyond me. He was a remarkable man.

"I really blew it, didn't I?" he said.

"Oh, I don't know," I replied. "From what I hear, you gave a very good accounting of yourself. It's a miracle you're still alive."

He chuckled once again. And winced again. "Shit. You call this *living*?"

"After a fashion."

"Yeah." He coughed. "What happens now?"

"I don't know yet. To some extent, that's up to you. Captain Kovalevski is postponing the disposition of your case until there is some clearer indication as to whether or not you will survive."

"Kovalevski? Not Character?"

"Yes, that's another thing," I said. "We can't exactly follow procedure at this point. You see, Sim Kovalevski wasn't willing to hand me over to the embassy, so the *Groan* is now officially a renegade ship. And there's the additional matter of our being pursued by a Shahin battle cruiser."

He grinned. "Sounds like I'm the least of your worries."

"Actually, that's not true. You're my number one concern right now. You see, I've resumed my old duties aboard the *Groan* and, since we have no doctor on board, as a paramed, I'm the closest thing. Trying to keep you alive is my responsibility. Ironic, isn't it?"

He watched me without responding for a while, then there was the barest glimmer of a smile. "You may have to take advantage of your convenient position," he said softly. "Because I'm not going to die on you."

"If you think I'm going to make sure you die of your wound, you're mistaken."

"No," he sighed, "you wouldn't. You're not the type."

"And you are? Tell me something, Creed, I know all the details of your capture. You could have easily killed those three. Why didn't you?"

"Fuck if I know."

I reached forward and wiped some of the sweat from his forehead. I rested my fingertips very lightly on his cranium. "It must be very lonely in there," I said.

"Pity, Dreyfus?"

"No. Not pity."

"Shit." He gasped and I knew that the pain was getting the better of him.

"I'm going to have to knock you out, Creed. I've done just about everything I can for you right now. The rest is up to you. And a higher power, if you believe in that. Either way, I can't have you thrashing around or you'll start to hemorrhage again."

"Yeah." He gritted his teeth. "Wake me when it's over, willya?"

Seconds later, he lay still, drugged into unconsciousness. It had been necessary to administer a dangerously high dose. He was fighting everything. I had no reason to want him to survive. After all, he had meant to kill me. It was strange. The other Alan Dreyfus would have killed him in a second. This one was doing everything in his power to save him.

"Will he live?" asked Cilix.

"I don't know."

"What will happen to him if he does?"

"I don't know the answer to that one either. The captain and I haven't discussed it."

"There will be pressure from the crew?"

"I'm certain of it."

"One in particular."

"Yes. Charlie Faen. If he will let me, I think that I can help him. Something happened between him and Steiger, I don't know what. I haven't had a chance to be with him. None of us have had much chance to do anything, yet. And we may never have the chance."

Both of us knew that the *Groan* had been designed primarily as a commercial vessel. We'd stand no chance against the Shahin ship. It was amazing that we had come this far.

There wasn't anything further that I could do for Steiger. I left him on life support and made my way, with Cilix, to the captain.

"How is he?" Kovalevski asked.

"He's holding the line," I said. "Whether or not he'll make it is anybody's guess at this point. He's fighting. It would be a shame to lose him."

The captain glanced at me. "You've changed, Alan."

"Yes."

His face was grim. "We're on borrowed time. We've all been very lucky so far."

"Have you had any success in raising that Shahin ship?"

He shook his head. "No. They refuse to answer. I wish I knew what they intend to do. They could catch us easily if they wanted to. So far, they've been content to merely follow us." He glanced at Cilix. "Do you drink?"

"I have developed the habit."

"Good. I've called Mustafa in. I think it's time that we all sat down and had a good, long talk." He fetched a bottle and some tumblers. Mustafa joined us shortly.

"I haven't yet had a chance to thank you for saving our lives," I said.

Mustafa shrugged. "You'd do the same for me," he said. Then he smiled. "Besides, do you have any idea how much the crew enjoyed it all? It was the closest most of them had come to the 'promise of adventure' since they read the recruiting brochures."

"Well, I'm afraid it's a long way from being over," I said. "There'll be a lot more than mere adventure where we're going."

"Yes, I've been meaning to ask you about that, navigator," Kovalevski smiled wanly. "Where *are* we going? What is this intrigue all about, anyway? You said that if we were sucessful in this venture you have planned, all will be forgiven and the Guild will welcome us all back with open arms. I never thought I would go so far in taking anyone on faith, Alan. Frankly, I'm terrified. If this goes beyond this room, I will personally throttle each of you, but the truth of the matter is that I feel as if I have lost all control: of the ship, of this situation, and of my senses. What in God's name have you stumbled upon that Lord Hhargoth's own ship pursues us?"

"I know that you must have a million questions, Sim," I said. "Just as I know that it's damn near impossible for you to ask them all. You know I'm grateful to you and the crew for what you've done. And I can express my gratitude in something far, far better than mere words. If Hhargoth gives me enough time, I intend to give each and every one of you a gift. A gift such as you could never imagine in your wildest dreams. As for what I've stumbled upon, I can show you. But brace yourselves for a shock: You know that Hhargoth deprived me of my arm. It was burned off just below the shoulder, here," I pointed to the place on my loose sleeve. "Cilix, will you help me with my shirt?"

Their eyes bulged as, a moment later, I stood bare chested before them.

"*Holy Christ*," Sim muttered.

Mustafa's jaw had gone slack. Both of them reached for the bottle at the same time.

It had happened much faster than I had thought it would. Though grossly out of proportion with the rest of my body, my arm was fully formed. The hand, the wrist, the fingers and the elbow, all the muscles, everything was normal, relatively speaking. The flesh was soft and pulpy-looking and the skin was red and heavily veined, but it was a normal arm and hand . . . normal, that is, for a child of about five or six years.

They were literally speechless—but were not beyond taking a long drink.

"I know how you must feel," I said. "Don't say anything. Not just yet. I'd like to send for Jil and Yuri. They can help me to complete my . . . explanation. But I must caution you. In order for all your questions to be answered, you must both be willing to bare your souls. To me, to Cilix, to them and to each other. There's no other way."

"Hell, I'm not even sure I know what that means," said Mustafa. "But if your friends can help to fill me in, I'm willing."

"I'm not certain about baring my soul," said Sim. "It all sounds rather dramatic. But after seeing that. . . ." He stared at my new arm, shaking his head in bewilderment. "If Mustafa's willing, then, by God, so am I. Go ahead."

When Jil and Yuri arrived, I locked us in and turned out the lights just to help the effect along. It really wasn't necessary, but I was feeling like a bit of a ham. I couldn't wait to "show off." We all sat down on the deck together, close to each other. Again, there was no need for it, but Jil and Yuri held their hands to reassure them. I relaxed, inhaled and exhaled, shut my eyes and brought us all together.

Once again, I found myself a child, romping in a creche, gurgling happily and babbling away in a tongue that I would never humanly be able to speak. My soft and cuddly playmates, my creche brothers and sisters were all around me and we stroked and hugged and pummeled each other, nipping playfully with our tiny, undeveloped teeth. One of them turned to me and began to recite awkwardly from the Koran, stumbling over the words.

I grew, shedding my first skin, staring proudly at the gleaming, iridescent new scales that felt soft and cool to my touch. I watched a beautiful and youthful Jil, dressed resplendently in a military-style cadet uniform, a brass visored shako tilted at a rakish angle on her head as she sat astride a white stallion, putting the animal through its paces and shouting in Russian with delight as she took her very first jump. She removed her shako with a flourish and waved at me.

I licked my lips and moaned with pleasure as I caressed the naked limbs of my very first girl, her lovely white skin like snow beside my coal black body. I entered her and encountered resistence. Confused, I pushed harder, then felt something give and Yuri cried out briefly, then hugged me to her and smothered me with kisses, whispering that it was all right. Her features seemed to swim before my eyes and they melted into those of young Sim, who clung to me and wept quietly. I kissed his hair and stroked him gently, twisting my body around so that my head was at his waist. I kissed him and felt his warm lips envelop me hesitantly. Fur began to sprout forth from his skin and we lapped at each other with curiously forked tongues.

It was the middle of the night and I got out of bed, dressing quietly so as not to wake my parents. I took my few most treasured possessions, which I had packed in secret, tiptoed silently through the house and stole away into the night. I saw a shape loom up out of the darkness and I passed out into Cilix' arms. When I woke up, I found myself in the cabin of my very first ship. I wore the uniform of the Guild proudly, dreaming of the day when the second lieutenant's bars would be replaced by the insignia of a captain.

I heard Jil's voice calling to me and I looked up, only it was John's face and he looked back at me with the dreamy gaze of Jil's painting.

I held Anthrus in my arms. He laughed and sank his teeth into the soft flesh of my arm, just below the bicep. Jil crawled to him, clutched at his tail, pulled him from me and placed him on her own black arm. Anthrus spat fire and the arm disintegrated into globules of blood and spattered gobbets of flesh and muscle tissue. I turned away and ran out into the streets, barely having the strength to put one foot before the other. In an alley, I found Sim curled up next to a pile of refuse, calling for his mother. I picked him up and laid him gently on the bed. Mustafa put his arm upon my shoulder and whispered, "Please, don't let him die." The scars upon our bodies healed as I dreamed nightmares populated by Shahin and Zharii. We awoke and started running for the stars.

Kovalevski was breathing heavily and his cheeks were streaked with tears. Mustafa sat still, stunned, shivering as Yuri held his hand in both of hers. Neither one of them could take their eyes from me.

We were on our way to Xerxes V.

"Sit down, Irina," said Patricia Character.

Irina sat down opposite the desk. She looked cool, composed, even haughty. Patricia knew her instantly. She smiled slightly, remembering her own youth and all the Irinas she had known.

"Do you know why you were brought here?" she asked.

Irina shook her head. "Am I under arrest? I haven't done anything."

"Where is Creed Steiger?"

"I don't know."

"You were living with him."

"Yes."

"And you don't know where he is?"

"He doesn't tell me where he goes and I don't ask."

"You could be protecting him."

"Why should I?"

"You would be in a lot of trouble if you were," Patricia said. "Steiger is wanted for murder."

Irina didn't even blink.

"You don't even care, do you?" asked Patricia.

"I didn't say that."

"You didn't have to. It's too bad in a way. I'd really hate to be in his place right now. The Shahin will not help him since he failed in his mission. Alan Dreyfus managed to make good his escape." She smiled dryly at Irina's reaction. "I am not without my sources," she said. "And what my sources don't tell me, my own experience and intuition do. I don't know what your relationship with those two was exactly, and I don't really want to know. I'm certain it was something pretty sordid and unsavory."

"May I go now?" asked Irina coldly.

"Yes, go. I have no more time to waste on you. I have a lot of work to do." Too bad, she thought, that she would not live to see its full fruition. That would really have been something.

Irina rose to leave.

"Oh, by the way," Patricia said, "I seriously doubt that Steiger, if he is still in the city, would be lunatic enough to go back to his old quarters. But, just in case, we're taking them over. I don't want you going back there, you'd only be in the way."

"Where am I supposed to go?"

"That's hardly my concern, my dear. Frankly, I couldn't care less."

"Thanks a lot, Ambassador," Irina sneered.

"Your sarcasm is wasted on me, my dear. I might have been disposed to help you, but you aren't exactly one of our most concerned citizens. I *could* suggest a couple of places if you're looking for work and a temporary place to stay, but I'm afraid you're too much of a whore to make an honest prostitute."

Irina's face went white. Her fingernails dug deeply into her palms as she shot Patricia a look of pure loathing.

"Out!" Patricia ordered.

Irina turned slowly and left. Once outside, her composure began to crack. Her lower lip started trembling uncontrollably, then tears began to come. "*Damn*," she whispered. Then, louder, "Damn, damn, *damn*!" She gave vent to her impotent anger in a torrent of scathing Russian obscenities. It seemed to help, a little, but not much.

Outside the gates of the embassy, Port City beckoned. She had no place to stay. She had no money. She was furious and she was hungry and she was alone. She took a deep breath and bit her lip nervously, swallowed, then squared her lovely shoulders and walked out through the gates.

Chapter Six

"And *I* say kill him!"

"At ease, Lieutenant," said the old man.

"Lieutenant!" Charlie Faen hissed. "That's a joke! What the hell does that mean now? We've all lost our commissions now. We're all of us criminals now, remember? I'm no more a lieutenant than you're a ship's captain!"

"I'm still the captain of this ship!" said Kovalevski, glaring at Faen. "And you are whatever I *say* you are. We all have responsibilities here; to the ship and to each other. Need I remind you that we are under battle conditions?"

"That's a joke too," said Charlie somewhat more calmly, though bitterly. "The Shahin are playing with us. Our ship is no match for theirs and you all know it."

"You could have stayed behind, Charlie," said Mustafa. "I thought that was what you wanted. Your commission used to mean a lot to you. What made you change your mind? Why did you stay aboard, instead of letting yourself be grounded with the others? That would have been the safest path to take."

"I—I don't know. I must have been crazy."

"Are you sure that's the reason, Charlie?" I asked. "Why don't you let me help you? Show me what's eating away at you. Let me in."

"Keep away from me!" he shrilled. "You may have half the crew mooning over you and following you around, but you stay away from me! Look at you! You've grown your arm back like some sort of—of *lizard*. You want to be like one of *them*!" He pointed ludicrously at some infinite point where he might have imagined the Shahin ship to be. "Don't think I don't know. You've been spending hours in the gym trying to turn that weird body of yours into some kind of superman, invading the minds of half the crew. You're a *freak*!"

"*That's enough!*" shouted Kovalevski.

"No," I said, "it's all right. Let him get it off his chest."

"Don't do me any favors, Alan," Charlie said. "I don't understand. What's *happened* to you? That man tried to kill you!"

"But he didn't."

"Only because we didn't give him a chance. And now you want to save his miserable life?"

"He spared yours, Charlie."

He had no answer for that. He looked wildly at us all, then stormed out.

"I'm afraid he's going to be a problem," said Kovalevski. "I should have made him stay behind with the others."

"He'll come around," said Mustafa. "He's young and he's scared. I'm sure he didn't mean all those things he said, Alan."

"Maybe so," I said, "but his point is well taken. I *have* been letting it go to my head."

"I don't know about that," said Mustafa. "Nobody's ever been through what you're going through right now. It's a great strain. After all, you're only human."

"Am I? I'm not so sure anymore." I raised my brand new arm and flexed it, feeling the power there. "Who's to say whether I'm a freak or human? Perhaps Charlie's right."

I had grown strong on the voyage. My arm was now fully grown and I was in better physical condition than I had ever been in my life. I was in complete and utter control of my body. As

soon as my arm had grown to match the other one, I had begun
training, anxious to see if what I had earlier suspected about my
body was true.

The discovery of my regenerative capabilities had shocked and
stunned my fellow crew members and even frightened a few of
them. But it fascinated several members of the crew who were
considerably more devoted to the cult of the body than most. At
the start, I felt somewhat intimidated by these men and women.
Despite my rapid recovery from my previous emaciated state, I
still looked like a victim of malnutrition when compared to them.

After my first two-hour workout, I felt sick and exhausted. I
was nauseous. I felt a pressure in my chest and every single muscle
in my body ached. The muscles spasmed with little jerks when
I tried to sleep. As a paramed, I understood it was normal, given
that I had never really taken proper care of my body before and
had, in fact, allowed it to be grievously abused. Still, understanding didn't make it easier.

The following ship's day, however, I felt better. Though still
slightly sore, I awoke feeling considerably refreshed and envi-
gorated. And, to my amazement, when I started exercising again,
I found that I had grown stronger, although there had been no
visible changes. I had no trouble with the weights I had used
before, and I was able to increase them. That certainly wasn't
normal, but then, what was normal for me? I had no way of
knowing, but I resolved to find out.

Each time, I found that I was stronger. The exercises strained
and taxed my muscles to their utmost, and they responded rapidly,
growing in size and strength. Soon I was eagerly sweating and
grimacing with the rest of my training partners, enjoying every
second of it. Not only was I getting results, but I found that it had
a calming, soothing, clearing effect on my mind, a therapy that
was very much in order, considering our circumstances. I found
that I could send blood to a muscle just by thinking about it. My
circulation improved and my heart became stronger, measurably
so, as my regimen forced the blood to pound through my arteries,
pumping up the muscle tissue and revitalizing it. I ended each
training period feeling robust, clear-headed, energized. As my
mass increased, so did my lung capacity, and my digestion improved. I treated my body as a medical experiment, carefully

monitoring all my functions and making certain that I ingested at least three hundred grams of protein every twenty-four hour period. The results were astonishing.

I soon surpassed all of my training partners in strength and size. With Jil urging me on, supporting me in my efforts like a relentless taskmaster, I was soon lifting two hundred kilograms and more. I had outgrown all of my old clothes. My arms measured almost sixty-two centimeters around. My chest was one hundred and fifty. My latissimus dorsi muscles fanned out from my back like wings. My waist became lean and trim and my abdominal muscles stood out in sharp relief. The lack of excess fat on my body made my veins stand out like maps of rivers. Running and doing calesthenics in the gel tank had increased my endurance and kept me supple. I found myself staring at my reflection in the mirror, not so much with narcissism as with disbelief. Was that really *me*? I did, indeed, resemble a Shahin warrior, only I was a great deal shorter in stature. There was no reason why the same effects could not be experienced by any human. It was a wonder that Hhargoth, knowing this no doubt, had not acted to destroy our ship.

His restraint was a mystery. It had the entire crew on edge.

And I had not been alone in regaining vigor. Creed Steiger had survived and was almost completely recovered. And now, his fate was to be settled.

It was a strange ethic, waiting for a man to recover, all the while knowing that it could be for nothing. With Steiger, the feeling was very strong indeed. He was convinced that we would kill him. And I couldn't resist the temptation to get through to him. . . .

I opened myself up to him slowly as he slept, controlling the intensity of the contact so as not to jar him. I thought that asleep, he would be able to undergo the experience easily, but once again I underestimated the control the man possessed, his resolve, the strength of his will.

The moment I made contact, his eyelids snapped open and his head jerked in my direction as he sat up abruptly. I backed away involuntarily, startled at the speed of his reactions.

His eyes bored into mine with fierce intensity. "What the hell are you doing?" he demanded.

"Trying to reach you," I said.

He frowned. "Don't get clever. What are you, a telepath or something?"

"Or something."

"You've tried to do this several times before," he said, "whatever the hell it is."

"Yes, though not completely."

"I *thought* I felt something screwy happening, like something nudging away at me, but I didn't know what was going on." He looked at me belligerently. "So it was you, was it? You're some kind of mutant, aren't you? I've been watching you sprout. All over. What kind of vitamins did you steal from Hhargoth?"

"No, I'm not a mutant. Not in the strictest sense of the word anyway. If you really want to know, I can show you. Wouldn't you like to know why you were sent to kill me?"

"I haven't exactly got much of a choice, have I?"

"Would you have given *me* a choice had you found me before my friends did?"

He smiled slowly. "Probably not. But then, I haven't been all that smart lately. Who knows, I might have done something stupid."

"I can establish the contact I want against your will," I said. "At least, I'm fairly certain that I can. But it would be easier for both of us if you were receptive."

"Why should I want to make it easier for you?" he demanded. "Hhargoth was scared half to death of you. And if that son-of-a-bitch was worried, I'm sure you can take care of yourself."

"Are *you* afraid of me, Creed?"

He paused, giving the matter thought. That was the measure of the man, I realized. He didn't live by any vainglorious concepts of machismo and heroics. Creed Steiger never lied to himself for an instant. In that lay his greatest strength: he accepted his mortality, he did not resist what *was*.

"No," he said after some consideration. "Maybe I should be, but I'm not. In some ways, I think, you and I have a lot in common, don't we? I sense that."

I smiled at him. "'To know oneself is to observe one's interaction with another person.'"

He laughed, suddenly. "You *are* a philosopher. Funny, what

you said is just a fancy way of expressing something I always felt in combat. It has to do with fear."

"How so?"

"You've never fought, have you?"

"Not in the way you mean, no."

"Men react to it in different ways. Some of them want to be heroes. They're usually the first to drop. Others are paralyzed with fear and they wind up defeating themselves. It pulls at them. Fear pulls, did you know that? I used to know a guy who was deathly afraid of heights. You couldn't get him near a balcony because he was afraid he'd fall. And, believe it or not, sooner or later he'd wind up on that balcony, looking over the edge. All on his own accord. I'd watch him looking down at the ground below, completely hypnotized, feeling the desire to jump. What ever you fear the most winds up getting you.

"I remember the first time I felt fear. It was in the academy during martial arts training. Yes, I know, if I went to the academy, why didn't I become an officer? It's a long story. Maybe I'll tell you sometime. Anyway, there was this guy in our class, a black African, about seven feet tall. Had long legs, like pile drivers. He could kick like you wouldn't believe. Amazingly strong. Every time we sparred, I was always afraid he'd catch me with those deadly feet of his, with that long reach. Sure enough, every time, I ran right into those kicks. I finally realized that being afraid of those hook kicks wasn't going to make any difference. He was still going to throw them and I was still going to get nailed, whether I was afraid or not. My being scared only gave him another weapon to use against me. It made him stronger.

"I decided to stop worrying about whether I was going to win or lose when I sparred with him. I was getting hurt anyway, so I saw no point in worrying about it. Just like your friends are probably going to kill me. I'm not going to lose any sleep over it. I just put the thought of pain right out of my mind. If he was going to hit me a glancing blow, I decided I was going to nail him solid. If he nailed me solid, I'd damn well break a few bones for him. The next time we sparred, I just stopped thinking because thinking got in my way. And wouldn't you know it? I beat him. I beat him every time."

I pursed my lips, thinking about what he had said. "You know, I envy you," I said. "I haven't reached that point yet.

> *Into a soul absolutely free*
> *From thoughts and emotion,*
> *Even the tiger finds no room*
> *To insert its fierce claws.*

I've become something of a student, lately," I grinned.

"What's that from?" he asked.

"It's a very old Taoist saying," I replied. "The old Taoist priests possessed a great deal of truth. We have forgotten much of it."

"You have that in your tapes here?" he asked.

I nodded.

"I'd like to take a look at some of that, if it's all right. Seems like I've got a lot of time on my hands."

"I'll arrange it."

"Thanks."

I turned to go.

"You're not going to try that probing trick of yours?" he asked.

I stopped and turned back to face him. "No, I don't think so. There really isn't any need, is there? We seem to be communicating very well. I still prefer talking, you know. We'll do this again soon. And I'll tell you all about my . . . mutation."

He looked relieved. "I'm anxious as hell to hear about it. I never cared for killing a man without knowing why." He chuckled. "You know, Alan, I can't say as I'm happy about the way things turned out since I wound up with the short end of the stick, but I'm glad I didn't kill you."

It was a mistake of course. I should have done it. I'm not sure why I didn't. I certainly enjoyed talking with Jil and Cilix and Yuri and the others. Jil and I, especially, were able to share and communicate very openly. Our shared experiences had only enhanced our relationship. I don't know what prevented me from trying it with Steiger. Perhaps it was fear or subconscious resentment of him, I didn't know. I wanted to know him and, at the same time, I was apprehensive. The fault for what had happened lay with me. I could have prevented it.

Charlie Faen leveled his weapon at Steiger.

"So?" said Creed. "I've been tried *in abstentia*, have I?"

"There's not going to be a trial," replied Charlie.

Creed raised his eyebrows. "You're acting on your own, Charlie? I applaud your initiative."

"Shut up!"

"Still trying to be a hero, huh, Charlie?"

"I said, *shut up*!"

"Don't tell me, let me guess. Alan's sticking up for me, isn't he? You're afraid they're going to let me live. I could be very useful to this ship since I'm probably one of the few veterans on board and I know the Shahin. Alan's being practical and the skipper's listening to him, isn't he?"

"Dreyfus is crazy. He's on some sort of insane ego trip and he's got half the people on this ship snowed. But not me. You're a killer, Steiger. You're dangerous, and God only knows we've got troubles enough."

"No, I see, you couldn't possibly let me live. A man like me. I stand for everything evil in your scheme of things, don't I? I'm just a soldier, but you're the patriot. You're the hero. You're an asshole, Charlie." He shook his head. "Why don't you go ahead and shoot, hero?"

With a lightning motion, Creed snapped out his arm, grabbing the container for his urine and dashing it in Charlie's face. As the acidic liquid hit his eyes, Charlie cried out and flinched, jerking instinctively away. Steiger launched himself from the bed.

I was summoned from my quarters by Kovalevski. I took my leave of Jil and went up to the bridge. The atmosphere, when I arrived there, was very tense.

"We've got trouble," Kovalevski said.

"The Shahin?"

"No. Steiger." He thumbed the intercom. "Alan's here," he said.

"Alan?" came Steiger's voice from the speaker.

"What is it, Creed? What's happened?"

"I'm afraid we've got ourselves a problem," he said wearily. "I'm not sure what we're going to do about it."

"He's killed Charlie," Kovalevski said heavily. "I've got a detail down there, but he's barricaded himself inside the sick bay and he's got a hostage. One of the corpsmen, Sarah." I paled; she had helped me treat him and was now his prisoner. "He's also got Charlie's gun."

"He tried to kill me, Alan," said Steiger's voice. "I had no choice."

"Damn it, Creed! Did you have to *kill* him?"

"I didn't mean to, Alan. I swear I didn't. I just jumped him and tried to get the gun away from him, but he broke his neck in the fall. But I don't expect anyone'll believe that."

"I believe you, Creed. Let me talk to Sarah." He put her on. "Did you see it?" I asked.

"No," she answered, "but his neck *is* broken. It *could* have happened like he said."

"Then, again," said Mustafa from behind me, "it could *not* have."

"Are *you* all right?" asked Kovalevski.

"Yes, sir," she replied. "He hasn't tried to harm me in any way."

"I will if I have to," said Steiger, "nothing personal, you understand."

"Yeah," she replied flatly.

"So where does that get you?" said Kovalevski. "If you harm her, whom are you going to hide behind?"

"You've got a point, Captain," he said, "but I'm betting that you're not going to sacrifice a member of your crew unnecessarily."

"See what sort of man you've been protecting?" he said, turning to me. "I can't do anything to him without harming the girl."

"We need him Sim."

"He tried to kill you!"

"We still need him."

"Not that badly."

"Yes. That badly. Where we're going, we're going to need all the help we can get. And there's still Hhargoth to contend with. Steiger knows those people better than anyone, Sim. He's served with them. He's got combat experience. Besides yourself and Mustafa, no one else on board has. Give the man a fair trial. Put him in double jeopardy. I can tell you if he's telling the truth and you can scan him at the same time. Better yet, I can reach in there and find out what he has on his mind. What have you got to lose?"

He thought a moment, then looked to Mustafa for a reaction. The exec nodded.

"All right," said Sim. "We'll do it your way."

Feeling relieved, I put my proposition to Steiger. My relief was short lived.

"Sorry, Alan," he replied. "No can do."

"But why? You've got nothing to lose! Be reasonable!"

"I've got everything to lose and I can't afford to be reasonable. I've got to look out for number one."

"Creed, why won't you trust me?"

He laughed.

"All right," said Kovalevski. "What now?"

I shook my head and shrugged, defeated. "I don't know. That's up to him, I guess. I tried."

"Steiger? This is the captain."

"I'm still here."

"What do you want?"

"I'll settle for getting out of this in one piece," he replied. "Where's the ship headed?"

Kovalevski hesitated, then shrugged. "Xerxes V."

There was silence on the other end. "That doesn't help me much," he said finally. "What little I've heard about that place ain't good. Is Hhargoth's ship still out there?"

"Yes."

"He doing anything?"

"No."

"Hmmmm, strange. That isn't like him. What do you suppose he's up to?"

"I wouldn't know," the skipper answered. "Are we going to discuss strategy?"

Steiger's chuckle emanated from the speaker. "Touchy aren't you?"

"Where the welfare of the ship and of my crew is concerned, yes," Kovalevski said grimly.

"Well, I don't blame you. I'm a mite concerned myself, actually. If this old bucket goes, so do I."

"I repeat, Steiger, what do you want?"

"I told you, Captain. I want to survive."

"What do you propose we do?"

"Frankly, Captain, I don't know. I'm fresh out of ideas. Looks like we've sorta got each other by the balls, doesn't it?"

Kovalevski angrily snapped off the intercom.

"The man's gotta sleep sometime," said Mustafa.

"I know," said Kovalevski, "but that doesn't help us. Any sound we'd make in breaking in would only serve to alert him."

"I was thinking of Sarah," said Mustafa. "She's a corpsman after all, and they *are* in sick bay. He's in a weakened condition and she's fit. When he finally drops off, all she has to do is slip him an injection. I think that we can count on her to do that, don't you?"

"Steiger isn't stupid," I said. "I'm sure that's occurred to him as well. She'd be taking an awful chance."

"She's a spacer," Mustafa replied. "She'll come through."

Many hours later, they sat staring at each other while the security detail outside the barricaded door was relieved.

"I'll bet you fall asleep before I do," Steiger said.

Sarah didn't answer. Instead, she rose to her feet and turned to the cabinets.

"What are you doing?"

"Taking inventory."

"You've already taken inventory twice."

"So I'll take it three times. What's it to you?"

"No, you won't." He gestured, vaguely, with the gun. "You're going to sit down and relax."

"It's only something to pass the time," she protested.

"Sorry," he said. "I'd much rather have you sitting down and doing nothing. Growing good and bored. And tired."

She sighed and sat down with an air of resignation.

"Thank you," said Creed.

"You're welcome," she replied.

He lit another cigarette. She had already told him that smoking was not allowed in sick bay. It seemed a silly thing to say under the circumstances.

"Mind if I have one of those?" she asked.

"I thought smoking wasn't allowed in here?" he said innocently.

"*Bastard*," she whispered under her breath.

"Look, Sarah," Steiger said not unkindly, "why not stop fighting and relax? You can barely keep your eyes open. Let's stop this silly game. I don't want to hurt you and I'm sure as hell not going to try and rape you or anything like that, so you might as well give up and get some shut-eye. I'm not about to let you try anything clever while I'm sleeping and I can easily outlast you. You'll only succeed in making yourself miserable."

"We'll see who outlasts whom," she said.

"Well, if you're going to be *that* way about it, I'm just going to have to *put* you to sleep." He started to get up.

"Just you try," she said, suddenly producing a laser scalpel.

Steiger stopped. "Inventory, huh? All right, that does it. I'm just going to have to figure out some way to restrain you and that's all there is to it."

"I'm warning you, Steiger," Sarah said, sounding suddenly very alert and in control, "don't come near me!"

"Shit," said Steiger. "That's what I get for trying to be a nice guy. I should have locked you up first thing."

The only problem was that he didn't see any immediate means of immobilizing her. He had never done duty in a sick bay and, though he knew that there must be *some* means of restraining patients, none fell readily to hand. There were no attachments on the beds that he could see, and in order to look for something suitable, he would have to take his eyes off Sarah. He was not about to do that, not while she was brandishing that nasty little scalpel. The only possible course of action open to him seemed to be to knock her unconscious and then search for something to hold her. He briefly regretted the lack of sheets or blankets on a space craft.

"Come on, now, Sarah," he said casually, "let me have that thing." He held out his hand.

She slashed at it and he withdrew it just in time.

"What *is* it with this ship?" he asked himself aloud. "Everybody on board wants to be a hero. Goddam it, Sarah, I've got a *gun*!" He held it up and shook it at her. "People are supposed to do what you tell them when you wave a gun at them."

"So go ahead and shoot me then" she said, still crouched, holding the scalpel. She seemed extremely energetic all of a sudden, áfter all that time. She had taken him in completely. He would have thought that she was just about ready to drop off. Hell, *he* felt tired!

"Look," he said, "will you give me that—" and, without warning, he threw his gun at her with all his might. Even as she flinched and it struck her in the shoulder, he was moving. His hand darted out and grasped her right wrist, the hand that held the scalpel.

She swore and twisted in his grasp and he cuffed her hard on the jaw. She crumpled. There was a slight, pittering sound, like tiny bits of gravel falling. He looked down. Pills.

"*Fuck!*" He struck himself in the forehead. "Am I an idiot! Inventory, my ass!"

"Sarah!" Someone's voice came through the intercom speaker. "Sarah, are you all right?"

Steiger walked over and pressed the button. "Nice try, friends, but it didn't work."

"Steiger! If you harmed her—"

"Relax, she's fine. Afraid she can't talk to you right now though. I've had to, uh, quiet her down a little."

"How do we know she's all right?"

"Well, you could take my word and wait a little while for her to come around or you could try breaking in here and maybe get Sarah and a couple of you killed. What's it going to be?"

There was no reply. And, as he reached out again to shut off the intercom, he noticed he'd been cut. The wound was small, but it was deep and, though partially cauterized, a small amount of blood was burbling forth. "Damn." He started rummaging through the supplies and finally found the spray-on plastic sealant. As he was covering the wound, he had an inspiration.

A short while later, Sarah lay stretched out on one of the beds, covered from the neck down in a full, hardened plastic body cast. That taken care of, he began his own inventory of the supplies.

When Kovalevski awakened from his sleep, he immediately checked with the security detail for a report on the current status of the situation in the sick bay.

"Steiger is still in control," he was told.

"Sarah wasn't able to hold out?"

"I'm not sure *what* happened, sir. She's still okay, we've been speaking with her, but he's put her in a full body cast so she can't move."

"Hell."

"And he's been up all the time."

"What? *Still?* He should be exhausted by now!"

"*You* tell him, sir. I'm sorry, Captain, I didn't mean that. It's just that he's got us all on edge. He's been acting real strange lately."

"What do you mean, strange? How?"

"Damned if I know, sir. It was quiet in there for a while, but lately, there's a lot of noise coming through. He's been moving around an awful lot and talking to himself and yelling—"

"What?"

"Listen for yourself, sir."

Kovalevski raised sick bay. "Steiger?"

"What do you want?"

He sounded manic, wound-up, irritated.

"What's going on in there?"

"What *should* be going on? Nothing! Leave me alone, what the hell do you want from me? You're driving me crazy, you and all those other assholes out there, all the time badgering me with questions, wanting to talk to Sarah all the time so I've had to move her next to the damn intercom and she won't shut up half the time, always whining and complaining and having to go to the head only she *can't* go to the head cause she can't fuckin' *move*, which is the way I want it, just fine with me, only she keeps saying how she's gotta pee and I tell her to cross her legs only she can't cross her legs cause she can't fuckin' *move....*" Steiger started giggling.

"What the hell...," muttered Kovalevski.

"He's stoned," I said.

"Oh, that's wonderful news," said Kovalevski, shaking his head wearily.

"Well, if you had to pick a place where you could hole up indefinitely with a hostage, you couldn't do much better than sick bay," I said. "He's got enough drugs down there to keep him flying indefinitely. The only thing I'm worried about is whether or not he knows enough about what he's doing to pull it off with a reasonable degree of safety."

"Are you kidding?"

"I wish I were. I seriously doubt that Creed knows enough about drugs to carry off a—for lack of a better way of putting it—a successful binge. He could wind up taking the wrong thing and overdosing, possibly going catatonic, perhaps sedating himself, causing some sort of brain damage, or even dying. On the other hand, we've got depressants down there that might make him quiet enough to allow us to break in. That's if he doesn't start hallucinating, which is something I'd rather not even think about."

"You mean he could hurt Sarah?" Kovalevski asked anxiously.

"Without meaning to, yes. I'm afraid that's a very distinct possibility."

The captain sighed. "As if we don't have troubles enough. We've *got* to get him out of there!"

"I agree," I said. "I only wish I knew how. He's justifiably paranoid right now. Leaving aside whatever it is he's been taking, he's killed Charlie Faen and he has no reason to expect anything but retribution from us. He's a hard man, Sim. A very suspicious man. Very bitter, though he hides it well enough. I couldn't think of a worse personality to subject to drugs."

"Maybe if you talked to him again. . . ."

"I'm going to have to. If for no other reason, to try and hold him down."

"Yes, do that," Kovalevski replied, his lips compressed grimly. "We're coming up on Xerxes V. Whatever it is that Hhargoth intends, he's going to do it soon. If we can't resolve this thing by then," he paused, taking a deep breath, "I'm going to send the men in."

"And Sarah?"

He shook his head. "Sarah knows the risks involved."

"There has to be another way."

"If you think of one, let me know."

Seventy-two hours later, Creed had tired of the little red pills and he started experimenting. The amphethyroids were making his heart race and he was hyperventilating.

"What are these?" he asked Sarah, who sat stretched out in the corner.

"You don't want those."

Steiger's eyes narrowed with suspicion. She had been driving him crazy with her constant suffering, so he had attacked the body cast, shattering it into a thousand fragments. Sarah wouldn't have moved had she been able to. All that time inside the cast had left her numb, but even if she had any feeling in her joints at all, she would have been petrified with fear at the sight of Steiger, eyes bulging, face sweating, screaming insanely, and pounding savagely at the cast with a nysteel mallet. Miraculously, she escaped the ordeal unscathed. Now, she half-sat, half-lay in the corner of the room, desperately trying to restore the circulation in her legs, not even thinking about the pain there. She was locked in a room with a screaming berserker who, at any moment, might see fit to cave her skull in. She had been doing her best to blend in with the wall and not attract his attention, but when she saw what he was holding, she summoned up every ounce of self-control that she possessed in order to remain calm.

"Believe me, you don't want those."

"Why not? What's wrong with 'em?" His voice had become a rapid staccato burst of sound.

"What is it, Sarah?" came Alan's voice over the intercom. He had been trying to talk Steiger "down" for what seemed like an infinity to her. There had been a bad moment when Steiger went crazy on the cast. If not for Alan, the whole thing would have gone up in smoke right then and there. And it could still. Sarah was afraid. She didn't want to die.

"Sarah, what's going on? Talk to me!" Alan's voice sounded strained, not surprisingly.

"You shut up!" screamed Steiger, pointing at her.

"Alan, he's found the atropine sulphate!" she shouted.

"I said shut up!" he screamed, shaking all over as if in a fever.

"Creed, listen to me," said Alan, his voice very calm, very soft, very soothing. "Atropine sulphate is very dangerous. I understand that you want to keep awake. It's perfectly all right with me for you to keep awake, I want you to believe that, really, but you don't want to take that stuff. It's vicious."

"Yeah, why should you want to help me? This sulphate stuff is probably just the thing, right? It's potent, huh? Just what I need!"

"Creed, listen, that stuff's bad. You're strung out. You're speeding like crazy already. Atropine sulphate is the active ingredient in belladonna, you know what that is, don't you? It's bad enough by itself. You don't know what you're doing. You have no pharmacological background at all. If you take that in your present condition, it'll blow your head clean off. That won't help you and it won't help me."

Sarah concentrated intensely on the interchange. She was exhausted. Completely drained and on the verge of collapse. She wanted to shut her eyes so badly.... Her head lolled forward on her chest and it seemed impossibly heavy. She had bitten her lip and blood was trickling down her chin. She tried to concentrate on the pain, so it would keep her awake, but even that was proving difficult.

Steiger was thoroughly crazed, gone deeply around the bend. In the early stages, he had struggled to maintain control, to hold onto some semblance of sanity, but all that was gone now, dispersed into a cacophonic, amphethyroid haze. And, to top it off, he had found some whiskey, whiskey that had no business even *being* there. She had passed it up in her inventory because it had been cleverly disguised as a container of rubbing alcohol. Sarah made a mental note, with her rapidly diminishing capacities, to find out who had hidden it there and, if she survived, to cut the bastard's balls off.

Steiger's innate paranoia was now in full bloom. He was frenetically pacing all around the room, never standing still for even an instant, waving the gun which he had earlier thrown at her, hammering at things, shouting and mumbling alternately, glancing at her constantly, and springing forward to see if she had moved.

Half the time, it seemed to her, he didn't even hear what Alan was saying to him. Several times he had shut off the intercom with a torrent of obscenities for accompaniment, only to turn it back on again seconds later, when the realization came that he could not shut Alan *off*, only prevent *himself* from being heard. He would pour forth a scathing stream of barely intelligible invective, much of which was gibberish, grow furious when Alan went on talking as if he hadn't heard him (which, of course, he hadn't), scream at the ceiling at the top of his lungs, and only then realize that he need only use the intercom to be heard. The way he kept smashing away at it, she was amazed that the unit continued to function.

The entire ship was aware of what was going on. They all knew about the Shahin ship that stalked them, they had learned something of the dangers which they could expect were they ever to reach Xerxes V, and they all knew that a dangerous lunatic in a deep, drug-induced psychosis had taken over sick bay and was holding one of their number hostage, having already killed Lieutenant Faen. They went about their duties briskly, efficiently, finding work where there was none. But they were all very, very quiet.

On the bridge, Alan was being fed subtler kinds of stimulants by Jil and Cilix while Yuri had taken over the job of keeping a constant line of communication open between the bridge and the security detail on duty outside the barricaded sick bay. Kovalevski, deprived of his navigator, had his hands full plotting an approach course and keeping careful track of the movements of Hhargoth's ship which, he had only just realized, had started slowly moving closer.

"Alan?"

"Just a moment, Captain," Jil told him.

"Creed! Creed, have you shut off the intercom again?"

"You three look a wreck," Kovalevski said.

Jil somehow managed a weary smile.

"He surely doesn't need both of you there with him," Sim said, constantly glancing back at his instruments and readout screens. Around them, the bridge crew acted as if they were completely oblivious of the drama being played out in their midst.

"Whether or not he does," said Jil, "both of us are here and here we will remain."

"This has gone on far too long," said Kovalevski. "This situation has gotten completely out of hand and it's all my fault. I should have sent the men in there immediately."

"We *can't* give up now!" she protested.

Kovalevski shook his head. "We're going to have to, I'm afraid. Tell Alan I need him. I'm going to send the security detail in there."

"And what of Sarah?" asked Cilix.

"I'm sorry," said Kovalevski.

Sarah's blurry eyes couldn't even focus on Steiger anymore. She never saw Steiger gobble up a handful of the atropine sulphate and, if she had, she couldn't have cared. She ceased hearing his ravings, and she never noticed when he abandoned his dialogue with Alan to cross the room to where she lay. Steiger, on the other hand, never even realized that she was incapable of hearing him.

"Shit. Shit. There's a whole goddam *universe* to hide in and I can't get away, I'm locked here in this fucking *room* and those embassy bastards are waiting on the other side to fry me, damn it, *me*, can you imagine? I'm all out of brandy and I can't find the fucking *music*, the *music*, I don't know where it is, you've got to show me, I looked everywhere, I don't know where it is,

I have to find it, I have to cover up the noise or else they'll *hear* me in here and they'll know just what I'm doing, I've got to make it *loud*, real *loud*, just *LOUD*...."

The atropine sulphate hit full force and Steiger reeled, as if physically struck.

"AHHHH, *GOD*!"

He dropped to one knee and started clawing at the floor. His whole body shivered and struggled to vomit out the invader, but he succeeded only in bringing up a stream of bilious ooze.

He struggled to his feet, swaying unsteadily, staring at the door and he could *see* them, see them waiting, guns ready, right through the walls, he could see them, poised and ready to leap. He dribbled on his shirt, jaw hanging slack, head swiveling around madly, looking for an avenue of escape.

Of course, the gun! He would blast his way right through the wall and escape into the streets. He held up his right hand, trying to stop its weaving motion. It seemed as if he had two hands. What? Two hands? Where did he get two hands? No, better check, perhaps there was a third one somewhere....

No time, no time, they were coming for him, have to act *NOW*!

He aimed his right hand at the far wall, completely unaware that the gun was gripped tightly in his left hand, which hung at his side, and he fired several bursts in rapid succession, making a large, gaping hole through which he could see into the adjoining compartment.

He knew they'd hear the shots, so he immediately launched himself through the hole and to safety.

He slammed into the wall face first. Bouncing back, completely oblivious of the fact that his nose was broken, he fell to the floor, wondering how he could possibly have missed a hole that size. He struggled to his feet and ran straight at the wall again, slammed into it, fell back, got up again and, like Quixote charging at the windmill, lurched into the wall once more. The gun went flying from his hand and skittered across the room. The wall was smeared with crimson.

The door had been forced open and the security detail swarmed into the room, weapons at the ready. They were confronted with the sight of Steiger sitting on the floor, his face a bloody mess. He squinted at them and raised his empty hand unsteadily and pointed it in their direction. He kept firing and couldn't understand why they didn't die. A groaning, droning sound was coming from between his parted lips.

The men froze in their tracks, bewildered by this sight. Alan entered. He sent three of the men to check on Sarah and the rest cautiously approached Creed. He let them get very near. They picked him up from off the floor and he seemed docile, limp, vaguely puzzled, and profoundly disoriented. Then, without warning, he exploded.

For a shockingly brief moment, there was mayhem. He flung them about as if they weighed nothing at all, screaming hoarsely in a berserker rage. He ran straight for the door and, this time, he didn't miss. They fired after him as he disappeared down the companionway, but it had all happened so quickly that he was out of sight before they knew what hit them.

Even as he hurtled through the ship, Kovalevski was alerted of his escape. But he had no time for him. Hhargoth was upon them. He barked out a quick order that Steiger was to be shot and went back to attempting his futile evasive manuevers. He knew that they were futile. He also knew that Hhargoth was now easily in the superior position, could easily destroy them, and still that moment did not come.

Alan returned to the bridge to beg him to rescind his order concerning Steiger. Kovalevski adamantly refused. And, at that moment, Hhargoth made contact.

"Stand by to be boarded."

Almost simultaneously, Kovalevski was made aware of one of the *Groan's* lighters leaving the ship, spinning crazily towards Xerxes V.

"Alan," he said, "get out of here. Get your friends down to the lighters now."

"But Sim—"

"I said *move*, Mister!" At the same time, he hailed the crew through the public address system. "This is the captain speaking. Abandon ship. Take what you can carry and proceed to the lighters immediately. Launch when ready."

Instantly, all personnel dropped what they were doing and quickly, effectively, moved to follow orders. Alan ran to collect the others.

Kovalevski was left alone on the bridge with a skeleton crew. He manuevered the *Groan* into orbit around the planet.

Hhargoth's ship came closer still.

Mustafa, in command of the evacuation, briskly supervised the loading of the lighters. The crew was well-trained and they knew to take only the essentials necessary for survival.

The boarding shuttles left the Shahin ship and began to cross the space that separated the two vessels. The main vessel remained in a position to fire upon the *Groan*, obliterating her if her captain attempted any last minute resistance.

Like seeds bursting from a pod, the lighters were launched from the *Titus Groan* toward Xerxes V. The large body of the ship hid them from the view of the Shahin vessel.

"All right," said Kovalevski to the bridge crew, "let's get out of here."

Unlike the fabled captains of song and legend, Sim Kovalevski knew that his first responsibility right now was to his crew and not the ship. The ship was safe enough in orbit. The Shahin would maintain it and, although the chance was small, the possibility still existed that they could retake the ship at some more opportune time. It wasn't very likely, true, but there was nothing to be gained in surrendering. Not to the Shahin. And they had come here for a purpose after all.

Moments before the enemy boarding party came in contact with the *Groan*, Kovalevski launched his lighter.

Green Xerxes loomed ahead of them. Like spoors that drifted on the wind, the remainder of the lighters could be seen descending, glittering like sparkling diamonds against the background of a verdant world much like their Earth.

And, as they descended, Kovalevski could make out the tiny dots that rose to meet them.

Shahin shuttles.

Chapter Seven

Steiger felt like he had died and gone to hell.

He had no idea how long he'd been unconscious, but consciousness was not a welcome state. His head felt as if it were the victim of a massive edema. There simply was no room inside his skull to contain the agony. It threatened to break through the bone and spill out. He knew that it was probably important to find out just exactly where in hell he was, and what the *situation* was, but it seemed like too much effort just then. Trying to concentrate was painful.

He remembered, albeit vaguely, drifting in and out of consciousness, brief spasms of lucidity during which he spoke to himself, only he couldn't remember what was said.

There were periods of being doubled over on the floor of the lighter, vomiting and not wanting to move, not being *able* to. Still, for some strange reason that he couldn't fathom, he would try to get up, making it to a half crouch and sinking back down to his knees again, suffused with failure.

He could barely recall what had happened in the sick bay up until the time. . . . *What* time? When did he lose control? He remembered some of it somewhat hazily. He had a vision of himself screaming at the top of his lungs and hammering away at Sarah— Good God! Had he killed her too? No, she had been shouting something afterward; he was certain he remembered that. Then there was something about him drinking from a bottle of rubbing alcohol. Was that possible? He tried not to dwell on that image.

The rest of it was a perfect blank.

He was *here*, wherever "here" was, and he was in a ship's lighter, although how that came to pass he had no idea whatsoever. And how much time had elapsed was also something he had no way of knowing.

There was a stubble on his face. He felt it, trying hard to think, knowing that it would give him some indication of how long he had been "away." Two days, three? Had he landed or was he drifting out in space? No, he had landed. Crashed. Xerxes V! Of course, of course, keep steady, Steiger, don't lose the thread. . . .

Where were the others? Why hadn't they pursued him?

"Oh, hell. . . ."

He didn't want to think about it. He wanted only to lie down and close his eyes and go to sleep. Escape the fuzzy, painful head and the empty, floating, vertiginous sensations that assailed him.

He felt a breeze and inhaled slowly, painfully, licking his dry and cracked lips to moisten them. That was when he discovered that two of his teeth were chipped and several others so loose that he could move them with his tongue. He took a slow inventory of his face, probing carefully with his hands like a blind person and he learned that his nose was not where it should have been. It had been mashed neatly, almost completely flattened against his face. The flesh was broken and the bone stuck through and, when he tried to move it, he felt no pain for some reason. But the crunching sound so unsettled him that he decided not to try it again. He put his hands down, for fear he would discover that one of his eyeballs was protruding from its socket, dangling by a thread.

The rest of him seemed to have fared somewhat better than his face. No major bones were broken, either in his arms or in his legs. He made little testing movements with his body. Everything responded . . . eventually. He was bruised, he was bloody and battered, and he might have fractured a few ribs, although he wasn't yet straight enough to be certain. But for all of that, he was reasonably functional. Physically. His mental capacities were another story. He had fried his brain to rare perfection and it wasn't up to working right just yet.

He dragged himself over to the jagged rupture in the hull of the lighter, fighting nausea all the way. The breeze seemed to make him feel a little better. It was pleasant, slightly humid, a bit cool. Creed stared out at the lush vegetation and lost himself in the pitter-pattering sound of raindrops.

Although he longed to go out in the rain, feel its refreshing coolness on his ruined face, rub himself in the large, moist leaves of the plants he saw, caution made him stay where he was, at least until his head was clear.

This was a place he didn't know much about. He was in no condition to expose himself to an alien environment. There wasn't much that he could do about the air, since he had already been breathing it for quite some time. If there were any organisms here that would prove inimical to his system, there wasn't much that he could do about it now.

He leaned his head back against the shattered hull and waited for the fog to go away. He drifted, grateful that the vomiting had stopped, wanting only to rest and wait for the feeling that was vaguely reminiscent of the sensation of falling to disappear.

A tiny lizard, no bigger than his little finger, crawled into the lighter and flapped its way across the floor, towards his foot. He noticed it and, without giving any thought to his action, casually raised his boot and crushed it beneath his heel. He closed his eyes and slept.

Dawn. A sparkling of dew. The leaves all glistened in the early morning light. Still damp from rain, they drooped and dribbled water, drop by drop, onto the mossy ground. The rosy sky above was clear and cloudless. Large birds with golden wingspans sailed on the wind currents, high above the trees, swooping down with incredible speed to pounce upon some tiny, unsuspecting animal.

Creed Steiger came awake suddenly with a jerk. His hand clawed for his weapon, only there was nothing there. He scuttled warily away from the rupture in the lighter's hull, cursing himself for his foolhardiness.

His mind was clear now. And it seethed with anger. Anger at himself for having lost control. He felt the pain of his injuries now, but he accepted it, putting it aside. There was a medipak aboard the lighter and he located it, but he set that aside too. There would be time for first aid later. He felt more at ease when he finally found the weapons. He broke out some emergency rations and ate a hurried breakfast. There was no telling when he'd need his strength.

Finally, he cleaned himself and applied some disinfectant, but there wasn't much that he could do to fix his nose or teeth. The bridge of his nose was so thoroughly shattered that it would require surgery. His cuts and bruises he tended to as best he could.

He went back to the gaping hole in the side of the lighter, checked the outside and, when he was satisfied that no immediate threat presented itself, he jumped down to the ground.

For the first time, he could see just how serious the crash had been. It was a miracle he had survived and not been hurt more seriously. He thanked whatever ingrained instinct it was that must have made him strap in before the ludicrous attempt at landing.

The lighter had come in diagonally, cutting a wide swath through the trees. They had saved him. The sheer density of the foliage slowed the passage of the landing craft. There had been some combustion, extinguished, no doubt, by the heavy rainfall. He could see the charred and blackened path the lighter had made as it came crashing through the forest.

He climbed up carefully onto the top of the ruined lighter in an attempt to orient himself. It didn't help him much.

From what little he could see, the jungle-like forest seemed to extend in all directions. An infinity of green. There was no sign of any kind of city, town, or village. No sign of civilization whatsoever. To the north, a range of mountains, not very high. In every other direction, nothing. It was as if he were the only one alive. Somewhere, he knew, were Kovalevski's people . . . unless they had been met in space by Hhargoth and destroyed. And somewhere, also, there were the surrogates. From what little he had learned of the creatures, he knew enough to fear them.

He decided to head for the mountains. He re-entered the broken lighter to gather together what few supplies there were. He found the lizard he had crushed beneath his boot the previous night.

It was a tiny thing. It didn't look full grown. Its skin was a mottled, yellowish green color, its head flat and triangular like a rattlesnake's. He shuddered inwardly, thinking that it or others like it might have attacked him while he slept.

He would have to be extremely careful. There was no telling what sort of creatures lurked here, blending in with the surroundings. And he had no way of knowing what he could use for food when the rations ran out. The game here would be plentiful, no doubt, but which creatures would he be able to eat safely? There really was no way for him to test whatever food he found except by trying it. He decided to cross that bridge when he came to it.

He had shifted gears now. Gone entirely was the sluggish illness of the previous night. He was awake, alert, and on his guard. He had been in tougher scrapes before. At least at the moment, no one was shooting at him.

As he walked, picking his way carefully through the undergrowth, he considered his position.

To all intents and purposes, he was alone and trapped. Stranded on a strange and very possibly hostile world. With no immediate means of escape. It made him feel a little frightened, but he felt sure he would survive. He always had before. This was like the old days. This was like war.

He knew the Shahin came here on a regular basis, unmindful of the quarantine. Finding them would be his best bet. His only course of action, in point of fact. There was something going on, something about which the Shahin were very secretive. If he could find out what it was, it might be worth something in bargaining with them. On the other hand, they might just decide to kill him to insure his silence. One thing was certain. His options were limited.

He conserved his energy, walking slowly, cautiously checking every step he made. He felt very much alive. He walked all day, taking careful stock of his surroundings. It was very peaceful. He found a tree which bore a large and tube-shaped fruit. He picked one, broke it open and sniffed the pulpy, fragrant meat. It did not smell offensive, which he knew meant nothing, so he chanced a small lick with his tongue. It tasted bland. He ate a very small amount and took the rest of it with him. If there were no ill effects after several hours, he would chance a little more. A little later in the day, he surprised some sort of animal. It had seen him, and it started leaping through the brush. He shot it.

He considered the body as it lay. "Damn, you're ugly," he said. "You probably taste like shit too."

He dressed it with some difficulty owing to its tough outer skin, then cut its flesh into sections that he could easily carry. Its blood, at least, was red, which could have been a promising indication. There was nothing very alien about the appearance of the meat. He made a small fire and cooked a piece. Although the taste was gamey, it went down without any difficulty.

About two hours later, he came down with stomach cramps and a severe case of diarrhea. He threw the remainder of the meat away in disgust and contented himself with the tubular fruit.

When it began to grow dim, he set about looking for a likely place to spend the night. Sleeping on the ground was out of the question. He thought about digging a pit for himself, something that he could conceivably cover over with branches, but that didn't seem very safe either. He saw potential danger everywhere.

He finally decided on sleeping in a tree. He selected a large, thick-boled tree that seemed to offer good camouflage. If he found a suitable berth up there, it would be almost impossible for him to be observed from the ground.

He shimmied up the tree until he reached the heavier, lower branches, and then he started climbing. He found a section where there was a fork and he used his belt to lash himself securely to the branch. It would hardly be comfortable, but comfort was a long way off from being his main concern. He had gone through hell and he had walked all day and wrecked his stomach on that miserable dog-like creature and he was tired and felt worn out and used up, and *still* there was no rest. He could not turn his mind off. There was white noise in his brain. It filled his head with static, with thoughts he didn't want to think. With memories he had no desire to recall.

Somebody was touching him.

He swung his fist, violently, heard a screech and at the same time found himself flailing desperately for balance, losing it and pitching over to one side. He didn't fall. He hung by his belt, face down, secured to the tree branch. He craned his neck, looking over his shoulder, weapon ready. A little farther up the tree on one of the higher branches, a little furry thing with eyes like a lemur watched him in terror. Its hairy little paws were pressed up against its mouth, and they made tiny scrubbing motions. It shivered, watching him. He chuckled.

"God damn. You scared the shit out of me, you little bastard."

He kicked out with his legs. thrashing awkwardly, hoping that his belt would hold him. If it broke, it was a long way down. He didn't think his face could stand any more flattening. His nose was already useless for breathing. He finally managed to twist himself around somewhat and work his way back to his precarious perch. He loosened his belt and freed himself from the branch. The little animal had not moved. It sat, as if paralyzed, except for the nervous little scrubbing motions it made with its paws.

"I guess I scared you about as much as you scared me," he said.

He put his gun away and took a good, long look at the little creature. It bore a superficial resemblance to a monkey. It was not much bigger than his fist and it was completely covered with green fur, allowing it to blend in perfectly with the leafy boughs. The eyes looked way to large for its tiny head and they never left him for an instant. It had a long prehensile tail, which it had wound around itself protectively.

"Cute looking little thing, aren't you? Where's your mother? Or are you supposed to be full grown?"

It stopped its scrubbing motions and looked at him inquisitively. It opened its little mouth and went "Yap-yap-yap-yap-yap."

Creed snorted and smiled in spite of himself. "Yeah, yap-yap-yap to you too. First friendly face I've seen around here. Well, don't worry, I won't swing at you again."

He reached over to his pack, which he had secured to another branch close beside him. He started to open it, then squinted, looked at it a little closer and grinned.

"Oho, been at this thing, have you?"

"Yap-yap-yap-yap-yap."

"Yeah, don't lie to me, you little shit, I know you've been at this pack. Couldn't open it, huh?"

It barked at him amiably.

"Terrific dialogue we're having here." He opened up the pack and removed some of the fruit. The creature sat up, anxiously, its eyes riveted to the stuff. Steiger popped a piece into his mouth.

"You hungry, there, Yap-yap? You want some of this?"

It chittered in reply.

He held out a piece. "Well, come on, I'm not about to climb up and give it to you."

It began climbing down to him hesitantly. He held his hand out, waiting. It came close to him, stopped, started with the scrubbing motions once again and, finally, reached out and touched his hand, then jerked back.

"That's right, Yap-yap. You be good and careful. You never know, this could be a trap. I might decide to wring your little neck and cook you up for breakfast."

It reached out its paw again, touched his hand briefly, and then jerked back again just as quickly. He didn't move. It repeated the process three more times, then decided to throw caution to the winds. It climbed up on Steiger's forearm, curling its tail around it tightly, faced his hand, and looked down at the piece of fruit. It looked back at him over his shoulder. Watching to see if he made a move, ready to spring off and escape.

"Yeah, you're no fool, are you? Well, go ahead, eat up, I ain't going to hurt you."

It grabbed up the piece of fruit and jumped off his hand, scampering up into the higher branches, yapping all the way. Steiger laughed.

"That was a quick friendship! All you wanted was breakfast, eh? And I went and saved you the trouble of cracking open one of those tubers. You made a good move, Yap-yap. Took what you wanted and then split. You'll do all right." He stared after it, no longer able to see the furry green creature for the leafy branches. He felt suddenly lonesome. "Yeah, you'll do all right," he said quietly.

"We meet again, Captain," Lokhrim said to Kovalevski, "only *this* time, you are not the one who gives the orders. And we are unhampered by the constraints of diplomacy."

"What do you want with my people?" demanded Kovalevski. "Where is Lord Hhargoth? I refuse to deal with underlings!"

"Do not be foolish, Captain," Lokhrim said easily. "I have no desire to see you hurt. I am perfectly willing to discuss this reasonably. The choice is yours."

Kovalevski stood shakily before Lokhrim. "Where is Hhargoth?" That got him a slap. He rose to his feet unsteadily.

"*Lord* Hhargoth. Or His Excellency or His Lordship. Those are the proper forms of address."

"Very well. Where is *Lord* Hhargoth?"

"His Excellency does not care for the company of Terrans," said Lokhrim. "He has become especially intolerant since meeting Alan Dreyfus. For the present, while His Excellency remains here, I will act as your liaison. However, that really means that I will be in charge of you and your crew. His Lordship does not care to hear any requests that you may want to make."

"All right," said Kovalevski. "In that case, may I *respectfully* inquire about the welfare of my crew?"

"They are all being well taken care of," Lokhrim assured him. "Naturally, we have had to segregate your people into small groups. It makes your people easier to manage, given our facilities here."

"You could have destroyed the ship. Why didn't you? What do you want with us?"

"Sit down, Captain," Lokhrim indicated a chair. Kovalevski sat. The chair made him feel like a midget since it was made to Shahin proportions. "I will be quite frank with you," Lokhrim continued, "in the hope that you will give me your co-operation. Co-operation is not necessary, of course, but it would make things simpler, both for me and for yourself."

"Get to the point, Lokhrim."

"Careful, Captain. There is a limit to my patience. I would advise you to cultivate yours." He appraised Kovalevski and, when he saw that the captain remained silent, he nodded and continued.

"To answer your questions, Captain, you are quite correct. We could have destroyed your ship easily. It would have been child's play. It would also have been wasteful. Your own obstinacy proved to be your undoing. We asked only for Dreyfus. Had you turned him over to us, none of this would have happened. As it is, it all worked out to our advantage. To *my* advantage.

"When your own government declared you outlaw, you became, as a Terran I have known would say, easy pickings. You forfeited the protection of your Guild. The *Titus Groan* is ours now. It is vastly inferior to our own ships, of course, but it is still useful and can be refitted. Even in the eyes of your own government, we have legal title. That is an answer, in part, to your question about why your ship was not destroyed.

"There is a second reason why your ship was not destroyed along with your crew and yourself. What has Dreyfus told you concerning surrogate lizards?"

"You've killed him, haven't you?" Kovalevski asked bitterly.

"No."

"Where is he?"

"I do not know. Unfortunately, not all of your people are accounted for. Some escaped, I do not know how many. I hope you will furnish me with that information. If any of them are still alive, I assure you, they would be much safer here than out in the wild. We are at war with them. Believe me, if the Zharii find your people before we do, they will eat them alive."

"You're insane if you think I'm going to help you capture my own crew."

"In that case, they are as good as dead," Lokhrim said without emotion. "Come with me," he said, rising. "I will attempt to convince you."

They left the room and walked down a short corridor. Outside, they crossed the huge compound to a group of buildings on the other side. The Shahin had cleared a large area to build their base. It was circular in shape, surrounded on all sides by huge walls. The shuttles were all grouped in the center of the compound. On the far side stood the captured lighters from the *Groan*. The base was a large, seemingly impregnable fortress.

The Shahin led him to a small room that contained a large, black cube. A guard was posted to one side.

Lokhrim led him up close. Keeping his eyes on Kovalevski, Lokhrim signalled the guard. The guard did something that Kovalevski didn't see and the blackness of the cube began to fade. As it paled to a smokey gray, Kovalevski could see that there was a figure inside, shadowy, curled up on the floor. Very quickly, the smokey gray hue of the cube faded away until the cube itself had dissolved. On the floor before him was a gangly, gawky form, bandy-legged, somewhat frog-like. It became aware of the light and, like lightning, leapt up to its feet and flung itself at Kovalevski with a blood-curdling scream.

Kovalevski yelled and threw up his arms, instinctively jumping backward. He fell and saw that the creature had struck something and bounced back. The cube, though all but invisible, was still there. He could see its walls where the creature made contact with them as it slammed against them again and again, trying to break free, howling like a demon from hell and slavering at the mouth. It was the most terrifying thing that he had ever seen.

"This one we have calmed somewhat with drugs," Lokhrim told him. "And it is only one. There are thousands more out in the wild. And this is what your people face."

"Why should you care what happens to us?" asked Kovalevski.

Lokhrim signaled to the guard again and the cube went black. Gradually, the screaming died down.

"We hunt the surrogates," Lokhrim told him. "Do you know why?"

Kovalevski did not reply.

"Of course you know," Lokhrim said, "else why would you have come here? Dreyfus learned our secret that treatments made with the surrogates as main ingredients make our warriors strong. You are a fool. Did you really hope to capture lizards on your own and have your Terran scientists attempt to duplicate the knowledge of our shamen?"

Kovalevski was amazed. He had to struggle to hide his incredulity. *The Shahin really didn't know!* Was it really possible?

"Dreyfus and your people are no threat to us now," continued Lokhrim. "You will never be able to tell anyone our secret. However, you may prove useful. And, if the plan succeeds, I will win back my commission."

"We need the lizards, but they are parasitical creatures, living off the Zharii, creatures such as the one you've seen. By themselves, the Zharii are vicious, mindless, lethal beings. But, under the guidance of the surrogates, they are a formidable enemy. Hurt them and the surrogate controllers make them continue, oblivious to pain. Deprive them of their legs and they will crawl to the attack, dragging themselves along the ground and howling in a killing frenzy. They are the surrogates' tool-making tools, providing them with the hands that nature did not give them. They have learned the art of warfare and they have made the hunting costly.

"But we have learned that surrogates can live off humans too. You and your crew will be our breeding stock. You will be the hosts for surrogates we can harvest. We will take good care of you and keep you well and make your existence as comfortable as possible and, if the idea proves to be a feasible one, we will endeavor to bring other Terrans here, such as would not be missed. You will be kept separate and allowed limited access to each other for purposes of socializing and mating. Make your choice, Captain. You can co-operate with me and remain in a supervisory capacity, seeing to the welfare of your people . . . or you can join the others in the experiment."

Kovalevski was stunned. He felt his skin crawl and his mouth went dry. "Mother of God," he breathed. "I might have expected something like this from you. You must be out of your mind."

"I will give you time to think about it," the Shahin said. "But not too much."

"Go to hell!"

"You may change your mind when you see the first lizard take one of your people."

I sat alone beneath the lighter, beside a small fire we had made, its glow hidden by the body of the landing craft. Above me, inside the lighter, a few members of our party were trying to get some rest. The others had formed a watch perimeter around the lighter. They were armed. They were afraid. I smoked a cigarette restlessly. Jil came and sat beside me.

"You should try to get some sleep," she said.

"I can't."

"You need rest."

"We all need our rest." I inhaled deeply, dragging the smoke into my lungs. "What have I done, Jil? What have I *done*?"

"You did what you had to do."

"Did I? It's all beyond me now. I felt like I was doing right, but now? . . . It all seemed so important."

"It *is* important."

I laughed in spite of myself. I put my arm around her and hugged her close to me.

"Did I ever tell you you're wonderful?"

"Not recently. You've been very self-involved."

"I know. I'm sorry."

We sat silently for a while. I opened up to her and brought her in. It was like making love. Like making love with someone you had known all your life, someone who complemented you perectly in every way. Someone who knew all your wants and needs and understood. We sat there in the still and quiet night as the cries of the night prowlers faded away. We went back into the past and met as children. We played together, watched each other grow. We learned. We hurt. We healed, we laughed and cried. If we both died in the next instant it would have been worth it. If only everyone could share like that. . . .

She made an abrupt, little mewling sound.

"What's wrong?"

"I wish you'd warn me before doing that! It took me by surprise, I wasn't ready."

"I'm sorry, that was selfish of me."

"Yes, it was, but I don't mind. Just let me know ahead of time before you do it again."

"All right, I promise." I sighed heavily, feeling at the same time contented and concerned. "What's going to happen to us, Lil?"

"It's already happened, hasn't it?" she said, looking up at me and smiling.

In spite of the Shahin dislike for Terrans, Kovalevski was being treated with a degree of courtesy. He felt like a prisoner of war whereas, in fact, he was nothing more or less than a kidnap victim. That was how he saw it. He had been kept apart from the others of his crew, given his own "quarters" which, naturally, he could not leave. He saw no opportunity for escape.

They had brought down as many of his possessions from the *Groan* as possible, making every effort to duplicate the atmosphere of his own ship's cabin. They treated him like an officer, even if their manner was visibly stiff and very forced. He had learned that he was in no position to make demands, so he made none. Lokhrim had stated his case very clearly. He knew what was expected of him. And he knew that he was being left alone so he could think.

What was there to think about?

Clearly, he would not be allowed to see any of his people until he made his decision. And on reflection, it was not an easy choice to make.

He agonized all night. At dawn, Lokhrim entered his room.

He stared at him impassively, his obsidian features expressionless.

"Have you chosen?"

"Yes." He shut his eyes and wearily lowered his head onto his arms.

Chapter Eight

Exhaustion, both mental and physical, had finally taken its toll and I slept. I don't recall when I fell asleep, but I awoke at dawn to the sound of Jil hissing. I came awake quickly and saw that she was staring out beyond the perimeter, her fur bristling.

"Alan, something's wrong!"

"What is it?"

"I don't know, a strange smell. Something's out there. More than one, it's very strong."

"Alert the others," I said. "We've heard nothing from the people on watch, but they haven't got your senses. I'd better see to them."

I ran quickly to the nearest watch post, a short distance away from the lighter. Banning should have seen or heard me coming. She didn't. I found her dead with an arrow in her throat. It had pierced her larynx and cracked the trachea wide open. While I was staring stupidly at all the blood, they made their move. There were too many of them. I didn't even have time to guess the size

147

of their force. An arrow struck my shoulder. Those who were still outside the lighter fell almost immediately.

I started running, but another arrow brought me down. It seemed to be hailing arrows. I found inadequate cover behind a bush and crouched there, firing in every conceivable direction. I was pinned, quite literally, to the spot. Out of the corner of my eye I saw that those who had taken refuge in the lighter were firing from within, attempting to get it airborne. The Zharii swarmed all over it.

One of the creatures landed on my back. I threw it off, fired, and then another was upon me and another and another. There was no time now to fire. I fought them with my hands and feet, swinging the rifle like a club. It hadn't been designed with anything quite so brutal in mind and it broke over a frog-shaped head. I wrenched free, bashing in a face, but now there were far too many of them. They brought me down by the sheer weight of numbers and, as I thrashed beneath them, I could hear the lighter lifting off. Panic-stricken, I opened up and desperately tried to reach Jil one last time.

And they all stopped as one.

Suddenly, I had inert bodies lying on top of me—as if someone had hit a switch and turned them all off at once. Slowly, they began to move, getting off me, giving me room, letting me sit up painfully.

It was my vision come to life. I was surrounded by them, but they did not touch me. They did not look so savage now. Their faces were expressionless, serene, detached. And each of the things had a lizard clinging to it, some had more than one.

The lighter was rising higher and higher, and I could see the bodies of the Zharii that still clung to it falling to the ground. The lighter had not been built for battle and was in the greatest jeopardy as long as it was in range of the Zharii's blasters. Besides, they probably thought that I was dead.

Perhaps I was. I was a pincushion of bloody broken shafts. It seemed that I was clearly going to die—if not right off, then painfully over a period of time. Dazed, uncomprehending, feeling pain with every move, I dragged myself to where the others had been. There were so many dead. . . .

Feeling dizzy, cold, I searched for Jil. The Zharii all stood by and watched silently. Then, amazingly, without any of them makıg a sound, they began to search the bodies too.

I was unable to move. Breathing heavily, I half-lay on the round, supporting myself on my arms, watching the bizarre ritual. And then it came to me. I realized that they had *heard* me.

I sank down to the ground, my face in the torn up dirt, "seeing" he bodies of our dead. Knowing that I lacked the strength to look, hey were doing it for me. So many images came to me so ast. . . . Banning, Stevens, Chien-li, Rostov, Boltonski, Habib, Agazzi, Cahill, Malik, Yuri—oh, God, Yuri. . . . The others had urvived, made good their escape in the lighter. Thank God, at east Jil and Cilix were alive still. Five of us left, out of fifteen. And it had all happened so fast, so incredibly, incredibly *fast*!

Everything was beginning to swim before my eyes. I felt their ouch on me, then some curious sensations, and I realized dimly hat they were pulling out the arrows slowly, carefully. I closed ny eyes and let the blackness take me.

Creed had found water.

Using the flash boiler from the medipak, he drank slowly, eplenishing his energy with the last of the rations. He sat on the ıank of the river, naked, waiting for his clothes to dry. Almost lreamily, he baited a line and began to fish. The first nibbler took he hook nicely, and after a brief struggle, surprising for a river ish, Creed landed his catch. It looked astonishingly like trout, ınly larger than any he had ever seen.

He needed to bathe, he realised, but he hesitated at first, eyeing he water gingerly. He finally went in, staying very close to the ıank, ready to jump out at the first sign of any hazard.

He ate a little of the fish, careful not to invite another upheaval n his digestive system. The fish tasted very good, but he resolved o wait at least two hours before he finished his dinner. The warm un felt good on his skin and he was tempted to simply lie back ın the grassy bank and close his eyes, but he didn't dare. He still ınew too little about this place.

As he stared at the water rushing by, he realized that he was ıeginning to enjoy himself.

He was completely on his own. His own master, totally alone, ınd he liked it. This was survival, distilled to its purest form.

Little by little, he felt himself starting to merge with the ecology ıf Xerxes. He felt himself starting to fit in. He had learned that there were five types of fruit that he could eat and six that he could not. His system would not tolerate the flesh of the dog-creatures, but it seemed to get along with the "trout" and with two types of berries he had found, as well as with the large eggs of the golden birds that nested high in the treetops. There was one plant with large spear-shaped leaves that left red welts on his skin if he brushed against them. And he had learned, through painful experience, to avoid the worm-like giant caterpillars that fastened to his skin like leeches. He had many more meetings with the little green monkeys that he shared his nighttime tree refuges with. He had started watching them carefully, having learned that the things they ate were things he could eat as well. Though their tastes did not completely agree, the things that they avoided, such as the golden birds, were things that he would do well to avoid also. The birds were much larger than he had realized and, while they did not attack him, they could be quite formidable in defending their nests when he climbed up to them to gather eggs. His hands were still covered with their claw marks from fending two of them off.

As he sat, resting on the bank of the river, he saw something floating downstream. When it floated nearer, he noticed that it looked like the body of a man.

He dove into the water and swam out to intercept it. It was not a man. He curled one arm around its neck and swam to shore, fighting the strong current. He dragged the body up onto the bank and squatted down beside it.

He frowned. "What are you supposed to be?" he mumbled aloud.

It was dead. He could not tell why at first. Its dimensions were somewhat similar to those of a human. It had two arms and two legs and the general appearance of the figure was the same, but there the similarity ended. It looked like some macabre cross between a human, a frog, and an ape. It was bloated from having been in the water for some time. Its skin was tough and leathery, somewhat slimey to the touch. It would be deceptively strong, he decided. The fingers on the hands were long, thin, and larger at the ends. It seemed to have no knuckles, nor did it have any fingernails. The legs were much longer than a human's and out of proportion, by his standards, with the trunk. It had no hair anywhere on its body. Still, he guessed that this was a male, although he was applying standards that might not mean anything on Xerxes.

The face was especially frog-like in appearance with the exception of the large teeth, more like fangs, in its cavernous mouth. Evidently, this thing ran down its prey and killed it with its teeth. It could probably jump very high and far. It looked dangerous and he hoped he would not run into any of its living relatives.

"Hmm, are you supposed to be the intelligent life form on this planet?" he mused. "No offence, but you don't look all that smart to me. Mean, but not smart. What the hell did you die of anyway?"

Then he saw that it had the scars of fang marks on its neck, arms, and chest. The bloating hid them so that he had to look very closely, but they were undeniably fang marks.

"A lizard maybe?" He sat back on the bank, thinking. "Yeah, it makes sense. If the damn things will attack humans, it makes sense they live off you frogs."

In a short while, the sun had dried him and he put on his clothes. At least he felt fresher now. He gathered up his pack and slung it over his shoulder, put on his boots and proceeded downstream, walking along the riverbank. He stopped and looked back at the body he had left lying on the ground behind him. Now he felt as if he had an enemy. He did not relish running into a group of those things.

He walked on, following the river for most of the rest of the day, looking for a likely place to cross. It was late in the day when he saw the bridge.

He stopped as soon as he saw it, staring at the primitive construction. It was made of wood, branches laced together by some sort of thongs or hemp.

"I'll be a son of a bitch," he said under his breath.

He approached the bridge carefully, but he could see no sign of its builders. It looked rickety, although he thought that it would easily hold his weight. He decided that he might as well take the risk. It swayed a little and creaked as he made his way across, but it held him. It was low, close to the water and the branches were all wet and slippery. He picked his footing with care and made it across without mishap. On the other side he found an honest-to-God trail.

Well, he thought, it beats fighting your way through the brush. This was the first sign of "civilization" he had seen. He wondered if the frog creatures could have been responsible. More likely, the surrogates, since they were sentient. But why would lizards have need for trails or bridges? It was puzzling.

"This place sure is full of surprises, ain't it?" The foliage neatly hid the trail, but the bridge was a dead giveaway. It made no sense.

Perhaps he was being too suspicious. Nevertheless, something just didn't feel right. He couldn't put his finger on it. But that old sense of paranoia was acting up again, and he had learned, in the past, not to ignore it when it did. He proceeded down the trail slowly, cautiously, keeping his eyes and ears wide open. What *was* it that kept bothering him? What didn't feel right?

And then he saw it. A trip wire. Not a wire, per se, but a thin, fragile length of hemp running across the path at approximately the height of his knees. If he had not been watching so carefully, he would not have seen it.

"What the hell. . . ."

He stepped to the far side of the path, then into the brush. He took his rifle and used it to break the line. With a *whooshing* sound, two giant, ball-shaped maces swept in powerful arcs down the trail lengthwise. Had he been walking there, there would have been no way to avoid them.

He watched them swinging back and forth like pendulums; their swing lessening each time. Two giant balls of what looked like dried mud and moss packed together, studded with razor sharp thorns and sharpened sticks.

"Jesus H. Christ!" He let out a long, slow breath, thankful for his instincts. "What the fuck is going *on* here?"

Without a shadow of a doubt, he knew that the entire trail was probably booby-trapped with similar, deadly devices. He had stumbled into some sort of jungle war.

Lokhrim came to see the new prisoners.

The search parties had found two of the Terran lighters. The crew of the first had been butchered mercilessly. The Zharii had been there first. The second lighter was caught when it made its escape from the Zharii. It had been forced to fly to the base camp. In it were two prisoners in particular whom Lokhrim was anxious to see. The Ophidian and the feline.

Jil looked up at the Shahin looming over her. She did not feel afraid. She felt empty.

"Where is Alan Dreyfus?" Lokhrim asked her.

She looked down. "Dead."

"Are you certain?"

"Yes, I'm certain," she replied in a small voice.

"How did he die?"

She didn't speak. Cilix came up beside her, placing an arm around her shoulder protectively. When he spoke his voice was flat, emotionless.

"We were attacked by the Zharii, *xothol*. We were barely able to escape. It happened very suddenly. Alan must have been among the first to fall."

"Good," said Lokhrim. He had not expected it to happen this way. He found himself feeling cheated. So much time, so much effort spent on trying to eliminate one man. . . .

"What are you going to do with us?" asked Cilix.

"The matter of the other Terrans has been settled," replied Lokhrim. "I have not yet decided what to do about the two of you. Where is the other, the Terran girl?"

"Her name was Yuri," Cilix said.

"I see." He could tell that this was a deeply felt personal loss for both of them. He almost expressed sympathy, but caught himself, feeling vaguely puzzled. They were not of the people. He turned away.

Lord Hhargoth was preparing to depart. He would be left in charge. It was a very large responsibility, a demonstration of faith in spite of his disgrace. His Excellency was giving him the chance to prove himself. It was more than he deserved. His entire future depended on the success or failure of the experiment. It was no time to begin showing weakness.

He turned back to face them. They looked defeated, pathetic. They had totally surrendered to their fate.

"Come along," he said to the guards, "bring them."

They followed behind as he made his way to his quarters. He was beginning to have thoughts he never had before. And he could not help himself. Alan Dreyfus had been an important part of his life, yet he had only seen him briefly, that first time when he came to them, looking like a barely animated corpse. And now it was over. He felt that he had missed something.

He bade them sit, then dismissed the guards.

"Are you hungry?" he asked.

Jil shook her head; Cilix said, "No, thank you, *xothol*."

"That is the second time you have called me that. How is it that you recognize my class?"

"I know that you are bondwarrior to Lord Hhargoth," Cilix replied without emotion. "None other could command from such a station. I was once in the service of 'the people'."

"Indeed? Why did you leave our service?"

"I don't enjoy cruelty."

"Ah, yes, of course, cruelty. Inferior species seem to find some solace in regarding strength as weakness and weakness as strength. I have never understood that."

"My name is Lokhrim," he said somewhat hesitantly. They sat silently, watching him, listening to him, but his eyes were averted. He seemed to be speaking his thoughts aloud, almost as if they weren't even there. "I was commanded to capture Alan Dreyfus. The remains of a surrogate were found. It affected His Lordship strangely. Answer me this, did Dreyfus find a way to free himself of the lizard?"

"Yes," spoke Jil.

"How was this done?" Lokrim leaned forward anxiously.

"He found strength within himself," said Jil.

"I do not understand."

"I don't expect you to."

"Do not play at words with me, feline," Lokhrim warned her. "You are not in a position to do so."

"I'll tell you how it happened," Cilix said. "But you won't believe me."

"Why should I not believe you?"

"Because in order to believe what happened, it would be necessary for you to accept the unacceptable. You don't know the full truth about the surrogates; that is self-evident. Your own elite have lied to you."

"You *dare* to insult the elite of the Shahin?"

"When you have no hope left, you dare anything." Cilix shrugged. And he told him what had happened. It was not as painful as he had thought it would be. Speaking about Alan seemed to bring him back to them. The memory of him was all that they had left.

Lokhrim listened without interrupting. When Cilix had finished, the Shahin laughed scornfully.

"You expect me to believe this?" he said. "What can you hope to gain by withholding the truth?"

"I said that you would not believe me," Cilix told him. "We are not the prisoners here. You are. A prisoner of your own system of belief."

"If you don't believe him," Jil burst forth, "why don't you ask your own man? Ask Creed Steiger. He'll tell you we're not lying!"

"Steiger? *Here*?"

"Isn't he with you?"

"Of course not. He came on your ship?"

"He was captured by the crew." said Cilix. "He escaped a short time before we, ourselves, fled. We thought that he had gone to you."

"I have not seen him. He is, no doubt, dead, along with Dreyfus. Most convenient for you."

Jil shook her head sadly. "He's told you the truth, you know. And you refuse to accept it. It doesn't even occur to you to test what he has told you, to find out for yourself. You prefer to blindly follow your superiors. You have the opportunity to find out for yourself just what the truth is. But you aren't going to take it, are you? You've already decided in advance what *your* truth is. And nothing will move you from that position because changing your position would mean accepting the possibility that you might have been wrong. That your leaders might not have told you the truth. That you have been a fool. And you just don't want to know, do you? You're afraid."

Lokhrim rose slowly to his feet. When he spoke, his voice was barely under control. There was cold fury in his eyes.

"I will test your 'truth', as you suggest. We will perform this little experiment and we will see what happens when one consumes a surrogate. And you and the Ophidian will be my subjects. We will see just how much you value *your* truth.

"Guards!" he shouted.

It didn't take long for Steiger to discover that the entire trail was a trap. Those deadly mud balls had been only a preamble. He spotted the covered-over pit easily enough. He guessed that there were probably sharpened stakes at the bottom. It had been well-hidden, but he had known what to look for. He avoided the catapults that sent spears and arrows hurtling down the trail. The most interesting device was a crude landmine fashioned from the thermal charge paks the Shahin used in their weapons.

Something was wrong.

All these tactics were familiar. They had been used to good effect in jungles on Earth in the past. Creed almost got the feeling the coincidence was studied, that someone was adapting Terran strategy to fit this world. Of course, it was possible that these tactics had been developed independently. Perhaps his imagination was working overtime.

Here were tricks that had been used in Korea, Viet Nam, South Africa, Honduras, China, Thailand. . . .

Steiger mumbled to himself as he moved forward slowly with painstaking care, high stepping through the brush. "If I didn't know better, I'd swear these lizards had Terran advisors." He chuckled, amused. "Hell, we'll send our boys anywhere."

Perhaps the thought wasn't so insane. True, the world was quarantined, but what better way to insure that a secret war be kept a secret? There was something here that the Shahin wanted. If they wanted it, why not the Terran Guild? But that didn't make sense. If the Shahin were at war with Earth, every living Terran would know about it. And then, why use such primitive, albeit effective, tactics?

Unless there were, in fact, Terran military advisors here and they were anxious to keep their involvement a secret so that the Shahin would not suspect. The Shahin would know nothing of Earth's military history. They would not recognize the strategy as he had. What a wild idea! Wouldn't that be something?

One instant, he was picking his way through the brush alongside the trail, the next, he felt the explosive impact of a body knocking him to the ground. He jumped to his feet, flinging off one creature and meeting another with a side kick to its abdomen. It doubled over, the wind knocked out of it. But, amazingly, it began getting back to its feet even as it was gasping for breath. And the first was already leaping back to the attack. Creed ducked underneath it as it passed over him. His fingers closed around its windpipe, and he gave a quick, savage pull, ripping out its throat. He was immediately knocked off his feet by the other.

Its fangs were in his shoulder. He reached around and grasped its head and twisted sharply, snapping its neck. It died instantly. He rose quickly to his feet, prying those teeth out of his shoulder and saw that the creature with its throat torn out, while rasping horribly and gushing rivers of blood, was *still* attempting to rise to its feet and come after him. He retrieved his fallen rifle and shot it.

Something was scampering up his leg. He swung his rifle and knocked the lizard off, smashing it with the stock. He heard a rustling in the leaves and turned, just in time to see the other lizard disappearing into the foliage. He started to fire, but decided against wasting the charge. Blood was seeping from the holes the creatures fangs had made in his shoulder. He quickly administered disinfectant and took an anti-toxin tablet, not knowing whether or not those fangs had introduced a poison into his bloodstream or whether or not the tablet would work if they had. He hoped for the best.

He was breathing heavily, but flushed with excitement. He always got a high off terror. His heart was pounding.

"What am I doing here? Boy, this isn't fun and games any longer. A guy can get himself killed around here!" He giggled nervously. "I'm scared. Jesus, I'm scared. I'd sooner take my chances somewhere else."

He paused reflectively. "Cheer up, Creed, things have been worse." He glanced up into the trees. "Hello? What's this?" He stood up and peered more intently into the trees. He gathered his things together and began to climb.

It was a well-camouflaged treehouse. An outpost. And those two creatures had been watching the trail.

"Guards, eh? I must be getting close to something. But what? Don't ask Creed, you probably don't really want to know."

From the treehouse, he found that he could see a good part of the trail and some of the surrounding brush on either side of it. And then he heard them.

They were moving quickly. He could hear them crashing through the jungle and they were not moving on the trail. He could see the shapes flashing by through the trees, moving with a great deal of speed. And he realized that there was another trail, not cleared as well as the one he had taken. His was a decoy trail that curled around, leading across the foothills. This second trail ran parallel to the decoy, but curled slowly in the opposite direction, leading high into the mountains. He used the scope sight on his rifle, aiming through the trees so that he could take a closer look.

They were the same sort of creatures as the two that had attacked him. There were more of them than he could count. Some were armed with spears or sharpened stakes and heavy branches with what looked like large thorns sticking out on all sides. Very nasty looking clubs. Others had primitive bows and quivers of arrows. And many of them wore weapons that he was all too familiar with. Captured Shahin blasters. He hoped that they wouldn't decide to change the guard or check on the treehouse. Then he saw several of them carrying a body. A human body. He dialed in the scope for greater magnification.

"Dreyfus!"

By the time he reached the ground, he could already hear their party receding into the distance. His mind was in high gear now. He was putting things together even as he struggled through the jungle separating the two trails. Part of him was now functioning automatically, remaining on the alert and watching out for any threat. The other part of him was clicking away like a computer, calculating, reasoning, considering options.

They were making no attempts to move stealthily. Which meant that they felt secure, knowing there was no enemy about. They had probably sent scouts ahead and the guards he had disposed of had not alerted them to his presence. Still, they were obviously in a great hurry to get someplace. Dreyfus had to be the reason.

His fear, the sense of panic that had him talking to himself, was present still, but it had been pushed to the back of his mind. It was always with him, that fear. Creed Steiger, the ruthlessly professional mercenary, who had been a hero at one time, who was now a murderer several times over, was, at heart, a coward. When other men were either taking chances, being foolhardy heroes, when other men were paralyzed with fear, Creed Steiger worked at the top of his capabilities. Because, even more than death, he was afraid of fear.

Since Dreyfus was here alive, that meant that Hhargoth had not destroyed the *Groan*. Or, if he had, it meant that there must have been survivors. He wasn't at all sure yet what that meant, but it was information to be filed away for future reference.

As he proceded cautiously down the trail, knowing that the Zharii were well ahead of him, he still kept a sharp eye out for any other traps or outposts. He didn't want to be surprised like that again.

He tried adding up everything that he had learned. There was something on Xerxes V of value to the Shahin and possibly of value to the Terran Guild as well. At least the Shahin thought so, for they had been very secretive about their visits to this world. A small handful of mercenaries who had been in their employ knew about this, but they also knew enough to be very careful about whom they shared their information with. Still, rumors could have reached the Earth authorities. It was possible.

Whatever it was that the Shahin wanted from this world involved the lizards. And the lizards were fighting back, using the Zharii and tactics that had once been known on Earth. Terran strategy. What did it mean? And where did Alan Dreyfus fit in with all of this?

He spotted another treehouse. He crept up to it silently, wriggling through the tall grass on his belly. He waited until he could be sure how many of them were up there. As before, there were two. He took one of them out with his first shot, being sure to aim at the lizard, so that it would be killed along with its host. The second one he killed as it dropped from the tree. It died in midair, falling heavily and lifelessly to the ground.

He would have to be very careful with his shooting now. There hadn't been many charge packs stored in the lighter, and he knew that he would most likely need them all very soon.

Night was fast approaching.

He was beginning to tire. His shoulder hurt where the beast had bitten him, and his legs were beginning to cramp from all the walking. Walking which was more like climbing now. He stopped briefly to gobble up the last of the tubular fruit and berries, which gave him at least the illusion of having acquired some more energy. He finished off his water, realizing that he might not find any more. He would have to subsist now on the stalks of the large thorn fronds from which he sucked a sickly flavored juice. The taste was vile, but it was moisture he was able to ingest.

The trail had now grown rocky. The going was considerably slower, climbing in earnest now, using the scrub trees and the vines to pull himself along when the incline became too steep. The Zharii were probably able to bound along this terrain like mountain goats. He didn't have the energy or the frame to duplicate such prowess, and he swore softly under his breath. Holding onto the spiney vines was making his hands raw. His clothes were torn in several places and sweat was making little rivulets through the dirt caked on his face.

And, finally, the trail ended.

He decided to continue in the same general direction, keeping to the cover of the rocks whenever he could. He almost didn't see the Zharii sitting on top of a large rock outcropping.

Raising his rifle, he dialed in the right degree of magnification and sighted in. He could not see clearly in the rapidly dimming light, so he switched to infrared. He could see only one of them. And there was no way for him to proceed any further without its seeing him. He looked carefully for the lizard, but he couldn't see it. Not good. Still, there was no choice. He fired, killing it.

When he reached the spot where its corpse lay, he could see no sign of a lizard. Perhaps there hadn't been one. But, of more immediate interest, was an entrance to a cave.

A natural formation by the look of it. And it appeared to lead down into the mountain. Caverns, he thought. That was where the Zharii had disappeared. And he felt certain that he had guessed correctly.

Should he follow them *in there*? They had taken Dreyfus in there and Dreyfus was still the key to all of this. Had always been. There seemed to be no other choice.

He took six steps inside the cavern. Six steps and then he stopped. This was more than crazy, it was suicide. He had a better chance with the Shahin. He hesitated, backed up a step, then turned to run from the cavern. The ground exploded at his feet.

He felt a searing blast of heat and splinters of rock flew up at him, cutting into his skin. He had been staggered by the impact and he brought his rifle up to fire, but another blast shook the ground at his feet and he fell. Four Zharii stood in the mouth of the cave between him and the night outside. Each of them held a Shahin thermal blaster. At such close range, they could not fail to miss. They could have thrown the guns and hit him. The implication was clear.

They stood motionless. His rifle was on the rocky floor by his side. He started to reach for it very slowly, and the Zharii raised their weapons. He drew his hand back, then slowly scuttled backwards away from them, leaving his weapon where it lay. They didn't move, as if expecting him to do something. He didn't know

hat it was. He just continued, slowly sliding backwards, facing
em. They began to move closer, following him into the cave.
ne on them bent down and picked up his rifle. Steiger froze,
aring at the Zharii, their faces totally blank and expressionless.
lizard clung to each of them. One of the Zharii motioned him
rise. He did so. There was no chance to try anything. He was
mpletely at their mercy. At least he was still alive.

He struggled to push the fear from his mind. It was no time
show them that he was afraid.

One of them went on ahead, the other three followed behind
teiger. They went deeper into the cave.

It soon grew so dark that he could barely see. They walked
almost total blackness. Further and further down. At times, he
ad to lean back slightly because of the incline of the rocky surface
low his feet. Several times he slipped on the slick surface, which
dn't seem to bother his captors at all. They waited until he
gained his footing and then continued on without sound.

Well, he thought, you got what you wanted, didn't you? There
as little hope of escape. Even if he managed to elude them, he
ould never find his way back to the surface through all the
visting, turning tunnels. He tried keeping track of the way they
ere taking him, but in a very short time he was completely
soriented.

It was very damp. Several times he knocked into large stal-
gmites that felt wet. The Zharii evidently could see perfectly well
the darkness. When they saw that he was having difficulty,
ey slowed their pace. They walked silently with only a faint
apping of their feet upon the stone. His own footsteps echoed
ally in the darkness. He could hear the steady dripping of water.
nd then he fell.

He landed with a loud splash into ice cold water that was over
s head. He floundered briefly, shocked, and then they pulled
m out. Guiding him, they set him onto solid surface and pro-
eded even more slowly. He could hear the lapping of water to
ther side of him. They were crossing on a narrow stone bridge,
e surface of which was slippery and uneven.

The tunnel was lit with a phosphorescent glow, making every-
ing look eerie and surreal. They took a branching tunnel to the
ft and began to climb. He realized that the entire mountain must

be honeycombed with tunnels, like a maze. The walls felt like granite, hard and cold. The moss growing on them seemed to be giving off the eerie light.

The tunnel began to grow wider. There was a greater profusion of rock formations here, some of them beautiful, veined with crystal that reflected light in shimmering patterns on the walls. The crystals themselves seemed to give off light. He realized, suddenly, what he was seeing. The entire cavern was shot through with the glowing crystalline formations.

Fire crystals.

He had never before seen them in their natural state. The crystals that a flamer would kill for if he could. The crystals that, when crushed and ingested, melted the mind and filled the whole body with sweet, inner warmth even as they destroyed the throat and vocal chords, gradually burned away the esophagus and the stomach lining and the villi in the intestines, causing the user to defecate blood and eventually die in horrible pain. The crystals that were so addictive that even the tiniest dose was enough to turn a man into a dying slave, wasting away slowly, gradually, corrupting like a living corpse.

The cavern was a drug trafficker's utopia. A mother lode of slow death.

They entered into a large chamber of the cavern that was, incredibly, filled with daylight. There was a huge fissure in the opposite wall, a crack through which a lighter could pass through. And a lighter had. He looked at it incredulously. It was old, probably it hadn't flown in years. It was scarred and battered and faded, covered over with dust and moss. As they approached it, he could barely make out the name of a ship lettered on its side. The *Iron Dream*.

A man came out from inside it.

They had halted, and the Zharii moved to stand on either side of Steiger with two of them behind. There were others in the chamber and they all watched him silently. He felt a tugging at his mind.

The man looked very old. His hair hung down to his shoulders and it was snowy white. His long beard and the simple robe he wore made him look like some sort of wizard king. Yet he walked confidently with a military bearing. He appeared spry and strong

His startlingly blue eyes met his, and he smiled, showing strong, even teeth.

"Welcome, Mr. Steiger," he said in a deep bass voice. He held out his hand and Creed took it, stunned. "My name is Andrick Dios. Late captain of the *Iron Dream*. You look pretty worn out. We'll see what we can do to find you a change of clothing and then I'd be honored if you'd join me for dinner."

Chapter Nine

They ate at a small table inside the lighter. Pieces of large red
and yellow fire crystals provided the illumination, and two Zharii
waited on them silently. Steiger had been dressed in a robe of
some kind of animal skin, laced together. He was naked underneath, his boots and the rest of his clothes set out to dry. They
drank a deliciously strong wine which Dios told him had been
made from the very berries Steiger had been eating. The meat
they ate was tough, but it had been soaked in some sort of seasoned
broth which made it easier to chew and, all in all, it wasn't bad
at all.

"What is this stuff?" asked Creed, pointing at the meat with
his fork.

"Zharii," answered Dios.

Steiger gagged, then choked. It was necessary for the old man
to reach around the table and pound him on the back several times.
He glared at the old man, then at the meat on his plate, then at
the Zharii attending them.

"That wasn't very funny," he said hopefully.

"I'm quite serious," replied Dios.

Steiger started to bring another morsel to his lips, but the sight of the creature watching them eating one of its fellows unnerved him. He pushed the plate away.

Dios laughed.

"You're not only eating Zharii," he said with a gleam in his eyes, "you're wearing it as well."

Steiger touched his robe distastefully. He looked up again at the two creatures standing by the hatch of the lighter. "Do, uh, *they* know about this?"

"They don't know anything, Mr. Steiger," Dios grinned. "In a way, the Zharii are the local equivalent of gophers. Rats, coyotes, call them what you will, the Zharii are varmints. Pests. They have no brains to speak of. Left on their own, the only thing that seems to drive them is a vociferous killer instinct. They'll attack anything that moves. The surrogates are their predators. To them, the Zharii are hosts, mounts, tools. The Zharii breed like rabbits, but the lizards keep their population down. The ecology on Xerxes works very well indeed. At least it did until the aliens came. You, myself, the Shahin. Especially the Shahin."

Creed poured himself some more wine. It was beginning to get the chill out of his body.

"I'd go easy on that, if I were you," cautioned Dios. "It can be pretty potent stuff if you're not used to it."

"Yeah, well right now, it's just what the doctor ordered." He drank, feeling one hundred per cent better. "You know, Captain Dios—"

"Just Dios will be fine," the other interrupted. Then, with a wry smile, he added, "I haven't been a captain for a great many years now."

"All right... Dios." Steiger paused, trying to collect his thoughts. "You know, I've got about a million questions and I can't figure out where to start. Well, I can think of two right off the bat. First, I suppose that I'm your prisoner. Not that I'm an ungrateful, uh, guest, but just what's going to happen to me now? And, second, what about Alan Dreyfus, the other man your Zharii... or your surrogates... brought in here?"

"All in good time," replied Dios. "Part of the torture of being my prisoner is having to put up with my conversation for a while

Communicating with the surrogates is accomplished rather differently. I haven't talked to anyone except myself in years."

Creed raised his glass and nodded at him. "Please, feel free. I've got nowhere special to go."

Dios chuckled. "I like you, Creed Steiger. And I know a great deal about you as well. You've probably guessed how I know by now, but I'll fill you in as I go along. It's a very long story actually. I'll try to give you an abbreviated version.

"The *Iron Dream* was the first ship, at least the first Earth ship, to discover Xerxes V. I was her captain then. Yes, I know that must seem impossible, I can see you've done some research. And I know why as well, but never mind for now. Bear with me.

"We thought at first that the Zharii were the dominant, intelligent species on this planet. We could not communicate with them, of course, but they seemed somehow to be able to understand us. What we saw was a very primitive life form, creatures that had a sort of tribal social structure, living in small villages composed mostly of thatched huts. Creatures that seemed to possess some sort of latent telepathic sense. They couldn't literally read our minds, but they seemed to understand who we were and what we wanted and how we felt. They were even able, right away, to differentiate among us as individuals. Clearly, a species with a great deal of promise.

"You can imagine how excited we were. I saw a promotion coming with this discovery. I couldn't wait to report our findings. Still, human nature being what it is, we had to meddle. We had to apply our own standards of judgment and analysis. Our own value systems. These poor creatures, who seemed so remarkably intelligent, were nevertheless at the mercy of a terrible affliction. Reptilian parasites that drained their blood, killing them, leaving cruel and ugly wounds on those still living. We resolved to help them rid themselves of these vile lizards since they couldn't or didn't know how to do it for themselves.

"There was one dissenting opinion. My medical officer, Jim Stires. He tried to convince me that the brains of the Zharii were underdeveloped, too small to support any kind of intelligence. He claimed that he had made some studies and his conclusion was that we weren't dealing with the Zharii, but with the parasites! I dismissed this as a ridiculous notion. Jim always had a wild imagination. It was one of the things I liked about him, rest his soul. I should have listened to him. But I couldn't accept the fact that a *lizard* was intelligent, that a superior being was some form of bloodsucking parasite.

At night, while they all slept, we went silently through their village, injecting little tranquilizer darts into all the lizards. We didn't want to take a chance on poisoning their bloodstreams, so we selected a nerve toxin, something that would cause the lizards to go into a comatose shock, numbing them completely and instantaneously. Then, we simply plucked them off the sleeping Zharii, although most of them dropped off by themselves and we simply crushed them with our boots."

He paused and swallowed heavily, obviously upset at the memory. He sipped some wine before he went on with his tale.

"Now I feel sick at the thought of what we had done. We were not freeing the Zharii from loathsome parasites. We were committing murder on a mass scale.

"In the morning, we were waiting for them anxiously, proud of the favor we had done them. We couldn't wait to see how gratefully they would respond. They responded with the most savage, brutal attack I had ever seen in my life. You simply can't imagine how terrible it was. No, perhaps you can. You've come up against several of them. But remember, the ones you fought were being controlled by surrogates. It was a fury under discipline. Dangerous, yes. Frightening, yes. But nothing like what we saw that day. I saw my people slaughtered in the most horrible way imaginable." His eyes were tightly shut and his voice sounded strained.

"They had their throats literally ripped out. Jugulars severed. Arms and legs torn off. Organs *pulled* out of their still living bodies and eaten. . . . It was a bloodbath. And I was the one responsible. I didn't know it then, of course. I was too busy fighting for my life and shitting in my pants from stark terror. They killed most of us. Those of us who were able, returned to the ship to lick our wounds.

"Then we returned and slaughtered them by the thousands, lizards and Zharii alike. You could smell the stink of burning flesh in the air. I can smell it still. They put up almost no resistence at first, almost as if they didn't understand what was happening to them. And then, they fought back. But, this time, we had come prepared. We killed. And we killed. And we killed. And we killed."

He paused again, covering his eyes with his hands, as if seeing the sight still. Creed sat motionless. He was like a man hypnotized. He realized that his own pulse was racing. He licked his lips, which suddenly felt very dry.

The old man sighed, seeming to collect himself. "I'm sorry," he said. "I just . . . well, never mind. I'll continue. We sustained casualties ourselves. There were very few who survived. The Zharii seemed to come from everywhere. There was no end to them. I, myself, was a casualty though not in the way you might think.

"I was attacked . . . and bitten . . . by a surrogate."

"Try to imagine the most wonderful drug imaginable. You've taken drugs, I know. Nothing as dangerous as the fire crystals all around us, but at least you'll have some idea what I'm talking about. Are you at all familiar with the mythology concerning vampires? Yes, I see you are. In very many ways, it's a good analogy. You become 'addicted' to the lizard's bite. The communion that you achieve with it is the most intimate experience imaginable. And it destroys you as well. The creatures do, after all, live off your blood. The blood of humans is slightly different from that of the Zharii, but the surrogates are able to assimilate it with no difficulty. Humans, however, are not as strong as the Zharii. They are not as resilient. It's difficult for the lizard to achieve a true symbiosis. Yet, just as a flamer will kill for his fire crystals, so will you go to any lengths to continue your relationship with the surrogate, even though it fills you with disgust.

"As I said, I was bitten by a lizard and I succumbed to it. I managed to hide it from my crew, those few who had survived. The effect of the experience on the survivors was terrible. They couldn't cope with it. I had Jim Stires take them all through inducement therapy, which helped their minds to blot out the experience. I refused the therapy, telling Jim I didn't need it, that I would have to remember it all in detail when I made my report. Besides, I didn't want him examining me because I didn't want him to discover the surrogate hiding underneath my uniform. Of course, he would have found out about it anyway as my health deteriorated, but, as it turned out, he didn't have the time. He commited suicide.

"I was left with a handful of spacers for a crew. Not even they survived. The inducement therapy failed to take hold. One of them became a gibbering idiot. Two went out the lock. It was as if the ship and I were cursed. By the time we were within communication range, there were only five of us left. *Only five!* Three women, two men, including myself.

"Except I was no longer myself. It became impossible to hide the surrogate from the others. They tried to kill it. I wouldn't let them. Then they tried to kill me. The surrogate defended itself. I killed them."

"*Christ*," whispered Steiger.

"I know what you must think. It isn't so."

"*You killed them?*"

"Just listen to me and I hope you'll understand. You see, I thought I had killed them. In a way, I mean. I had been the instrument, but the will had been the surrogate's. I was left alone on the *Iron Dream*. I felt like the character in Coleridge's poem, *The Rime of the Ancient Mariner*."

He shut his eyes and slowly, ponderously, started to recite.

> Alone, alone, all, all alone,
> Alone on a wide, wide sea!
> And never a saint took pity on
> My soul in agony.
>
> The many men, so beautiful!
> And they all dead did lie:
> And a thousand thousand slimy things
> Lived on; and so did I.
>
> I looked upon the rotting sea,
> And drew my eyes away;
> I looked upon the rotting deck,
> And there the dead men lay.
>
> I looked to heaven and tried to pray;
> But or ever a prayer had gusht,
> A wicked whisper came, and made
> My heart as dry as dust.
>
> I closed my lids, and kept them close,
> And the balls like pulses beat;
> For the sky and the sea, and the sea and the sky
> Lay like a load on my weary eye,
> And the dead were at my feet.

The cold sweat melted from their limbs,
Nor rot nor reek did they:
The look with which they looked on me
Had never passed away.

An orphan's curse would drag to hell
A spirit from on high;
But oh! more horrible than that
Is a curse in a dead man's eye!
Seven days, seven nights, I saw that curse,
And yet I could not die.

Steiger's eyes were downcast, looking at the surface of the table. The way the old man had said those words, he seemed to feel them. As if he had been there with him. He tried not to look at Dios.

"You see," said Dios finally, "I wanted nothing better than to die. I longed for it with all my soul. But the surrogate wanted me to live. Not only to insure its own survival, but mine. Because, believe it or not, it *cared* for me. It knew what I was feeling. And, besides that, it had a mission.

"Yes, a mission. I learned, then, a great deal about the surrogates. And about myself as well. It sought to ease my mind even as it drained my body. As it was forced to do, in order to survive. But it took very little. It cared for me at its own expense. I knew that it was weak.

"It's mission was to protect its species. Protect them from outsiders like ourselves. The surrogates are highly sentient creatures. In some ways, many ways, they are very much advanced. Our equals. In some respects, incredible as it may seem, they are our superiors.

"Being what they are, they have no need of civilization as we know it, or any of its trappings. They were living a peaceful, simple existence. Until we came along.

"Their reaction to what had happened was much like ours. They didn't really understand at first. They saw that we could not communicate as they did, so they kept their distance, both out of caution and because they were ignorant of our ways. They felt sorry for us because we could not share each other as they did, and they didn't wish to intrude. Amazing, isn't it? They accepted us openly, trustingly. And we responded by murdering them in their sleep. Out of ignorance. Out of our own conceit. We reaped the whirlwind.

"They, too, reacted out of fear. They sent one of their . . . well, elders would be as close as I could describe it . . . to attach itself to me. To try to use me to insure that what had happened would never happen again.

"Xerxes V became a quarantined world. I know because I arranged it. I won't go into all the details of the report that I communicated, but suffice it to say that I made Xerxes V sound like a purgatory not even Dante could have dreamed of. Virulent bacteria, hostile plant and animal life, inhospitable atmosphere, no mineralogical value, etc., etc., etc. It was the greatest lie I ever told. A part of it was that the *Iron Dream* had become a plague ship. In the commander's judgment, it could not return. All of us were dropping like flies and even I was dying. That, at least, wasn't all that far from the truth.

"The logs and records of the *Iron Dream* are classified. They don't really know what happened to the ship or to myself. I told them that my dying act would be to send it into a sun. And I did. *This* sun." He pointed to where the viewport of the lighter had once been, where now was just an empty space. Through it, they could see the sun beginning to rise through the fissure in the cavern. It was dawn already. A beautiful dawn.

"I brought with me everything I could. I decided that this place would be as good a place to die as any. And the lizard wanted to come home.

"However, in the time that we were away, there had been a new development. The Shahin had come. And they had brought even worse destruction.

"At first, they were only interested in the fire crystals. They have been found on several other planets in this system, but nowhere in such quantity as on Xerxes V. You can imagine how delighted they must have been. None of them would ever touch the stuff themselves, but any of them would be all to happy to sell it. And with what they've found on Xerxes, they must have cornered the market."

"I didn't know they were involved in that," said Creed.

"No, I'm sure you didn't. There are a lot of things about the Shahin that even the authorities aren't aware of. Including the total war being fought on Xerxes V. When I returned to this world, the surrogates were being slaughtered. They fought back as best they could, but they knew nothing of war. I had to help them somehow. I did what I could, but I wasn't much of a man anymore. The surrogates no longer used me as a host and they were able, to some degree, to fill the emptiness I felt at the cessation of that relationship . . . yes, even though it would have killed me, I missed it. It can be that powerful. But my health was failing. I could never get my strength back. And my will had been, to a large extent, extinguished. Not by them, but by myself. By my own knowledge of what I had done. It seemed hopeless. And then something astonishing happened.

"Somehow, the Shahin had learned that they could evolve themselves a step further by consuming a surrogate lizard. There is something, evidently, about the lizards' body chemistry that must trigger certain latent abilities. Lord knows, I'm not a biochemist and I know nothing of genetic engineering, so I haven't got the faintest idea *how* it works, but the results were nothing short of miraculous. The Shahin discovered that they could develop regenerative abilities, greater growth and muscularity, sharper, faster reflexes and a limited empathic sense. Instead of killing the surrogates indiscriminately, they started hunting them.

"There was little I could do to help them. I was dying, and they needed me alive to direct the fight against the Shahin.

"One of them volunteered to be sacrificed. I later learned that there had been many, many, volunteers. So one of them gave up its life and they served its remains to me in my food. Had I known, I would never have allowed it, but while a human or a Shahin cannot deceive a surrogate, a surrogate can deceive a human.

"I didn't die. Instead, I discovered that a human can react to the consumption of a surrogate to an even greater degree than can a Shahin. I am now like them. I share consciousness with them. In all respects, except the physical, I am *one* of them. I have been here with them these many years, fighting. Fighting to save their race. I don't know exactly how long it's been, I've lost track over the years, but by my nearest reckoning, I would guess that I am somewhere in the vicinity of two hundred Earth-years old. For all I know, unless I'm killed, I may never die."

I lay on a pallet of dried grass, thinking about what a terrible tragicomedy of errors it had all been. It all seemed so pointless and unnecessary and I could not see where it all would lead.

They had brought me to a cavern and made me comfortable, gave me food to eat and wine to drink and treated my wounds with healing herbs. I would heal. Was already healing. To my great fortune, none of the wounds had been fatal. I had lost a lot of blood, but I would survive. All I really needed was time to rest and allow my body to take care of itself.

Meeting Andrick Dios and *being* with him had been the most meaningful experience of my entire life. Everything was clear now. And I had been so wrong. So very, very wrong.

He was a lonely man.

Not lonely in the sense that he was all alone because he wasn't. The lizards were his friends. But they could not provide him with the one thing that he missed most of all . . . human companionship.

He did not know that we had come to Xerxes. Seeing me was as much of a shock for him as seeing him was for me. Until we met, I had been helpless. The surrogates had tried to communicate with me, but I could not handle such a massive influx and I collapsed under the strain. They drew back, understanding, then one came to prod me, to "feel me out" when I revived. This time, I felt a presence, but there was no sharing of experience. It was confusing. When Dios came to me, all my confusion went away.

He was so much more skilled in the use of his abilities than I was that it was a humbling experience. In the long run, Charlie Faen had been proved right. I *had* let it go to my head and I realized that I had felt myself to be superior when, in fact, I hadn't really understood at all. In that respect, I was still just like an infant, only I had attempted running before I had fully learned to crawl.

I lived through Andrick's experience along with him, felt what he had felt, learned what he had learned, all the while, he brought me through it carefully, gently, compassionately, not simply opening the floodgates as I had done with Sim and Jil and Cilix and the others. The result was knowledge in its purest form. It was not a shocking, almost sexual invasion of the persona as I had known it. Instead, it was a slow, serene coming together. It was more complete. It was more fulfilling. It was like a perfectly frank and objective dialogue between two souls. When it was over, I felt as if a huge burden had been taken from me.

Then he brought one of them to me. They did not use names; they had no need of them since they all knew each other, knew each other in the most complete sense of the word. But I learned that this one had a very high standing in their society. She was ... well, the closest human term would be a "matriarch," except there were a number of them who did not rule so much as guide the others in certain social activities. We established a rapport and, while Dios "listened," I learned the full story.

The surrogates had been desperate. Beset by the Shahin, they were too slowly learning the questionable art of warfare and they fought always at a disadvantage, despite the frenzy of the Zharii. They had no modern weapons and, while Dios was a fine strategist, it simply wasn't enough.

They had managed, over a period of time, to capture a number of Shahin. And I knew that it must have been no easy task. Those Shahin became controlled by surrogates. The surrogate that became, in the end, mine had been selected to make a daring bid to obtain as host the captain of a Shahin vessel. But first it was necessary for it to find a way on board. No opportunity presented itself for a long time, but finally it was able to attack a Shahin warrior during a skirmish. To help insure the success of the plan, a pregnant female had been selected. In this fashion, its offspring would be born aboard the ship, and there would be two surrogates trying to reach the captain.

Once that was accomplished, with the captain in thrall to the surrogates, it was intended that the lizard use the captain to order a shuttle from the ship down to a designated area far from the Shahin base. There, the Shahin prisoners, already under the control of the surrogates, would overpower those on the shuttle and use it to gain entry to the ship. They would then take control of the ship and use it to attack the Shahin base. And Dios would take command of the ship, using it against any more that came. It was a bold plan, but it never succeeded.

The surrogates had no way of knowing that the mercenaries were really nothing more than a sort of high class chattel aboard the Shahin ships. The Shahin who had been bitten had, no doubt, been discovered and killed. John was not so lucky.

Poor John. I wondered what he was really like. The surrogate had made a bad choice in him. Alone in an alien universe, it had been unlucky enough to choose for a host a man for whom, finally, not even the Shahin had been able to find a use. It must have despaired of ever seeing its home again. Their sense of community was very strong. Alone, the lizard had, no doubt, gone at the very least half mad.

And a simple twist of fate brought it to me.

If it had tried to tell me what the real situation was, if it had tried to *show* me . . . but then, it had. And I was too busy feeling sorry for myself to pay any attention. Even so, I probably would not have believed it anyway. I had already cast it in its evil role. In retrospect, I couldn't blame it. It *had* to be ruthless. After all, it had been sent to save its race. I could only blame myself.

"I feel sorrow that your friends were killed," the matriarch communicated to me. *"We had no way to reach your people safely, and we were afraid. Afraid that you had come to hunt us, like the others."*

"We sought to escape being hunted ourselves," I told it, "but we were no different from the Shahin. We, too, came to hunt."

"You did not know. You did not understand."

"What difference would it have made? Others will come. They're bound to. Xanfru will be sure to bring them. I suppose that certain things, such as greed and lust and selfishness, are common to many species. You have something that they want. And it doesn't matter that they will have to kill to take it. They'll win. They always do."

I felt tired and they both felt my need for sleep. They left me. When I awoke, already feeling stronger, the first thing that I saw was Steiger.

"Creed!"

"Hello, Alan," he smiled. "Surprised?"

"It's getting so that very little surprises me anymore. I'm beginning to believe that you and I are indestructible."

"You are, maybe, but me, I'm feeling definitely mortal these days. What happened to the others?"

"I don't know." I shook my head. "A lot are dead. Many have been taken prisoner by the Shahin. I don't know what to do. It's all been my fault."

He was silent for a long moment. Then he came and sat beside me. "Did I ever tell you why I never got around to becoming an officer?" he asked. "No, I'm sure I didn't. The only time we really got to talk, there was a wall between us and I was so throughly twisted nothing would have made any sense. I'd like to be able to have a normal conversation with somebody. The old man keeps peeking inside. He probably can't help himself, so I don't really mind. Well, maybe I do, but so what? At least the lizards keep their distance. Go figure, they have no privacy themselves, and yet they understand my need for it. Most people could learn something from them."

"A lot of things, I'm sure."

"Yeah. I guess so. Well, you shouldn't feel so bad. I went through it too. It's really pretty simple. I never became an officer because I was scared."

"You?"

"Yeah, me. Swear to God. I've been scared most of my life. I didn't want to be put in the position of having to make decisions because I was afraid of making the wrong decisions. It's easier when you've got to follow orders. Then it's not your worry and you can bitch about the wrong decisions other people have made." He put his hand up to the back of his neck and rubbed wearily. "There was just one problem though. A couple of problems actually. I wasn't much good at following orders and I made the wrong decisions anyway."

I laughed. After all that had happened, it felt good to laugh. It felt terrific.

Steiger laughed too, but it was somewhat forced. He cut it short.

"Boy, some screwy friendship this is going to be. I haven't had a friend in a long time. That bastard, Lokhrim, was about as close as I came. And I started out to kill you. No hard feelings, right?"

"No, Creed, no hard feelings."

He began to chuckle. It wasn't a chuckle of amusement though.

"Shit," he said. "I fucked up so bad. . . ."

"We all do."

"Yeah, only I made a career out of it. I don't know. . . . I wish that I could start all over. Right from the beginning, straight out of the womb. Pop out of the hatch and greet the daylight with a smile and a cheery wave and go off to make my fortune."

I watched him as he leaned against the rock wall, talking into it. He turned around and stared at me, a strange, hard look in his eyes.

"You know what the right decision for me would be right now? To haul my ass out of here and run straight to the Shahin and sell them everything I know for a ticket out of here!"

"Is that what you're going to do?"

"It's what I should do. It's what I have to do!" He exhaled loudly. "And I ain't going to do it, God damn it. I'm going to wind up fighting for a bunch of fuckin' frogs and lizards, for crying out loud."

"Why?"

He looked at me, "You know, you're being pretty square about staying out of my head. I know it's not exactly that, it's sharing feelings or whatever, but just the same, I want you to know that I appreciate it. You're okay, Alan, you really are."

"You haven't answered my question."

"Yeah. Yeah, I know I haven't. I'll tell you why if you really want to know. Because I always make the wrong decisions, that's why. Because they've got a war here and that's the only thing I'm good for! An honest-to-God, for-real war. And it's the only one around. It's the only one I've got."

"I have a feeling that you might not be picking the winning side," I said.

"Maybe so, but at least they've got no fucking officers!"

He turned and walked rapidly from the chamber. I could hear his footsteps receding in the tunnel.

Jil stared at the plate with horror.

"Eat," commanded Lokhrim.

"Please. . . ."

"Eat it!"

She took a small piece and put it in her mouth. Feeling revulsion, she gagged and felt the gorge rising in her throat. She vomited.

"Again," said Lokhrim. "You too," he said to Cilix. The Ophidian sat, stonily staring at his plate. Jil's race, though different in appearance from the human and the Shahin species, was at least closely similar to them in body chemistry. His was vastly different. There was no telling how the lizard flesh would affect him. And, in truth, he did not really care. He sat and ate quietly, ignoring the vile taste of the meat. Jil had difficulty keeping it down. Twice, she threw up. Cilix felt very tired.

In a short while, Jil began to shiver and heave. He began to feel strange. Jil was soon sweating copiously, shaking like a leaf and mewling pitifully, her fur damp and stringy. She finally passed out. Lokhrim had her removed from the room. They were left alone, watching each other. Cilix began to feel cramps in his stomach. His body fought to vomit out the alien flesh, he fought to keep it down. He sat, with dignity, staring at Lokhrim. When evening came, he died.

Kovalevski refused to admit defeat. But he didn't see any way for them to escape. The Shahin had been most thorough in their preparations for his crew. To all intents and purposes, they were in a prison camp, completely isolated. The others were allowed no freedom of movement whatsoever. They were strictly confined. He, at least, was able to move about the base somewhat, but his movements were restricted and he was never left alone. They kept him under constant guard.

Lokhrim did not feel that administering to the needs of his crew required Kovalevski to communicate with them. They saw him, knew that he was working with the Shahin, and he had no chance to speak with them to try to explain his painful decision. Lokhrim appreciated the value of placing him in such a position. Shahin were experienced with the needs of humans from having employed human mercenaries. In that respect, Kovalevski really wasn't needed. But using the captain removed from Lokhrim the burden of having to monitor their welfare. After all, if they were to be experimental breeding stock, it would be necessary to insure that they last as long as possible. And that was something that Kovalevski would be much more concerned about than Lokhrim.

Twenty of the *Groan's* crew had been selected at random to be the first subjects of the experiment. These twenty, Lokhrim hoped, would give him some indication of how long the humans would last until they weakened and died from being hosts to surrogates. He had learned that a human could live for a very long time indeed with a surrogate that had enough time to establish a symbiotic rapport with its host. But the nature of this experiment was different.

The Terrans would all be exposed to several at once, pregnant ones and young ones, newly born. Each of them would be exposed to a different number or lizards to establish exactly how many surrogates a human could support at one time without lethal dam-

age. As soon as the lizards attained a reasonable size, they wou
all be "harvested" and the human would be given an opportuni
to receive rest and care, building up strength *and* need—since tl
relationship had been proven to be an addictive one—while anoth
human took the place of the first. It was like rotating crop
Lokhrim felt certain that it would work.

Already, Lord Hhargoth was pleased. Soon he would take tl
ship and depart, leaving Lokhrim in charge of the base. And the:
was every indication that Lokhrim would be left behind as
officer. Lokhrim was satisfied.

Kovalevski was destroyed.

He had been present during one of the experiments, watchin
through a transparent partition made out of the same material
the black cube in which he had seen his first Zharii. Lokhrim an
two others stood beside him as the material faded, its blacknes
ebbing to transparency, revealing one of Sim's young female crev
members inside. It was a small room, completely bare of fur
nishings of any sort. A floor, four walls, and a ceiling. She wa
badly frightened. She saw Sim and ran to him, calling out hi
name. He couldn't really hear her. She sounded very far away.

Sim tried to shout to her, but it was evident that she couldn
hear him any better than he could hear her. Lokhrim and the other
merely stood and watched silently. Lokhrim signaled to one o
the other Shahin who then left them.

The lizards were introduced into her room. Four of them. An
two were pregnant. Their bodies bulged visibly. She screamed.

The lizards hesitated at first. Kovalevski was puzzled by this
even as he was horrified at what was about to happen. It wa
almost as if her screaming had frightened the creatures. They mad
no move towards her. Had Kovalevski known the truth about th
lizards, he would have realized that they had sensed her terror
her very helplessness. He would have realized that the surrogate:
would *know* that she, too, was a captive, away from her natural
environment and kept apart from her fellow beings. But the sur
rogates had been prisoners for a long time. They were hungry and
they were very weak. The pregnant females were especially in
need. They began to move towards her.

Kovalevski couldn't watch.

He shut his eyes and turned his face away, tried to leave, but
Lokhrim restrained him.

"Look," he said.

"I can't," gasped Kovalevski. "Dear God, I can't, please, please, I beg of you, don't make me!"

"Look."

"NO!"

The Shahin grabbed Kovalevski's struggling form and held him with his arms pinned behind his back. He turned him so that he faced into the room.

Kovalevski tried to kick back with his feet, keeping his eyes shut tightly all the while, but it was to no avail.

Lokhrim placed his fingers on Sim's temples. He began to press slowly, deliberately increasing the pressure.

"Open your eyes."

"No," Sim gasped with pain. "No, I can't, I won't. . . ."

Lokhrim pressed harder. "Open your eyes."

The pressure became unbearable. Kovalevski felt as if his head was being slowly crushed. He cried out in pain, redoubling his struggles in the Shahin's grasp, but he couldn't break free. He tried to shake his head, but it was clamped, as if in a vice, between Lokhrim's hands.

He couldn't take it anymore. He opened his eyes.

She was crouched down on hands and knees. The four lizards had fastened onto her and they were feeding. There were no Zharii. There was no one, nothing else. They were starved almost to the point of death and the females had their young to think of. And there was no other source of food.

One of them clung to her neck. The others had fastened onto her arms and legs. She had been stripped of almost all her clothing before being placed in the room and Kovalevski could see where they had clung to her flesh, could see their fangs imbedded in her skin, could see the tiny rivulets of blood trickling down her neck and arms and legs where their claws had sunk in to take a hold.

He moaned pathetically and began to sob.

Lokhrim nodded to the Shahin who held him and the other led him away, half dragging him. Lokhrim was satisfied. A few more such sessions and the Terran captain would be completely pliable.

Chapter Ten

The surrogates met in council.

Creed slept and I did not attend. I would have been welcome to meet with their "elders," but I found that I could only sustain communication with a few of them at any one time. Only Dios, whose many years of experience with them had sharpened and refined his abilities, could attend and tell me what transpired. I could not handle such a massive input and became instantly lost. It was a jarring experience. I still had much to learn.

I kept thinking about Jil as well as Cilix and Sim and all my other friends. What had happened to them? Were they still alive? So many had died, so very many. . . .

I tried to feel hate for the Shahin, but I found that I could not hate them. Strange though it may seem, it simply wasn't in me. I realized that we had to fight them somehow, but I couldn't bring myself to feel hate. Neither did the lizards hate them.

They understood that they had to kill in order to survive. That, after all, was part of nature. They had been killing the Zharii for centuries in order to survive, it was a part of their way of life, the natural balance. The Shahin were just a recent element added to the equation of survival. They would have to kill them too if they could, only in a different way. Death was a part of life.

Perhaps I was learning to accept things the way that they did. I was able to feel anger and outrage, but hate? No. Even though they had done everything that they had done, I was able to accept it. What else was I to do? Allow myself to become consumed by the desire for revenge? There was no satisfaction to be found in that. And it would only harm me in the end. It wasn't a matter of forgiving them. Forgiveness did not enter into it. After all, they were only doing what I would have done myself.

I had led Sim and the others here in the hopes of obtaining for them the thing that I had come to accidentally. And then I would have given it to the Guild as well. The surrogates were a superior race. A unique and even noble race, yet if killing them meant that humans would be able to reach a higher plane of existence. . . .

We would have found a way to justify it. We always did.

Creed came running into my chamber. He was sniffling from a cold. My own increased resistance, like that of Andrick's, prevented the damp from causing me anything more than some minor discomfort. Creed was not so fortunate.

He was a strange man. I had nothing to fear from him anymore, but I still respected his desire to be left alone. He was very jealous of his privacy, very protective of his self-imposed isolation. He had spent a lifetime building up barriers. He would not be breached. I wondered how he felt. But he had obviously reached a stage of crisis in his life and he didn't want to attempt it alone. In the last analysis, all he had was me. The man whom, once, he had set out to kill.

"Creed," I said, rising to my feet. "I thought you were asleep."

"I couldn't sleep," he said, slightly out of breath from running through the tunnels. "Besides, it looks like all hell's broken loose."

"What do you mean?"

"Come on, I'll show you."

He ran back the way he came and I followed. We sped through the dripping caverns, from one tunnel to the next, until we came to the large chamber with the fissure in it, the one where Andrick had his ancient lighter. We ran over to the giant opening in the cavern wall and he pointed outside.

The dark night sky was all lit up with sporadic flashes of light in the distance. Steiger pointed in the direction where Andrick had said the Shahin base camp lay.

"It started a little while ago," he said. "A while before it happened, I was standing here, just trying to get some warm breeze on my skin when the whole sky was lit up with a ball of fire. Up there. I'll bet you anything it was the Shahin ship being destroyed. They've come, just like you said they would. The Shahin base is under attack."

"How many ships, do you think?"

He shook his head. "I don't know. One, two, maybe three? Who knows? But if they're ours . . . well, Terran Guild ships, I mean . . . they're military craft. They'll be attacking with fighter shuttles. If the Shahin were able to get any of their own up in the air, it must be quite a sight."

"We've got to tell Andrick," I said.

"I know," Andrick replied, joining us from behind.

"What are you going to do?" I asked. "What have they decided?"

"They have decided what to do," he answered. He shook his head sadly, then shrugged. "We will have to fight one enemy at a time. For now, they fight each other."

"But our people are at that base," I protested. "The survivors from the *Titus*! They're our people, Andrick! Those are *our* people attacking that base!"

"*Your* people, perhaps," said Dios. "I don't really think of myself as one of them anymore. I don't trust them anymore— nothing against you, Alan, or you, Creed, but you've reminded me of things I'd sooner forget. I understand how you feel. But how can you do anything? How can the surrogates do anything? What did you think they came here for?"

"You're right. I'd forgotten. But perhaps I can convince them. . . ."

"Do you really think they'll listen?"

"I can try."

"Then you must go to them. I will ask my friends to take you. But if there will be fighting still, they will not help the Terrans."

"I understand."

"You should go as well, Creed. I can see what's troubling you—"

"God damn it, Dios, mind your own business, will you?" He sighed, then grinned at my startled look. "He can't help himself, I guess," he said. "He's got no manners, not like you. Been with those frogs and surrogates too long. In case you've forgotten, I'm sort of stuck between a rock and a hard place. The Shahin won't be able to do much without their ship and I'm still wanted by the Terran Guild for murder, remember?"

"Are you going to stay?"

"Not me. Things have changed now. Besides, this fucking cold is killing me," he sniffed. "Let's just pretend I'm someone else, okay? I'll be Joe Donovan, a merchant spacer. Who knows? I might even get away with it long enough to let me come up with some other angle. What the hell, it's worth a try. Besides, I'm missing a bloody good fight."

"You're crazy."

"So? What else is new?"

"There's just one thing that bothers me, Creed. Whose side will you fight on?"

He shrugged. "I'll figure that out when we get there."

When we arrived, the aerial attack was over.

The Shahin base was a shambles. Almost all of our lighters had been destroyed along with many of the Shahin shuttles. The wreckage was everywhere. The walls and many of the buildings had been destroyed. The forces of the Terran Guild had landed and they were mopping up. They would have a great deal of mopping up to do. The Shahin were badly battered and many of them had been killed, but they were savage fighters and they would make a stand to the last.

It was an indescribable chaos. The memory of that sight will be forever etched in my mind. If it wasn't for Creed, taking over and barking orders at me, yes, like an officer, ironically enough, I would have been completely helpless. But then, Creed was in his element.

We found Sim Kovalevski. He glanced quickly at Steiger, then at me. He seemed disoriented, confused.

"Sim!" I shouted. "Jil, where's Jil? Is she here? Is she alive?"

He nodded, numbly and pointed to a shattered building. We ran towards it with crossfire all around us. The Shahin survivors had taken refuge in some of the ruined buildings and the fighting was fierce. Creed had found a blaster. We made it, somehow, to the ruin Sim had pointed out to us and fought our way through the rubble. A Shahin soldier stumbled out of the room and Creed shot him. He exploded in a mess of blood and entrails.

We found Jil.

She was sitting in a room that had half the ceiling missing. She and a handful of the crew from the *Groan* huddled there together. She was covered with dust and her fur was filthy and matted. Blood had caked on it from a large cut over one eye. Many of the others had been hurt as well. There were eleven of them there. Two were dead.

Lokhrim was there too.

They had taken his weapon away from him. He sat quietly, looking somewhat dazed, beside Jil. He looked up at us . . . *and smiled*.

Creed lowered his weapon. "What the hell. . . ."

Jil looked up at me and brought me in. *She* brought me in and we were together once again. In that instant, we lived through all that we had gone through while we had been apart, thinking each other dead. And then I knew. I understood.

The Shahin detested being close to humans. And Jil brought Lokhrim closer than any Shahin had ever been before.

The Shahin finally were defeated. They had fought hard and bravely, but all had died. Even Lokhrim. When they came and found us, they shot Lokhrim the moment they laid eyes on him before any of us could stop them.

I tried to convince them not to hunt the surrogates, but, as Andrick Dios had predicted, they wouldn't listen. So the Shahin were replaced by our people. It made little difference to the surrogates. Another species, the same sort of persecution and oppression. Only they had less success than the Shahin, which is to say, they had no success at all. They killed many Zharii, but they were unable to get their hands on a single lizard or a single lizard corpse. I knew why, for Dios had told me, communicating in our private way, what the surrogates had decided before we had left.

They knew they could not win. And they did not want to see

Xerxes V become a battleground between two other species, humans and Shahin. They didn't wish to see Xerxes spoiled. So they had decided to stop breeding.

It would be a long time before they all died out. They fought on, for life was precious to them, but they modified their strategy, doing what before would have been unthinkable to them. Rather than be killed and eaten or captured and then killed and eaten, they commanded the Zharii to consume them instead. The Zharii ate their dead and any Zharii that was captured gobbled its lizard down before it could be taken. It didn't take long before the Zharii overran the planet. Those that had eaten their lizards became more formidable, more intelligent. In time, as they interbred, the Zharii would become a sentient species.

War between the Terrans and the Shahin was avoided, but just barely. There were other battles and other skirmishes, but when they realized that they were fighting over a prize that would be denied to both of them, they stopped. The humans left Xerxes V. The Shahin returned and killed Zharii by the thousands as they resumed the mining of the fire crystals. But the Zharii bred fast and they bred true and they were becoming stronger and more intelligent, evolving faster owing to the survival of the fittest. In another century or two, if the demand for fire crystals still remained, the Shahin would be negotiating trade with them.

We never found Andrick Dios. I have no idea what happened to him. Perhaps Dios is there still, perhaps he's dead. I don't know. I think about him every now and then and wonder about a lot of things.

"Joe Donovan" came back with us. When we made port it was discovered who he really was, but he was long gone by then. I think about Creed Steiger too. I never saw him again. I wonder if he ever found whatever it was he was looking for.

Sim Kovalevski had to be hospitalized. I tried to communicate with him once again, after it was all over, but either I couldn't reach him or I wasn't skilled enough. He had withdrawn after losing most of his crew and I wasn't able to bring him out. Eventually, after long and proper treatment, he recovered. He retained his rank, but he was never able to command a ship again. He was given administrative duties and when I tried to see him, he refused me. I couldn't blame him. The memory was painful.

Only Jil and I are left. We came through it, survived. And we have a long, long time ahead in which to be together. The old Alan Dreyfus might have felt bitter and remorseful. The old Alan Dreyfus might have felt, in part, responsible for the dying out of an entire race of sentient beings. I felt none of these things. I accepted what was and resolved to live with it. The old Alan Dreyfus would not have understood. But I was different then.

There was one other thing that I felt I had to do. On the ship returning from Xerxes V, Creed had told me about a part of a poem that Dios had recited to him. It must have had a very powerful effect on him, for he remembered most of it. Either that, or Dios left it in his mind somehow. I still don't know the full extent of what I can do. Everything will come, in time. I looked up the poem that Creed had mentioned. I would not have thought him to be the sort of man to be impressed by poetry, but this particular one had a lot to teach. It had been written a long time ago, in 1797, and it told the story of a seaman who had gone through a terrible ordeal. In more ways than one, it was *our* story too. I committed it to memory, but one passage in particular stands out. It comes very near the end.

> *Forthwith this frame of mine was wrenched*
> *With a woeful agony,*
> *Which forced me to begin this tale;*
> *And then it left me free.*
>
> *Since then, at an uncertain hour.*
> *That agony returns;*
> *And til my ghastly tale is told,*
> *This heart within me burns.*
>
> *I pass, like night, from land to land;*
> *I have strange power of speech;*
> *That moment that his face I see,*
> *I know the man that must hear me:*
> *To him my tale I teach.*

Afterward

As I write these words, it is about a quarter after nine in the p.m. and I am at my psychedelic Underwood (really, it's green and red and sky blue and purple and orange and pink and yellow...) a machine that's not quite twice my age. I have just returned from a meeting with my editor, John Silbersack, and my agent, Adele Leone, both good people and good friends. We looked at some sketches for what will be the cover of this book. And we changed the title. Sometimes the title that the author originally wanted doesn't make it for one reason or another. When a portion of this work first appeared in *Galaxy* magazine, then edited by J. J. Pierce (who was attempting to perform the task of Sisyphus with that magazine), it was called "The Surrogate Mouth." I thought it was a good title. I still think it's a good title, but what do I know? I just wrote the damn thing. Anyway, the title *Journey From Flesh* was taken from a Theodore Roethke poem "The Shape of Fire." What's all this leading up to? Well, it's leading up to the answer to a very popular question. *Where do you get your ideas?*

I constantly hear the "old, established pros" complaining about being asked that question and, frankly, I don't know why it bugs them. As writers, they should be pleased that someone's even paying attention. Now this happens to be my first novel. I've done a few short stories and some magazine articles, but I'm still new at this, friends, I'm no big deal. I have, in the past, held down jobs that some people might consider a big deal. I've been a disc jockey, a radio engineer, I've worked in a recording studio at the United Nations, I've been an armed guard, a rock musician, a straight bartender in a predominantly gay bar, and a host of other things. One would think that people would ask questions about those jobs. But, no. They usually say something like, "Oh, that must have been interesting" and then continue on with whatever they were talking about. Folks are so blasé these days. Yet, if I answer the question "What do you do?" with "I'm a writer," it doesn't matter that they never heard of me. If it's not the first question, "Where do you get your ideas?" comes right after "What name do you write under?" I kinda like it. It's my cue to do an hour or two on my favorite subject. This, then, is a little something extra.

Journey From Flesh has an interesting history. The title came first—that is the original title; see why I had to explain? At the time, it had nothing to do with the story.

I was driving home one night in a borrowed car (I rarely drive cars, I'm partial to motorcycles) with my friend, Richard McEnroe, who is also a writer. The conversation turned to an annoying, but I suppose a necessary evil, telephone answering machines. Richard called them "surrogate mouths." It struck me as a great title for a story and then and there, right in the car, we thrashed out an idea for a story about a telephone answering machine that develops sentience. Anyway, it was going to be a short, clever little satire, and you watch, I'll bet someone writes it sooner or later, if they haven't already.

I started to write the story. And I couldn't have cared less. It went absolutely nowhere. I kept getting up from the typewriter, smoking cigarettes, turning on the radio, going out to burn up the road on my bike, but nothing doing. I just couldn't get into it. Except that the title kept doing strange things in my mind.

About that time, a song started going through my head, God only knows why. I first heard it several years ago when I was a disc jockey on a small FM station. The song was called "Junkie John" and it was written and performed by Tim Dawe on an album called *Penrod*. It was about an addict in the East Village during the old coffee house days. In the song, there is a line that goes, "When Junkie John walked into a room, you got the feeling somebody just left." Tim, if you're out there, I'm giving you credit for the line and for having an influence on me in the writing of this book. Indirectly, your song was what started the wheels turning. I recalled the image that the lyrics and the music called forth to my mind. A man, a very human and vulnerable man, who had a haunted, powerful presence. Whose need was so great that it was a palpable thing, that it repelled people. As John Kay of *Steppenwolf* once sang in a song called "The Pusher" (written by Hoyt Axton), he was a man who had "tombstones in his eyes." I wanted to write about that man.

So I started cooking. I'm very much what might be called a "method writer." I never plot. It drives a lot of people crazy that write that way (and I'm sure at least one reviewer will say that my work reads that way!), but the way I do it is to create a character that seems real to me . . . and then jump inside his head. Needless to say, I sometimes get very flakey while I'm working. I never have any kind of control over my characters. Steiger drove me crazy. He was *supposed* to be a minor character, but the s.o.b. simply wouldn't behave. You understand, I really had no choice in the matter. I lift weights and I know karate, but Creed's a *mean* bastard and I refused to fuck with him.

The nice thing about writing science fiction is that, although most people think allegory went out with Spenser, it's still around in SF and doing very well, thank you. There is, of course, the obvious allegory, that of drugs. And somebody found Jungian archetypes in it, but I've never read Jung, so go figure. Aside from that, there is human greed, conceit, sexual manipulation, and the illusion that we are not "in control."

The "communication" that happens in the story isn't really so farfetched a notion. My brother and I can often "call" each other's reactions to any given thing in advance, though we don't always agree. Lovers or spouses who have been together for a length of time and share direct communication and intimacy (I *don't* mean sex) can often "read" each other. I'm reasonably certain that you, yourself, have probably experienced something on this level with someone who is close to you. Joe South might have called it the "walk-a-mile-in-my-shoes" effect. The surrogates all have this. I think we do too, only we've tuned it out. Another possible interpretation might be, "Eat the apple that the serpent offers you and you will gain knowledge. Eat the serpent and you will understand that knowledge."

The use of Samuel Taylor Coleridge's *The Rime of the Ancient Mariner* came quite naturally. If you haven't read it, go to it. Coleridge was a fascinating man. He was a friend of Wordsworth's, a contemporary of Goethe, and his work influenced Shelley. I find it ironic that a man who was supposed to have been weak-willed, neurotic, self-indulgent, and addicted to opium has given us what is, perhaps, one of the finest works on the meaning of responsibility and redemption written in the English language.

See, that's another thing about writers. We're constantly jumping off each other's shoulders. Not that I would be idiot enough to put myself in the same league as Coleridge, only that I mean to say that inspiration comes not only from observing, as the Moody Blues sang, "with the eyes of a child," but from reading the works of others and responding. I've been influenced by everyone from Harlan Ellison to the Beowulf poet. (I really should have put that the other way around, Harlan. Sorry.) And I am grateful to all the writers, both living and dead, to whom I have listened.

And I am especially grateful to *you* for listening to me. Thank you.

Nicholas Yermakov
Merrick, New York

About the Author

Nicholas Valentin Yermakov was born in New York City on September 30, 1951. Although born in the United States, English is his second language, the first being Russian. He attended American and Hofstra Universities, majoring in English Literature and Communications. He recently became a full-time writer and his short stories have appeared in *The Magazine of Fantasy and Science Fiction, Galaxy, Heavy Metal, Chrysalis* and *The Berkley Showcase*, along with non-fiction articles in various other magazines.

Nick is single and currently lives in Merrick, Long Island. He is an avid motorcyclist, a member of the American Motorcyclist Association and Cross Island Motorcycle Club. He is also a member of the Science Fiction Writers of America and his upcoming novels are *An Affair of Honor* and *Clique. Journey from Flesh* is his first novel.

MS READ-a-thon—
a simple way to start
youngsters reading

Boys and girls between 6 and 14 can join the MS READ-a-thon and help find a cure for Multiple Sclerosis by reading books. And they get two rewards — the enjoyment of reading, and the great feeling that comes from helping others.

Parents and educators: For complete information call your local MS chapter. Or mail the coupon below.

Kids can help, too!